I0778408

Cover art by Felix Tindall

The Ties That Bind

ROBERT J. HALLIWELL

TRIPLE SCALE PUBLISHING

Contents

For Adam, who has given me more love and support than I thought one person could possibly give.

For my found family, thank you for seeing me for who I really am, even when I couldn't.

CHAPTER ONE

Alone

Alone. That was the word that kept running through Zoey's mind as she watched the rays of dappled sunlight play against the drab concrete that zoomed by outside. Despite the two silent figures sitting in the front of the charcoal-gray sedan, despite the few friends who she'd managed to retain over the past year promising to reach out once she had settled in, Zoey had never been more alone in all her fourteen years. No matter how many times people told her it was a chance to start over, the best option for everyone, Zoey couldn't see her situation as anything but a sentence to solitary confinement.

As if on cue, the figure in the front passenger seat turned and, wearing a smile that was far too full of pity for Zoey's liking, said, "Zoey, as hard as this all must be, I hope you know that your Uncle Will and I have been looking forward to having you."

Zoey had to ponder the sincerity of that statement. While it was true that she and Aunt Carol were family, the two of them were total strangers to one another. She wasn't even her real aunt. She was her great-aunt, younger sister to her grandmother on her mother's side. Zoey only had one hazy memory of the woman. It comprised a hurried kiss on the cheek before rushing off for a bunch of meaningless chatter with her grandma in the other room. It seemed unlikely that taking in some random fourteen-year-old girl could be a cause for celebration for any two people, let alone a pair who were well into their sixties.

"I hope it's not too much trouble," was all that Zoey could think to mutter back, her fawn-brown eyes still focused on the flickering sunlight on the other side of the window.

A sad smile played at the corners of Zoey's mouth at the soft, but audible exhalation that escaped her uncle. In what Zoey could only assume was a hasty attempt to cover the awkward moment, the car filled with the sound of clattering beads and bangles, Aunt Carol adjusting further in her seat. Sparing a glance in her direction, Zoey caught the briefest trace of annoyance ripple across the well-lined features on her aunt's face. With a sigh of her own, Aunt Carol pushed a long flyaway gray hair behind her ear and hitched a look of determined cheer on her face.

"It's no trouble, really. We've got more room than we know what to do with in that big, old house," said Aunt Carol, her voice a shade too sincere. "And, as much as I love your uncle, it can get a bit lonely with just the two of us."

Though there was no huff this time, Zoey was certain that Uncle Will had rolled his eyes hard enough to flip the car right there on the interstate. She let the statement hang before deciding that not answering would only invite further half-true affirmations from her aunt.

"Well, I'll try not to get in the way too much at least. I'll have school and homework and all that to keep me busy."

"Oh, I'm sure you'll have more than just school and homework to keep yourself entertained. You'll have all the friends you're bound to make. I've looked into it and there's lots of clubs for you to join once school starts up," gushed Aunt Carol, latching onto the minimal response with almost indecent verve. "You know, it's a bit of a blessing that all this unpleasantness happened over the summer. You'll have a fresh start with high school, just like everyone else."

Zoey had to bite the inside of her cheek to keep her from spitting out a furious retort at her aunt. As used to her situation being twisted this way and that as she was, no one had ever chalked up the destruction of Zoey's life to mere "unpleasantness."".

For the first time since the drive began, Zoey locked eyes with her aunt, hoping that the raging storm behind her gaze would express the words she knew better than to utter. Her soft brown eyes bored viciously into Aunt Carol's misty gray until not a trace of a smile remained on the older woman's face.

"I only mean, I hope that getting away from your old setting will be good for you."

With that, Aunt Carol turned in her seat and the previous uncomfortable, yet familiar, silence fell upon the car once again. Through the resonant thump of her raging heart, Zoey had to admit, at least in the privacy of her own head, that Aunt Carol just might be right. The problems she faced back home were made worse by how many people felt it was their business. Teachers, her friends' parents, and more than a couple of kids her own age. They all seemed remarkably well informed about what was going on in her life, without having any idea as to what it actually meant.

Two years ago, Zoey's dad had gotten in the way of a drunk driver doing seventy when he should have been doing twenty. The inebriated monster behind the wheel had walked away with a couple of broken bones and a sentence of fifteen years. Zoey's father hadn't been so lucky.

Her mom had done what Zoey felt was her best at first. She worked a full five days a week, kept the house in order, and even managed to find some time to spend with her. Zoey had done what she could to help out, but at twelve years old, there was only so much she could do. She started to get the feeling that her mom resented her for not being more self-sufficient. For not doing more. As time went on, it even felt as though her mom was upset at her for grieving the loss of her father as much as she was.

The cracks had begun to show slowly, spreading through their lives like strands on a spider's web. Drinks out with her friends on weekends where she stayed out later than usual. Ordering out more often than not because she was too tired to cook. These simple acts progressed over time to more worrying events. Missing shifts to instead lie in her curtain-darkened room until well past noon. Forgetting to buy groceries or leave money for Zoey to order something for herself. The nights out bled into the weekdays. The hours grew later, the days of missed work more numerous. Zoey began having to do more for herself. Doing her best, but failing to keep things in order without a shred of guidance from the stranger who had replaced her mother.

It continued on like this for nearly two years before Zoey's mother had admitted that she had problems that were too big for any one person to solve. It was decided that, for her mom to have the best chance of regaining herself, she needed to be able to focus on herself as much as possible. This left the few adults left in Zoey's life with the burden of deciding what to do with her.

Six hours ago her great-aunt and uncle had shown up to take her away from the only world she'd ever known. After a series of unimaginably awkward smalltalk, her unknown relatives helped her carry down the two oversized suitcases she'd managed to cram full of everything important to her. With barely enough reprieve to give Charlie one last scratch behind the ears, it was time to go.

She thought of everything she was expected to give up for this plan to work. Her sense of home, the dog her father had given her for her eighth birthday, and, of course, any relationship with her own mother. Bitterly, she thought that between the two, Charlie was more likely to miss her. But she'd return in time. People kept assuring her of that. Time would make things better. Time would make her mother stronger, would give Zoey room to heal. It was the best plan they had. The plan for future happiness. The sentence binding her to her new life.

"Well . . . I know it's not the one you're used to, but we're nearly home," said Aunt Carol, though she'd been saying that since they first crossed into Connecticut. "I'm sure you'll love the place. Much more room than your old house, you know. Your new bedroom is twice the size of the one I saw when we picked you up. It's an old house with plenty of character, in some ways, maybe a little too—"

Aunt Carol's words trailed off, following another frustrated huff from Uncle Will.

"Oh, Will, I know you don't believe, but how else do you explain—well, I guess I won't say anymore and let Zoey make up her own mind. But I'm hopeful that I'll have someone to talk to about everything."

Zoey took a moment to try to work out what Aunt Carol was talking about. The house had too much personality? Wanting to have someone to talk to about it? She wasn't sure what either of those leading statements might mean. What she did know, however, was that if she wanted to find out, she would need to re-enter the conversation. Despite the boredom born from the nearly silent six-hour car ride, Zoey wasn't in the mood for continued conversation, and so, she let the comments hang in the air between them.

Seeming to recognize defeat, Aunt Carol let out a sigh and turned back in her seat, leaving Zoey free to be alone once more.

CHAPTER TWO

Rules

Despite the mingled sense of dread and apathy that she felt toward her new home, Zoey peered out through the inky blackness outside the car. Night had fallen several hours ago, and the car glided up a lampless street surrounded by houses on either side. It gave Zoey an impression that was eerie, yet peaceful. The brief glimpses that the sedan's headlights provided told Zoey just how far away from her old life she was.

She had always considered the two-bedroom home she'd grown up in to be fairly standard. It was the only thing she'd ever known. Most of her friends lived in similar houses, give or take a couple hundred square feet. What little she could see of the homes rising up on either side of her made her old house seem tiny by comparison.

With a muffled crunch of rain-soaked gravel, the car came to a stop in a darkened driveway. A set of motion-activated floodlights took the place of the car's headlights. Zoey's heart gave a nervous flutter as she took her first look at the place that would be her home for the foreseeable future.

Through the stark shadows cast by the floodlights, Zoey could see what her aunt had meant about her liking the place. It would be hard for anyone to not be at least a little impressed.

It was an old Victorian, with three stories of rich brown wood rising into the night sky, complete with a turret worthy of a teenage witch. While there was a modern touch here or there, the house looked as though it had fallen out of a grander era. She wouldn't be comfortable calling it a mansion exactly, but it was about as close as a place could get without crossing that threshold.

"Oh, it's good to be home," said aunt Carol from somewhere to Zoey's left, accompanied as always by the sound of clattering bracelets. "If you grab one of your suitcases I'm sure your uncle will be happy to take the other. Then we can get you all settled into your new room before we turn in for the night."

Not looking toward the huffy grunt that escaped her uncle, Zoey gave a curt nod and pulled one of her suitcases out of the back of the car. Following her aunt's lead, Zoey pulled half of everything she owned over an uneven cobbled path. Dense flowers flanked the path that led up toward the back of the house. A set of double doors with large, stained glass panes waited for them on the other end of a wooden patio. With the click of a lock and a blast of cool, sweet-smelling air, Aunt Carol pushed the doors open and strode inside. Once the lights flickered on, they revealed a grand kitchen, complete with a substantial floating island.

Zoey stepped inside, then, looking around, took a moment to work her way out of her well-worn Converse. She didn't think that tracking dirt through the room would get her new life off to a good start. Aunt Carol paid her own shoes no mind. She marched forward, her soft brown clogs beating out an even pace beneath her flowing wrap dress.

"No need to take your shoes off. I'm not much of a stickler for formalities like that, despite what the old place might lead you to believe," said Aunt Carol, flipping on lights as she walked deeper into the house.

Feeling that stopping to put her shoes back on would only make things more awkward, Zoey nodded and mumbled, "Alright," before shuffling forward.

"I'm afraid the full tour will have to wait until tomorrow. I'm sure you're excited to see the place, but after a drive like that, I think we could all do with some rest. Nighttime doesn't do the place justice anyway. It all looks much better with some nice cheerful sunshine."

Aunt Carol turned on her heel and waved her bony hand towards Zoey before making her way up a wide staircase. With a glance over her shoulder as she followed her aunt, Zoey confirmed what her ears had already picked up on. Uncle Will and her second suitcase weren't following their strange little procession. She could only assume that he was taking a break from the uncomfortable aura that poured in from all sides. He wasn't exactly subtle, and Zoey couldn't really blame him for it. She was a "troubled teen" with whom he didn't share any meaningful connection. Her presence in his life could hardly be expected to be a welcome one.

The thought gave her a moment's pause and in it a tiny spark of hope bubbled up inside her. She decided she had to give Aunt Carol at least some credit. She could easily reflect her husband's chilly disposition to Zoey's presence in her life. Quite to the contrary, it was obvious that she was making a sincere, if somewhat overzealous, attempt to make her feel welcome.

"There's a bathroom down the hall and to your left, the door on the right's a spare room. Down the hall from that's a little TV room that doesn't get used all that much, and your room's just over here," chirped Aunt Carol, snapping Zoey from her introspection.

Following Aunt Carol's hand, Zoey's eyes fell upon a four-panel door. It was stained a rich mahogany and was fitted with a brass handle, complete with quintessential keyhole. Her aunt pressed down on the handle and pushed open the door. There was a gentle click of a flipped switch, and a rounded overhead light flickered to life, bathing the room in a soft, white glow.

Like the rest of the house, her room was impressive. Her aunt had been right, it was at least twice as large as the one she had back home. The gleaming hardwood floor stood in a stark yet pleasant contrast to the cool gray walls, which were themselves lined with decorative, snow-white molding. A large bay window complete with a carpeted bench overlooked the front lawn. Curiously, a glittering, indigo dreamcatcher about the size of her head dangled from the center of this window. A small collection of glittering purple crystals lay in a neat pile on the center of the cushion beneath it.

"Well? Didn't I tell you that you'd like your room?" said Aunt Carol, correctly interpreting Zoey's silence.

"It's a lot nicer than my old room, that's for sure," replied Zoey, taking in the large four poster bed, which sat in pride of place atop a Persian rug against the same wall as the door.

"We can put your suitcases in here for now," said Aunt Carol, walking over to a heavy wooden door that swung open to reveal a narrow, walk-in closet. "I cleaned everything out for you. Feel free to put your things wherever you'd like. The hope chest at the foot of your bed is yours to use, too."

The hope chest in question was large enough that two people Zoey's size could fit curled up inside if they were so moved to. It was a solid, but beautifully worked thing, with carved vines and flowers arcing in graceful loops and swirls around the lower half. An ornamental brass latch hung around a square peg that held the mirror-smooth lid in place. Zoey could tell from the worn quality of it that it was old, though immaculately maintained. An object from Aunt Carol's past, or going back even further, a genuine family heirloom.

"Everything in here's so . . . fancy," mumbled Zoey, thinking how out of place her things would look in such a fine room.

"I don't know about that, but it is a lovely old house, isn't it? If it's missing one thing though, it's a bit of a youthful presence to help fill it up."

Not knowing how to react to such a flowery view of her presence, Zoey took a few tentative steps deeper into the room. It had been stripped bare, save for the furniture and a few touches here and there. There was a shoulder-height bookcase that sat on the wall opposite the bay window. It was devoid of all but a small collection of books that took up half of the top shelf. Glancing at the titles, she judged them to be self-help books with a largely new age leaning. *The Healing Power of Mother Earth* and *Manifesting Joy Through Meditation* stood out particularly to her.

Not wanting to think about how these specific volumes had been left in the room for her benefit, Zoey moved her mind toward her still-forming opinion of her aunt. The books, the crystals, her aunt's sunny disposition, and flowy, technicolor style of dress. Her aunt was a hippy, or at least someone who had enjoyed the '60s and hadn't quite found a way of letting them go.

"I guess I should go get my other suitcase and start unpacking," said Zoey, taking a few steps back toward the door.

Aunt Carol, beating her to the punch, shook her head. "Let me go see what's keeping your uncle. You just get settled and I'll send him up in a minute." Aunt Carol made to leave the room before giving a little jump. "Oh! I almost forgot." She reached deep into her pockets and produced a shining silver something that she thrust with a grin into Zoey's hands.

Surprised by the sudden gift, Zoey fumbled for a few moments before realizing what it was. A set of keys sat in her hand, strung through a shining silver hoop with a gaudy pink crystal that dangled from a short golden chain.

"Oh, uh, thanks . . ." said Zoey, unsure.

"I know this is all new to you, but I hope you'll make yourself right at home," replied Aunt Carol with a smile.

Before Zoey could respond, her aunt left the room with a whirl of her glittering pashmina. Zoey breathed a sigh of relief. Grateful to be away from her aunt and uncle for the first time in over nine hours, she tossed the keys inside her bedside table. She took a moment to give the room an appraising once-over. It didn't feel like home by any stretch of the imagination. But maybe that was a good thing? If this was supposed to be a fresh start, then different was probably best.

She made her way to her suitcase and got it set up to unpack. A moment later, she wished she hadn't. A framed picture sat atop a stack of folded t-shirts within. She had forgotten all about it. It had been a last minute addition, shoved hastily in moments before it had been time to go. The picture showed a tall woman with shoulder length auburn hair and wide, kind eyes and a powerfully built man with a toothy grin and a slightly crooked nose. They had their arms around an eleven year old Zoey at her elementary school graduation. A perfect moment captured forever behind a pane of glass.

She didn't know why she'd decided to take this painful reminder with her. She hated everything about the picture. Hated how much her parents she saw in her own smiling face. Her eyes were the same shade of brown as her mothers, as was her hair, though hers only came down to the nape of her neck. She had mercifully been spared her father's crooked nose, but saw him in her smile. Her parents had towered over her back then. Now she stood at the same height as her mom

Zoey blinked the haze from her eyes and shoved the picture along with the stack of t-shirts into her top dresser drawer. Before she could take anything else from her suitcase a shiver traveled up her spine. A pair of voices had risen from downstairs, muffled by the floor that divided them. They weren't exactly shouting, but they were raised in conflict. It was a sound she had come to know well over the last couple of years. It was the sound of people discussing her. Discussing what to do with her. Discussing what was wrong with her. It had been sounds like that which had led her here.

Doing her best to ignore the muffled spat, along with the pinpricks of gooseflesh now breaking out over her arms, Zoey forced her attention back to her suitcase. She took extra care to first choose an item, then imagine where it would look best before placing it there. Her movements were slow, methodical, focused. The voices downstairs faded into meaningless sound. It was just her in her new room, getting her things in order.

She continued on like this until the odd clutter of objects that made up the topmost layer of her suitcase had been placed in their new homes. Beneath this, her fingers came into contact with a collection of jeans.

Zoey was so deep into her self-imposed distraction that she didn't notice the presence behind her until a small cough hit her ears. She turned her gaze from the pair of jeans in her hands and up to her uncle looking down at her. Zoey sprang up off the floor so fast that it might have been electrified. Several seconds of silence passed between them, each one longer than the last.

Zoey's hand twitched as she tucked a strand of her chestnut bob behind her ear. "T-thanks for bringing up my suitcase. I was going to get it, but Aunt Carol said you would . . ." said Zoey, her sentence dropping off as the chill coming from her uncle sucked the air from the room.

"That's part of what I wanted to talk to you about," said her uncle, letting go of the suitcase to fold his arms across his chest. From his severe side-part to the dress pants and button-up that were still crisp and wrinkle-free, his stern demeanor remained unruffled even after the nine-hour car ride. "My wife has certain ideas of what's best for you, and as much as I love her, I can't say that I agree. She's the kind of person who sees the best in everyone, to the point that, a lot of the time, I think she sees things that aren't actually there. We both agree that this is going to be your home for as long as your mother needs to get her act together. But it will not be a free pass for you to go on missing school and causing trouble."

Zoey was about to return her uncle's unkindness with a great deal of colorful interest before she caught herself. He was the adult here. She could sling all the angry words she wanted, and he'd still be the one with all the power. More than that, to snap at the first unkind thing he said to her would only prove his opinion of her right. She wasn't about to give anyone that satisfaction. Instead, she took a slow, deep breath and, making sure not to look away from his steel-gray eyes, hitched a smile on her face.

"I'm not going to cause any trouble. I know I'm on thin ice. I'll tread carefully."

A look of something satisfyingly similar to annoyance flashed across her uncle's face. In the time it took Zoey to give herself a smug, mental pat on the back, however, his expression reverted to its usual stern state.

"I hope for your sake that's true." He unfolded his arms, his expression severe as ever. "Look, it's late and we're all tired, but we need to get some ground rules laid down. Your grandma told your aunt and I that you have a habit of staying up 'till all hours of the night and that stops here. Bedtime is eleven. That means in bed, lights out, and going to sleep. No reading, no texting, no listening to music. If you can't fall asleep at a regular time, it just means you're not doing enough in the day to get yourself tired. So to help with that, you're expected to be up and out of bed by eight every morning, school or not. I've also got a list of chores you'll be responsible for. Are we clear?"

With a brief glance toward the small cluster of amethysts by the window and a well-suppressed smirk, Zoey gave a nod before replying, "Crystal."

A look of what Zoey could only assume was consternation at her lack of protest crossed her uncle's face. He opened his mouth as if to add more to his list, but instead, furrowed his brow and left the room with a curt "Goodnight."

Zoey turned back to her suitcase and shrugged. Aunt Carol was right, unpacking could wait for the morning. She picked out a pair of shorts and an oversized t-shirt, then zipped up her suitcases and pulled them into the closet. She let the smile she'd been repressing spread across her face as she began changing. She knew her uncle wasn't bluffing. Her life was set to be more than a little strict going forward. But denying him what she was sure he thought was going to be a shouting match was, sadly, the most fun she'd had in a long time.

CHAPTER THREE

Tea

A clipped shout and the sensation of falling. That was how Zoey found herself hurled back to wakefulness. She sat stark upright in bed, breath ragged, body shining with a thin sheen of sweat. Heart hammering out of her chest, her eyes darted rapidly around the near pitch-black room, trying to make sense of what she was seeing. The unfamiliar bedding, the strange proportions of the room, none of it did anything to calm the surge of terror coursing through her. Her hands gripped at the covers, her legs tensed. Every nerve in her body was ready to send her tearing away from the danger that pressed in from all sides.

She had all but let the covers fly when her desperately searching gaze fell upon a faint glimmer of purple. A trace of misty moonlight had fallen over the small pile of amethysts resting beneath the bay window. The world came out of its cruel focus of her panic, latching on to the logic the new age nonsense provided. This was her bedroom in Aunt Carol's house. She remembered getting into bed, snuggling down under the covers, and then . . .

Zoey let out a long, frustrated sigh. Though it had already begun to fade from the forefront of her mind, she now remembered a handful of the details of the dream that had woken her. She and her dad in the old family car. The sound of laughter. The warmth of her father's love. Screeching tires. Then shattering glass and an impact. It was an oldie but a goodie as far as her nightmares went. She didn't know why her mind insisted on replaying it. She hadn't even been in the car with her father when it happened.

"Useless thing," grumbled Zoey, eyes locked on the dreamcatcher by her window.

She knew there wasn't any use in her trying to go back to sleep, not for a couple of hours anyway. With her uncle's words echoing in her mind, she pulled her phone off the bedside table and flipped it open. It was ten past midnight. She hadn't even been afforded a full hour's sleep before being rocketed back to an all too uncomfortable wakefulness. It wasn't as though the reoccurrence of the dream shocked her, but some part of her had hoped that things might be different in her new setting. At least for a while.

As much as her last interaction with her uncle had been something of a victory, she knew better than to think that meant what he said didn't stand. She had taken his list of rules seriously, but she figured she had at least a couple of strikes before there'd be any major consequences. In her current state, desperately wanting to get out of her room and away from her nightmare, that thought was enough. She slid out of bed and crept toward the door.

She had all but pressed down on the handle when she clocked the chill air running over her exposed arms and legs. Whatever AC unit her aunt and uncle had was doing serious work. While the air was soothing to her nightmare-hot skin, she'd be shivering in minutes in her current clothes.

Zoey crept across her bedroom and opened the closet door as quietly as she could. After a moment's rummaging, she produced a pale green hoodie that she pulled on over her nightshirt. Significantly snugglier than she was before, Zoey walked back to her bedroom door and, holding her breath, eased it open.

Zoey squinted in the darkness. She realized she didn't know where her aunt and uncle's bedroom was. It was possible it was on the same floor as hers, but the staircase that brought them up from the first floor continued on to another story. Accepting that venturing out of her bedroom was going to carry some risk either way, Zoey headed downstairs.

Despite her still restless and now nervous state, Zoey took in a deep, relaxing breath. Even through all the anxiety it caused her, she had come to appreciate aspects of the dead of night. There was something tranquil about the heavy darkness outside, like a weighty blanket on a cold winter's night. It carried a sense of stillness and solitude with it, as though the night itself was a place for her alone to enjoy.

The trip to the kitchen was less troublesome than Zoey thought it might have been. A couple of the floorboards gave slight squeaks of protest, and the fourth step down groaned so loudly that she skipped over it. Once on the ground floor, she made her way to the kitchen, thankful for the layers of wood separating her from her aunt and uncle's bedroom.

It took her a few tries, one involving a cupboard full of pots and pans that screeched in complaint when opened, but Zoey found a cabinet full of cups. She pulled a tall glass from among its brothers and filled it up under the icy gush of water from the sink. She took a long, steady pull from the glass and sighed. The cool liquid spread its comfort out from her throat and into the very core of her being, driving away the last lingering remnants of her nightmare-fueled panic.

With continued care to make as little noise as possible, Zoey pulled out a chair surrounding a scrubbed wooden table and sat down. She took small sips of the chilly water and steered her thoughts away from continued anxiety, focusing on the stillness and quiet of the night. Try as she might, her mind refused to empty.

If she was back at home, the next move would be to try her mom's cell phone. There would be a slim chance that she'd answer. If she did, her mother would give either a vague forecast for her return home or drunkenly reprimand Zoey over not being in bed so late on a school night. More often than not, it would instead be a torturous series of rings followed by her mom's voice telling her to please leave a message. After that, she'd settle down on the couch with Charlie, the one guardian who hadn't abandoned her. She'd pick out a good book or flip on the TV, ready to while away the hours until her body calmed down enough for sleep, or her mom came home.

As none of those actions were advisable in her current situation, she stayed in her chair, taking small, calming sips of water. It didn't take long for slim tendrils of anxiety to wrap themselves back around her mind, though. She knew the stars and moon behind the scattered clouds outside were the same as the ones she knew from back home, and yet the dark and stillness of the night felt different in her new setting. The gentle whir of air being pumped through the house, the rustle of tree limbs outside, even the sound of her own breathing were like jarring notes in an otherwise familiar song.

Counting on the sturdy layers of wood between her and her aunt's bedroom to muffle her footsteps, Zoey pulled away from the table and wandered out of the kitchen. She was immediately met with two options: a door similar to the one that led to her bedroom to her right, and a narrow, shabbier one to her left. Opting for the left, Zoey pulled it open and was greeted with a gentle blast of musty air. The faint illumination provided by the spotty rays of moonlight from outside was enough to show the first couple of steps of a lopsided staircase. It descended at an ominous angle, down into a thick, inky blackness. Deciding that she had seen enough horror movies to know better, Zoey closed the door with a click and headed through the door opposite.

She tiptoed through a dining room with a substantial table at the center, surrounded by six hardback wooden chairs. From there, she strolled into the largest room she'd seen so far in the house. Zoey supposed if it were owned by other people it would be the family room, complete with couch, chairs, and television. Instead, the room was a bizarre split that was at odds with both the rest of the house and itself.

On one side of the room sat a stubby table. Every inch of its surface was covered in an array of glittering gems, half-melted candles, bundles of dried herbs, leather pouches, sticks of half-burned incense, and thin metal trinkets etched with intricate, swirling designs. A spherical wicker chair hung suspended from the ceiling above a garish mandala rug. There was zero doubt that this part of the room was of her Aunt Carol's design.

The other half was much more orderly and, as far as Zoey could see through the darkness, lacked any of the new age trinkets that so dominated the other. A grand piano with a sleek and shining finish so black that it stood out against the haze of night, took up most of the space. She thought for a moment that the piano must belong to her uncle, but she couldn't see him doing anything as joyful or expressive as making music. Resisting the temptation to lift the key lid and plunk out a couple of notes, Zoey strolled out of the strangely split room. She found herself back in the hallway that led to the kitchen.

Across the hall from her was an office, illuminated by the lights shining on several electronic devices. A click and muffled shuffling came from the kitchen. Zoey jumped in place and quickly stifled a cry of surprise. With the most feline steps she could manage, she crept toward the kitchen. A warm, flickering light was dancing somewhere from within, sending strange shadows dancing up and down the part of the wall that Zoey could see.

Getting as close to the door frame as she dared, Zoey craned her neck to the side and breathed a sigh of relief. Her aunt was sitting at the kitchen table facing away from the door, dressed in a fluffy purple bathrobe. Her long flyaway hair was bundled neatly in a glittering wrap that was dotted with silver and gold crescent moons.

Zoey couldn't help but laugh to herself. In the handful of seconds since she heard the click of what she now realized was the stove, her mind had imagined any number of possibilities. Her uncle sitting in place of her aunt or some dark, nightmarish creature prowling through the kitchen had both flicked to the forefront of her mind. Given those options, her aunt enjoying a late-night cup of tea was about as benign an outcome as she could have hoped for.

She considered her options from her hidden spot in the hallway. As much as she was unknown, Zoey thought there was little risk of Aunt Carol exploding at her being out of bed past curfew. Sneaking back to her room risked her making a sound and alerting her aunt. Then she'd wind up in the same situation, just with some extra awkwardness thrown in on top of everything. Zoey took a sip from the glass still held loosely in her hand and stepped into the kitchen with a tentative "Aunt Carol?"

Her aunt gave an almost imperceptible jump, and without turning, replied, "Zoey, I thought you might be up and about." The smile on her lips was evident.

"Oh, uh, sorry. I couldn't sleep. I hope I didn't wake you."

"Not at all, dear. I'd gotten into bed a while ago and realized my mind was a little too busy to turn off for the evening. It's not uncommon. I've got my own little ritual for it, which I have to admit, I often find myself enjoying," said Aunt Carol.

Zoey's body began to relax as she sat down at the table across from her aunt. "I know what you mean. I don't like it when I can't sleep. But being the only person awake, sometimes it feels like . . ."

"Like you're in your own little world?" supplied her aunt, still smiling.

Zoey nodded, somewhere between touched and impressed. This was the first time an adult had ever been on anything resembling the same page as her about something like this. "You said you thought it was me. Did you hear me walking around?"

"Oh, no, you were quiet as a kitty cat," said Aunt Carol. She reached her arm out and with one of her long, bony fingers tapped a faint, dark ring on the scrubbed table. "I've been accused of seeing things before, but water rings have never been among them."

"I'm sorry, I didn't think a—"

"No need to apologize. It's a table, it's meant to have bumps and bruises—it gives it character. I doubt this one will stick around, but if it does, it will just be a pleasant reminder of the first night you spent in the house."

"Do you really want a stain to remember me by?" asked Zoey, unsure if Aunt Carol was putting her on or not.

Aunt Carol traced her fingers along the wood grain on the table, a misty smile on her face. "Like I said, imperfections give things character. This knick over here," she continued, indicating a deep slash about an inch in length, "is from the first time I ever made my own pickled beets. Those little tubers are a lot tougher than they look and the knife got away from me. And this spot is from just earlier this year. I had a friend over for fondue. There was cheese, there was wine, and just a little bit of a fire."

Aunt Carol's trip down kitchen table memory lane was interrupted as a high, tinny whistle filled the room. With surprising speed and grace, Aunt Carol stood up and took the kettle off the heat before its shrieking reached its peak. Without so much as a look toward the cupboards, she opened one up and produced two glazed clay mugs. "Tea, dear? I've got all kinds, but I'm thinking a nice classic chamomile for tonight," asked Aunt Carol, producing a tall tin and two small infusers from another cupboard.

"Sure, I'll try some tea."

Aunt Carol bustled around the kitchen, deftly opening cupboards and retrieving objects from inside with a series of soft clatters. A minute later, she was shuffling back to the well-worn table with two steaming mugs of tea in hand. She set them down before turning back to the countertop. Next second she was at the table holding a small, flowered plate with several cookies in one hand and a small jar in the other.

"I figured if we're going to do midnight tea, we might as well do it right," said Aunt Carol, picking up a cookie from the plate and taking a healthy-sized bite. "These sugar cookies came out pretty well if I do say so myself. Everyone seems to like them, but they don't disappear quite as fast as the chocolate chips."

Zoey took a cookie and gave it a tentative bite. "Pretty well" was a bit of an understatement in her mind. A light sugary sweetness spread across her tongue, tempered with rich creamy butter, just the right hint of vanilla, and something else that Zoey couldn't quite place. Whether it was because it had been so long since she'd had anything as picket fence as a homemade cookie, or because Aunt Carol had a bit of a knack with flour and sugar, Zoey wasn't sure, but she reached out and set another cookie on the saucer with her tea.

"So, you gave yourself a little tour of the house? Just down here, or did you take a look around the second floor, too?"

"Just down here. I didn't want to wake you or Uncle Will, especially since I don't think I'm supposed to be out of bed this late," replied Zoey, setting down her half-eaten cookie and stirring her tea with the infuser.

Aunt Carol pursed her lips slightly, still holding the half-eaten cookie between her thumb and forefinger. "I love my husband dearly, but he's got certain ideas about things that I just don't agree with."

"Ideas about curfews? Or about taking in messed-up teens?" asked Zoey.

"A little bit of both, to be honest. Not that he isn't in agreement about having you here . . . It's just, he sees things as black and white most of the time, while I tend to deal in shades of gray. For example, I hope you won't mind me saying that I don't think for a moment that you're all that messed up. I think the word grieving would be a better fit, or maybe just hurting, if we want to get right down to the core of things."

Zoey's cheeks flushed as a hazy blur pushed in at the edges of her vision. Staring determinately at the mug of tea in front of her, she blinked away the unexpected wetness in her eyes. She couldn't remember the last time someone had spoken out against the idea of her being some willfully awful kid.

While Zoey appreciated her aunt's sympathetic take on the situation, she couldn't begin to think of how to respond to what she said. Instead, she gave her tea another stir, eyes fixed on the swirling, steaming liquid. It took several long seconds before Aunt Carol seemed to decide that Zoey wasn't going to respond, the silence broken only by the soft tinkling of the infuser against the mug.

"But we don't need to talk about that right now. Just know that he and I have talked, and I'm pretty sure I've got him convinced to ease up on the whole sleep situation. I agree that we need to get you on a better schedule before school starts, but that's over a month away. I don't see why you shouldn't be free to enjoy the summer and keep some off-color hours every now and then, at least until we get closer to school starting."

"Thanks for that," replied Zoey, looking up at Aunt Carol. "It's not like I really want to be awake so late, it was just . . . hard to fall asleep at my house sometimes."

"I can certainly understand that, given everything you've been through. Look at me, plenty older than you, no real strife in my life to speak of, and here I am eating cookies in my kitchen well past midnight. But enough about that, I'm curious since you've looked around a bit. What do you think of the house?"

"Well, I haven't seen it all," began Zoey, taking the steeper out and wrapping her hands around the mug, taking in its warmth, "but it's nice, and big. A lot bigger than my house."

"Did you notice anything odd at all?" asked Aunt Carol, taking the lid off the small jar and stirring honey into her tea with a tiny silver spoon.

Zoey scrunched up her face at the question. The house was larger than hers, a little different to be sure, but odd? "I don't know about odd, but the, uh, piano and meditation room stuck out. Is that all you or is it sort of half yours, half Uncle Will's?"

Zoey wasn't sure if she was imagining it, but she thought a look of something like disappointment had flashed across her aunt's face for the briefest of moments.

"Oh, that's all me," replied Aunt Carol before giving a small jump. "I can't believe I didn't mention it. Sometimes I don't know how I get by in this world, as much as I forget. I teach piano for a little something to do while Will's at work."

"He still works?" asked Zoey. She had assumed that they were retired, given the comfortable life they seemed to live.

"Don't get me started on that," said Aunt Carol, a look of good-natured exasperation visible on her face. "He could have retired a couple of years ago if he wanted, but he likes to think the firm can't get by without him. Not that he isn't useful to them. He helped build that place from the ground up, after all. I think he's just having some trouble passing the torch."

"Change is a bit hard sometimes."

"Yes, but some changes are for the best. Even ones we think might not be in the moment can turn out to be absolutely fabulous in hindsight," said Aunt Carol thoughtfully. "But, I got in the way of your answer. Do you like the piano? Some of my students are pretty talented, so you should have some nice pieces to listen to. A few of them are quite young, though, so I'm afraid you're going to put up with some sloppy scales and choppy renditions of "Twinkle Twinkle Little Star" if you stay in the house while I teach."

"I think the piano is pretty, and those kids would have a leg up on me, so no judgment here."

"If you'd like, I could start giving you lessons. I don't like to toot my own horn, but I've produced some fine students in the end, and I can't see why you'd be any different."

"It could be fun to try, I guess. But the last instrument I played was the recorder back in grade four," said Zoey, remembering with some fondness the shrieking plastic instrument she and her classmates had all been taught to play.

"You know, a lot of my students come to me with even less experience than that, so you've got a leg up already."

Zoey gave a small nod, and after stirring her own spoonful of honey into the tea, mirrored her aunt in taking a sip. The sweet, floral liquid coaxed a small, satisfied sigh out of her as she drank. She took the moment of relaxation to clock how different her situation was from only a few short days ago. Chatty as Aunt Carol was, it wasn't in a bad way. For the past year, it felt like every adult was talking at her, rather than to her. This was the first genuine conversation she'd had with someone over fifteen since all the issues between her and her mother started.

The two of them sat in silence for a while after that, taking bites of cookies and small sips of tea. As odd as it should have been to sit there, having tea in the middle of the night with a near stranger, it felt strangely natural. Tea and cookies were a lot better than waking up in a dead sweat, alone in a house with nothing but Charlie and the TV to keep her from spiraling.

Whether it was the tea or the company, Zoey's eyelids were growing heavy in a way that often took most of the night to achieve after a bad dream. Stifling a yawn, she glanced over her shoulder at the stove's clock and was shocked to see that it had been less than an hour since she'd woken up.

Undeceived by her suppressed yawn, Aunt Carol glanced at the clock herself. "If you go to bed now, you'll probably be able to get some good sleep and still wake up at a decent time."

Feeling that Aunt Carol might be onto something, Zoey sipped the last of her tea and stood up from the table. She had taken a couple of steps toward the stairs when she paused, hand on the empty door frame. "Aunt Carol?" she asked tentatively.

"Yes, Zoey dear?"

"I, uh, just wanted to say thank you. For- you know," Zoey fumbled with the word "everything," before "the tea," rushed out in its place.

"Oh, it was my pleasure. I enjoyed the company."

Zoey had once again started toward the stairs when a soft exclamation from her aunt pulled her up short.

"Before I forget. You're welcome to have as many cookies as you want, but could you be sure to remember just how many you have and let me know? I like to keep track."

Zoey paused with one foot still in the air, her sleepy mind trying to make sense of why her aunt would care about something like that. Assuming that there must be a rational root to her question, and wanting to get up to bed, Zoey gave a hesitant "Sure" before heading back upstairs.

Shuffling back to her room, Zoey suppressed another yawn with the back of her hand. Strange as Aunt Carol was, Zoey decided it was, at large, a good kind of strange. It probably worked in her favor that her aunt was a bit of an airy-fairy person. It was good that she was the type to make her own pickles and, for whatever reason, count the number of cookies that people ate. There weren't many people in their sixties who'd take in fourteen-year-olds. There were even fewer who'd be half as welcoming as she'd been so far.

Still warm from the tea and conversation, Zoey slipped off her hoodie and curled up under the covers. Then, for the first time in a long time, she drifted off into a deep, dreamless sleep.

CHAPTER FOUR

Signs

Zoey's eyes fluttered open as she left the unfamiliar embrace of a good night's sleep. With the quality of the light now spilling through the broad bay window, noon couldn't be too far away. She rubbed some of the sleep from her eyes. When was the last time she'd felt so rested after a night that included a nightmare-induced wake-up?

The sound of morning birds brought a smile to Zoey's face. She propped herself up on her elbow and flipped her cellphone open. Her heart fluttered. She had an unread message from her mom. Her thumb hovered over the button to open it but faltered at the point of follow-through. A voice whispered in her head.

What if she's saying she's sorry? Maybe she wants you back home.

Even if the message contained such a plea, and she knew it didn't, she wouldn't accept it. A small, gnarled part of her heart wanted to hurt her. She wanted her mom to want her back in her life, for the simple pleasure of telling her no. Let her mom be the one to spend sleepless nights with a racing mind and lonely heart.

Tossing her phone from both her hand and her thoughts, Zoey sank down into the plush mattress. An unexpected lightness filled her heart at the thought of the day ahead. It was sure to be weird, and maybe a bit awkward, but it felt as though it might be freeing. There would be no arguing with her mom. No stab of pain as she watched one of her former heroes fall apart with each passing day. She didn't know if she'd go so far as to say the day was bound to be good. But it would at least be different, and that was good enough for her.

Zoey glanced towards the books she'd unpacked last night. It would be all too easy for her to curl up and lose herself in one of the worlds they contained. Instead, she planted her hands against her bed and forced herself up. She'd believed Aunt Carol when she'd said Uncle Will's rules wouldn't be a factor just yet, but she didn't think that lazing around in bed all day was in her best interest.

She let her legs dangle over the side of the bed and listened for signs of activity in the house. Aside from the faint murmur of a TV playing somewhere nearby, the place sounded much as it had last night. Taking the lack of grumbling voices as a good sign, Zoey got out of bed with a content sigh. It didn't take her long to find where the sounds of the TV were coming from. Across the hall stood a mirror image of her bedroom door. The muffled strings of music and chattering voices were coming from the other side. Hoping it would lead to Aunt Carol rather than her uncle, she gave a soft knock.

"Aunt Carol? Uncle Will?"

After waiting several moments with no answer, Zoey pushed the door open. The room inside was smaller than any of the others she'd been in so far. It comprised little more than an overstuffed, cream-colored couch and a large entertainment center housing a boxy black TV. It was tuned to some colorful kids' show. It was one that she recognized from the weekends of her past. She sat down and focused. She smiled as remembered her parents having to tell her to turn the volume down pretty much every Saturday morning. Zoey grinned and turned the sound up several notches.

It was one of those shows that revolved around the power of friendship. How friendship and teamwork were enough to overcome any problem. It was something that she'd taken to heart in her younger years. Life, as it turned out, was a lot more complicated. Friendship didn't manifest sparkles or lasers that solved your problems. Few issues could be solved in a twenty-minute span, not including commercial breaks. She let herself believe in the saccharine words coming out of the TV for the rest of the episode, however.

When the credits rolled and an excited voice told Zoey to stay tuned for more thrilling episodes of all her favorite shows, she clicked off the TV. Her stomach growled. Thinking of at least grabbing another of Aunt Carol's cookies, Zoey heeded the call of hunger and headed for the stairs. The fourth step gave the loud and proper groan that she'd denied it the previous night. She set a course straight for the kitchen, hoping there would be something there for her to eat. She stopped short of pulling the fridge open. The idea felt weird to her, going through someone else's fridge without asking first. Much as Aunt Carol insisted she make herself at home, a single night's sleep was hardly enough time for Zoey to stop feeling like a guest.

"Aunt Carol? Uncle Will?" she called again, more loudly than she had upstairs.

With no reply to be heard, Zoey's heart gave an involuntary flutter. Cursing herself, she strode through the first floor, taking the same path as last night. It was the middle of the day. She had seen Aunt Carol just last night, and to be quite honest, she didn't want to see Uncle Will.

There was no reason for her heart to be racing like this. She made her way through the entire first floor with no sign of either of her relations.

The tightness in her chest was beginning to demand that she go check out the other floors when a door opened and closed from somewhere at the back of the house. Flush with embarrassment, Zoey headed back to the kitchen and was greeted by the sight of Aunt Carol. She was wearing a flowing green wrap dress, accompanied again by a great many beads and bangles up and down her arms. She was peeling a pair of flowery gardening gloves off her bony hands when she spotted Zoey.

"Zoey dear, I was just about to come and see if you were up," said Aunt Carol from beneath her ludicrous sun hat.

"Hey, sorry for sleeping in," said Zoey, the apology slipping out on reflex. "I've actually been up for a bit."

"No need to apologize. Yesterday was exhausting," replied Aunt Carol as she removed her floppy sun hat. "I was just thinking about lunch myself if you wanted to join me."

"Lunch sounds good to me," said Zoey, the empty feeling in her stomach overcoming any sense of awkwardness she might have felt over the offer.

A quarter of an hour's work and chatter later, she and Aunt Carol were sitting down at the kitchen table, enjoying their lunch of soup and sandwiches. Zoey wasn't sure if Aunt Carol was trying to impress her or if this was just the way she and Uncle Will lived, but everything about lunch was an upgrade to what she was used to. The fanciest form that either of those offerings took at Zoey's house was something along the lines of ham and cheese with the "good bread" and chunky-style soup.

Those old standbys felt shabby compared to what Aunt Carol had whipped up. Thin slices of tender roast beef and crisp leaves of Butter lettuce piled high on crusty French bread and spread with a hint of horseradish. The soup was a hearty vegetable concoction with a rich tomato base that, though she'd never say it out loud, felt like a warm hug with every spoonful. Aunt Carol informed her between mouthfuls that it was not only homemade, but she'd grown most of the vegetables herself.

"So, do you have any idea what you're going to do with the rest of the day?" asked Aunt Carol as they reached the end of their meal.

"I guess just finish unpacking then hang out around the house, if that's OK," said Zoey, swallowing her last spoonful of soup.

"That sounds like a fine plan to me. I've got a couple of my younger students coming by today, so it's probably best you be at least a floor away from that," replied Aunt Carol with a tinkling laugh.

Zoey returned her aunt's laugh and, after thanking her for the delicious lunch, headed back upstairs. As she passed by the closed door to the TV room, she paused for a moment. She could hear the sounds of muffled voices and faint strings of music. She was almost certain that she'd turned the TV off before she'd headed downstairs. Sure enough, when she pushed open the door, the TV was on, still fixed to the same kid-friendly channel. She grabbed the remote off the couch and pressed the volume button. As she had thought, it was lower than where she remembered leaving it.

Blaming it on an old, unfamiliar TV on the fritz, Zoey clicked it off before tossing the remote back down on the couch. After pausing for several seconds to make sure that the TV was well and truly off, Zoey headed back to her room.

She spent the next hour emptying her overstuffed suitcases, scattering their contents throughout her room as pleasingly as she could. She was right when she'd thought her things would look a little weird in their new setting. Somehow antique hope chests and Persian rugs didn't go with crinkled band posters and stacks of pirated CDs. In the same vein, the small collection of horror and dark fantasy novels she'd thought to bring along felt more than a little out of place among the new age volumes that Aunt Carol had left out for her.

Sometime in the last fifteen minutes of the room's redecoration, sounds of Aunt Carol's first lesson began floating their way throughout the house. Zoey thought that Aunt Carol might have been right after all. She was sure she could have done a better job than the person who was currently putting fingers to keys. The tiny feeling of superiority didn't last long. There was every chance in the world that the student in question was somewhere in the single-digit age range.

With her room looking as good as it was likely to, Zoey grabbed her well-worn copy of *Carrie* and flopped down onto her four-poster bed. She couldn't remember where she'd left off when she'd last picked up the tattered, dog-eared novel. Not one to lament reading a classic over again, Zoey flipped to the beginning and did her best to lose herself in the world within the pages.

Carrie hadn't even used her powers for the first time when a loud creak pulled Zoey back to reality. It had come somewhere between choppy attempts at whatever song Aunt Carol was trying to work her student through, or she was sure she wouldn't have heard it.

"Hello?" Zoey asked, sitting up a little straighter, her ears listening hard for a reply.

No reply came, though Zoey was almost sure that she'd heard a couple of softer creaks before the piano started back up again. Zoey slid out of bed and poked her head out of her room, looking up and down the empty hallway.

"Uncle Will?" she called again, a little more loudly now that the music had resumed.

Zoey followed the lack of reply over toward the stairs and was greeted by nothing but air between her and the first landing. Frowning, Zoey walked down the first three stairs and, with her mind focused on the sound she'd heard, pressed her foot down on the fourth. There was no doubt. The pained groan it gave was what she'd heard from her bedroom.

Sure that there was a logical explanation, Zoey continued on downstairs and crossed the kitchen. She peered through one of the stained glass windows at the back door and could make out one very empty driveway. Either Uncle Will had come home, sprinted from the house, and sped away like a maniac, or the sound hadn't come from him. Zoey stood there listening to the distressed strains of music coming from the other room, playing with the thought of asking Aunt Carol about what she'd heard.

Excuse me, Aunt Carol, but the TV was on earlier when I thought I turned it off and then there was a creaking sound. Do you know what that's about?

Zoey scoffed. If it sounded that stupid in her head, she could only imagine how utterly absurd it would sound out loud. Sometimes houses creaked and groaned. This house was a lot older than hers, so it made sense that it would make unfamiliar sounds. Even if it wasn't an ambient creak, what did she think that meant the alternative was?

Thinking that maybe she should switch to *Goosebumps* since she was acting like a scared little kid, Zoey headed back upstairs to grab her book. She told herself she was taking her little reading session outside because it was such a beautiful day. As she skipped the fourth step on her way downstairs, however, she couldn't bring herself to believe that.

Zoey whiled away the rest of Aunt Carol's lesson sitting on an old porch swing out at the front of the house. The quaint little seat presented Zoey with a pleasant view of the sleepy street. It was a little hard to see the other houses from her spot due to the vast amount of plant life that surrounded them. Each magnificent house was bordered by towering trees and either well-manicured hedges or various kinds of flowering shrubs. The greenery that surrounded Aunt Carol and Uncle Will's house fell into the latter. Zoey thought she sensed Aunt Carol's influence in the rhubarb-colored roses that covered the border between the front lawn and the sidewalk.

With the distractions of her new surroundings, Zoey had made little headway in her book by the time the lesson was over. A small boy who looked to be about eight walked out the front door shortly after the sounds of the piano stopped. She could tell from his expression that he hadn't expected to find anyone else on the porch. Zoey remembered feeling that way when she was the boy's age. Back then, anyone over the age of twelve had been as good as an adult to her.

A few moments after the boy disappeared from sight, the piano started back up. The notes that flowed out into the glorious day surrounding Zoey were so unlike the choppy jumble preceding them that she had trouble believing they were coming from the same instrument. The piece Aunt Carol had chosen started soft and simple. It grew in depth as the notes poured on, and soon Zoey sat adrift in a sea of sound that she couldn't quite describe.

Her book forgotten on the swing, Zoey walked back into the house, careful not to make a sound and risk stopping the performance. Something welled up inside Zoey as she stood in the hallway, the richness of the piece no longer tempered by layers of wood and plaster. It was hopeful, yet somehow sorrowful at the same time. The music was without her and kept her grounded in the moment, but it drew her inward, lost in a sea of emotion. Memories of better times, of wistful days she'd thought long forgotten, all bubbled up in her as the song went on.

Zoey had never given the piano much thought before. Classical music, as a whole, struck her as far too serious and stuffy. The music she liked came with a good beat and catchy lyrics. Though there were no words to accompany her aunt's piece, she thought the notes sang.

By the time the song was over, a strange heaviness had settled in Zoey's chest. She wasn't sure if she wished the song could have gone on longer, or was glad that it was over.

"What was that song called?" asked Zoey, walking into the piano room.

Aunt Carol started and turned around, her look of shock softening when she saw Zoey.

"Oh, Zoey dear, you snuck up on me there," said Aunt Carol, her hand patting her chest.

"I'm sorry," replied Zoey, only now remembering that she'd taken extra care to remain silent when she came back inside.

"It's alright. I was starting to droop a bit and that did me better than a shot of espresso."

Zoey let out an awkward chuckle and walked further into the room. "Well, I'm glad I could be of service."

"So I take it you liked the song?" asked Aunt Carol, plunking out a handful of the notes that made up the melody with her gaze half fixed on Zoey.

"Yeah. It was really beautiful, but sort of sad, too."

"Now that you mention it, it was an odd choice for such a cheerful day," said Aunt Carol. "It's called 'Clair de Lune' by Debussy."

"What's it about?" asked Zoey, hoping for some clarity on the feelings it brought up in her.

"Well, I suppose the only one who really knew that is Debussy, and he's long gone." Aunt Carol continued playing out bits of the melody with her right hand. "Instead of guessing at what it's about, can I ask how it made you feel?"

Zoey opened and closed her mouth a few times, finding no words to say. Aunt Carol knew a lot more about music than she did, and she didn't want to say anything stupid. More than that, though, she wasn't sure how the piece made her feel.

"*Clair de Lune* means 'Moonlight' in French," continued Aunt Carol. "So, it always reminds me of those drizzly evenings where the clouds don't quite cover the moon. Where everything is still and fresh, waiting for a new day to dawn. thinking you might want some lessons?"

"Would it be ok if I sort of just played around with it on my own for a bit?" asked Zoey, thankful for the slight shift in the topic.

"You're welcome to play the piano as much as you'd like. Just don't take any food or drinks near it and make sure your hands are clean before you play."

"Thank you," replied Zoey. "I promise to wash my hands before I even think about touching it."

"Since you're interested, let me get you a couple of beginner books. I'm not sure how far you'd get without at least some basics."

Before Zoey could protest, Aunt Carol had already risen from her seat. She flipped open the piano bench and rummaged around before producing a sizable book titled *Adult All-In-One Course*. With a genuine smile and bustling of beads, Aunt Carol thrust the book toward Zoey.

"That's a great place for anyone your age to start, I'd say. If you need any help with anything in it though, just let me know. I'd be absolutely thrilled to help."

Zoey was saved the necessity of answering by a series of swift, gentle knocks on the front door. Aunt Carol strode off to answer the knocks, giving Zoey time to scamper out of the piano room and back upstairs.

She'd only just gotten back inside her bedroom and shut the door behind her when music filled the house again.

Zoey flung the book onto her bed before falling down beside it. She wasn't sure how, but she couldn't shake the feeling that she'd just been assigned homework, and during summer break at that. Strings of broken scales floated up from the lesson going on downstairs. She shrugged and held the book out in front of her with both arms. Thinking there were any number of worse things to be stuck doing over the summer, she flipped to the first page. Between the music and trying to make sense of the first bit of sheet music she'd seen since fourth grade, Zoey didn't even hear the groaning creek that came from the stairs outside her room.

CHAPTER FIVE

Séance

Zoey was midway through the copy of *Carrie* that she'd retrieved from outside when there came a knock at her bedroom door. Setting her book aside, she turned down the volume on the mix CD she'd chosen to accompany her reading and pulled the door open. She was unsurprised to see Aunt Carol on the other side. What did surprise her was the odd, anxious expression on her face.

"Zoey dear, sorry to bother you. I just had a question I wanted to ask," said Aunt Carol, her words carrying with them a sense of urgency Zoey hadn't heard before.

"Uh, sure," replied Zoey, her mind immediately trying to figure out what she could have done to cause Aunt Carol's anxious state. "Is everything ok?"

"Everything's fine, maybe better than fine. I think. If you didn't take them then that means I was right."

"Aunt Carol?"

"I know this must sound strange, but I need to check with you. Did you have any cookies since last night?"

Feeling both confused and a little annoyed that she'd let Aunt Carol get her worked up about sugar cookies of all things, Zoey gave her head a shake. "No, the only food I had today was the soup and sandwiches we had at lunch."

Something like a look of triumph flickered across Aunt Carol's face before transforming into an expression of nervous excitement. Walking into Zoey's room, Aunt Carol sat down on the edge of the bed and began fiddling with one of the glittering rings on her index finger.

"Zoey, I know you haven't even been here a full day yet, but have you noticed anything strange since you moved in? Anything at all."

Zoey opened her mouth to reply, then hesitated. She had previously decided against telling her aunt about the slightly strange events she'd experienced that morning. In the moment she was sure that Aunt Carol would find her concerns laughable. Now, when faced with the idea that her aunt was bound to take her every word as gospel, Zoey felt hesitant to utter them.

"Zoey?" asked Aunt Carol, her jittery excitement falling away slightly in favor of one of concern. "Did something happen?"

Spurred forward by a strange desire to make sure Aunt Carol didn't worry about her, Zoey gave her head another shake. "No. I mean, not really." She gave a deep sigh. "When I woke up this morning the TV was on, tuned to some stupid kids show. I'm sure I turned it off before I went downstairs for lunch. But then when I came up here to finish unpacking, it was back on and the volume was lower than I left it."

Aunt Carol's eyes widened at Zoey's confession, silently urging her to continue.

"And then when I was reading in my room, I thought I heard someone on the stairs, but when I went to check, there wasn't anyone there."

"Your Uncle Will, he doesn't see these things, or chooses to ignore them. I just knew you'd believe."

"Believe what?"

"Believe that we aren't alone in this house."

An uncomfortable silence filled the room despite the soft music still playing from Zoey's boombox. Aunt Carol was looking up at her with an expression of such wide-eyed sincerity that Zoey couldn't bring herself to laugh. Sure, she had thought that the TV turning back on and the creaking was weird. Maybe even a little, tiny part of her had thought that it might have been something in the vein of the supernatural. That was the thing, though, it was a tiny part of her. Zoey could tell with zero effort that Aunt Carol believed her statement with every facet of her crystal-loving heart.

"Not alone, like there's a ghost or something?" asked Zoey, once the silence between them had stretched on as long as she could stand.

"Exactly," replied Aunt Carol, nodding vigorously. "I don't claim to know exactly what it is, but I'm sure that there's something, or someone, in this house other than the people we can see."

"Because a TV turned itself back on and I heard a creak on the stairs?" asked Zoey, hoping hearing it stated so plainly might make Aunt Carol realize how absurd it sounded.

"If it was just that, I'd probably be on your Uncle Will's side. The odd creak here or there, electronics doing strange things, that would be a little odd, but I wouldn't jump straight to an otherworldly presence."

"So there's been other, uh, events?"

"Plenty," began Aunt Carol, her beringed fingers still twiddling nervously in her lap, "but here's the strange thing. I've lived in this house for almost forty years now, and it's only in the last few weeks that these things have started to happen."

Zoey couldn't help but think, unkind as it was, that the reason behind this mysterious fact was that Aunt Carol was starting to see things in her old age. That, or she was getting bored despite her piano, crystals, and garden.

"Aunt Carol, you're not just messing with me, are you?"

"What? Of course not," replied Aunt Carol, looking a little offended. "I wouldn't joke about something like this. I even waited until I had proof to show you."

"Does this proof have something to do with cookies?" asked Zoey, unable to feel anything less than fully ridiculous as the words left her mouth.

"Exactly!" exclaimed Aunt Carol, jumping off the bed. "There were twenty-two sugar cookies in the jar before your uncle and I went to pick you up. By the time we got back, there were only twenty. Then we had four last night and I gave two to each of my students today. So there should have been twelve left, but when I counted them just now, there were only nine."

Zoey thought about this for a moment. It was certainly a little bit odd, but it didn't make her mind go straight to the supernatural. Even if she did believe in ghosts, she wasn't sure she could kid herself into believing in a spirit with a sweet tooth.

"Are you sure Uncle Will isn't taking them and not telling you? Maybe he just doesn't want to admit how much he likes them."

Aunt Carol shook her head vigorously. "My husband isn't one for sweet things, but he is big on following rules. I asked him to tell me whenever he took one and, on the odd occasion when he has, he's told me."

"And you don't think it's rats or something?"

"I thought maybe that at first, too," replied Aunt Carol, starting to pace the room in small, shuffling steps. "But I can't see how they'd get the lid back on the jar even if they'd managed to get it open. It's not just the cookies either. I've heard creaks, found doors I'm sure I'd left open shut, and sometimes, I'd swear I can feel someone's eyes on me, especially when I'm playing the piano."

"So, it's a ghost that loves cookies and music?" asked Zoey. She hoped the absurdity of her question might bring Aunt Carol back down to earth.

"I don't know. I just know it has to be something. I've always believed that there's so much more to this world than what we can see, hear, and touch. This is proof."

"Alright, but ghost cookies?"

"I know it's hard to take it seriously when you think of it like that, but I honestly think there's some other presence in the house."

"Alright," said Zoey, caught somewhere between humoring and believing her aunt. "Do we need to be worried? Maybe call a young priest and an old priest?"

Aunt Carol pursed her lips. "Whatever it is, I'm almost certain it's not malevolent. Even when I feel like I'm being watched, it doesn't feel dark, or dangerous. No, I don't think we need to worry about it. I do want to understand it, though."

"Are you thinking a séance tonight instead of tea and cookies?"

"I don't see why it has to be either/or," replied Aunt Carol, her nervous air lessening enough for her to let out a soft chuckle. "I don't think it should be at night, though. I don't know why, but the creaks, the feeling of being watched, they don't seem to happen nearly as much after sunset."

"Isn't that the opposite of how things like this usually work?" asked Zoey. The idea of the supernatural growing in strength at night had been reinforced in her mind by countless books and movies.

"I suppose so. Strange as it may be, I think our best chance at making some kind of contact is in the daylight hours. Right now, if you're not scared."

Zoey was feeling a great many things in the moment, but fear wasn't among them. Worst case scenario, they reached out into the supposed aether, nothing happened, and things would be awkward. Things were already pretty awkward as far as Zoey was concerned, so she couldn't see how a little bit more would hurt.

"Alright, if you have an idea, I'm down to help out. It beats reading about Carrie going full metal bonkers on her classmates for the hundredth time anyway."

"Oh, Zoey, *Carrie*? I wish you'd read something a little more uplifting than that," replied Aunt Carol, the irony of her chiding Zoey over her penchant for horror seemingly lost on her. "Let's go down to the kitchen. I'll just need a few minutes and then we can try an idea I had. I would have done it weeks ago, but it felt silly to do it by myself."

Several minutes later, Zoey was sitting at the kitchen table once again. Aunt Carol had already bustled in and out of the room twice, setting up an array of half-melted purple candles and a spattering of yet more amethysts.

"Is that why I've got those amethysts in my room? You wanted the spirit to talk to me or something?" asked Zoey, picking up one of the purple crystals.

"Oh no, I put those there because I thought they might help you get a good night's sleep."

"Good sleep, talking to ghosts, can they do anything else?" asked Zoey, endeavoring to keep her tone conversational rather than judgmental.

"They can do all sorts of things beyond that. They don't call them the all-purpose stone for nothing you know."

"I actually didn't know that," said Zoey, having never given the glittering rocks much thought outside of appreciating their beauty. "How do you know about this stuff anyway?"

"Well, I made my way through the sixties with a fairly open mind, so I picked up quite a few things back then. The rest I've learned through the years by talking to some very wise people and reading more books on the subject than I should probably admit to."

Zoey thought of the handful of volumes that had been left in her bedroom. She hadn't realized they were just the tip of the proverbial iceberg. With a flick of a match against the side of its decorative box, Aunt Carol deftly lit a long stick of incense. Its smell was caught somewhere between musty and overly floral and made Zoey's head feel immediately heavy.

"Aunt Carol, I don't know how else to ask this," said Zoey, squinting her eyes up against the thick plume of smoke now issuing from the smoldering incense, "but are you a witch?"

"I'm not Wiccan, no. I don't go so far as to think we're casting a spell or anything like that. I'm just doing what I know to help create a centered, calm environment to open up communication between us and the unseen."

Unable to see a difference between identifying as a witch and the load of spiritual mumbo jumbo Aunt Carol had uttered, Zoey nodded. She had to wonder if her aunt would be so outspoken in her strange beliefs if Uncle Will were around. As much as they still didn't make sense as a couple, it did seem to Zoey as though her uncle had a grounding effect on her aunt.

"I just need to run and grab the spirit board from the basement and we should be ready to go. I've done everything that I can think of anyway," said Aunt Carol thoughtfully.

"Are you sure going into the basement alone is a good idea? I mean, aren't we sort of in horror movie territory here?"

Aunt Carol shook her head. "I know you don't believe the same way I do, but try not to poke fun. This isn't a horror movie, and I don't have any reason to be afraid of my own basement."

With that, Aunt Carol left the kitchen again. Zoey heard the basement door open followed by the sounds of Aunt Carol's moccasins descending the rickety staircase.

"Hey, Spirit, if you're really here, just try not to do anything too creepy, alright?" said Zoey acerbically, still doing her best to not breathe in too much of the incense that now hung thickly throughout the room.

Aunt Carol stepped back into the kitchen a few moments later. She was holding a box that looked like any number of ones that Zoey had seen every game night growing up. Her aunt opened the cover and pulled out a quintessential ouija board, complete with a triangular pointer.

"Parker Brothers?" asked Zoey skeptically as Aunt Carol sat down.

"It's the intention that matters with things like this," replied Aunt Carol, her cheeks not showing the faintest trace of blush.

With no trace of preamble, Aunt Carol snapped her eyes closed and let out a low, melodic hum. Zoey's eyes darted away from her aunt. She hoped she wasn't expected to join in. She watched Aunt Carol reach her hands forward to rest delicately on one corner of the plastic pointer. Zoey placed the tips of her fingers on the opposite side and in an attempt to feel less awkward, closed her eyes as well.

Aunt Caron began to pull the pointer in large, swooping circles around the board. "Spirit, we call out to you. Please, reach out and communicate with us."

Zoey opened one eye to stare down at the triangular pointer and stifled a snort. Given the fact that she'd initially refrained from mentioning the TV and creaking to Aunt Carol, she could hardly believe what she was doing. As much as she thought the little ritual they were attempting was a distinct waste of time, Zoey couldn't deny that a tiny part of her desperately wanted it to be real. If Aunt Carol was right, if there was more to the world than birth, death, and then the void, then maybe her dad wasn't totally lost to her after all. Watching her aunt stare fervently at the pointer through the haze of heavily perfumed smoke, however, Zoey wasn't about to let herself get her hopes up.

"Spirit, we've both sensed your presence. We've both seen your signs. Please, tell us what it is you want. How have you come to be here?"

This continued on for some time, their fingers pushing the pointer around the spirit board in wide, slow circles, waiting for some force to change its course. Aunt Carol alternated between humming and intoning question after question to thin air. Zoey watched the trail of ash grow longer, crumble, and fall from the incense to the wooden holder beneath it. When enough time had passed that nearly half the incense stick had crumbled to dust, Aunt Carol finally removed her hands from the pointer and gave a frustrated huff.

"I don't understand why it's not reaching out."

By this point Zoey didn't particularly care about the answer. She was longing to get away from the smoke and her aunt's rhythmic humming. She shook her head "I don't know how any of this is supposed to work, but it's been nearly half an hour. Maybe there's no answer because there's not anything here to give an answer?"

Aunt Carol's face fell so much it sent off a pang of guilt inside Zoey. She looked like a child who'd just heard an adult say there was no such thing as Santa Claus.

"Don't give up on this just yet, Zoey. I know you don't believe like I do, but I know you do believe, deep down."

Zoey's face flushed a bit at that. Sure, a small part of her wanted what Aunt Carol was saying to be true, but that wasn't the same thing as actually believing. She somehow didn't like someone she'd known for less than forty-eight hours telling her how she felt. A small, bitter voice in her head saw no difference between Aunt Carol insisting upon this and the adults back home telling her that she was a troubled child.

"I'll keep an ear out for creaks and stuff, but I think I'm going to go back to my room and read now, OK?"

Aunt Carol scrutinized Zoey's face as if she was trying to delve behind the politely neutral mask that she'd fixed on it. "I think we can agree that this," her aunt began, gesturing to their makeshift little ritual, "isn't an exact science. I hope you'll keep an open enough mind to try this with me again?"

Not seeing how she could say no, Zoey nodded. "Maybe a different incense next time, though, this one's a little strong."

"Oh, do you not like patchouli and sandalwood? It's one of my favorites," replied Aunt Carol, stubbing the smoldering stick on its holder.

Taking this as a sign that their ritual had come to an end, Zoey got up from the table and took a couple of tentative steps toward the staircase. "Maybe it's an acquired taste."

"You know, you might be right about that. The entire world kind of smelled that way back in the sixties, so it was either learn to love it or stop breathing," said Aunt Carol, returning to her usual chipper manner with almost concerning swiftness.

"Do you want me to help you clean up?" asked Zoey, taking another hopeful half-step toward the stairs.

"Oh no, it won't take more than a couple of minutes anyway," said Aunt Carol, placing the spirit board back in its box. "I'll be starting on dinner soon, though. If you want something to do, you could help with that."

As her culinary prowess consisted of little more than dishes like Hamburger Helper, Zoey smiled awkwardly. "I could try, but I might just get in the way. My dad actually did most of the cooking."

An all too familiar shard pierced Zoey's heart. Even after two years, hearing her dad referred to in the past tense was painful. Hearing it slip out casually in her own voice was its own gentle agony.

"Oh, I didn't know that," replied Aunt Carol, pausing in the act of adding an amethyst to the small cluster gathered in her arms. "If you'd like to learn, I'd be happy to teach you a thing or two. It might make you feel a bit closer to him."

Something in Zoey recoiled at the idea, forcing out a quick shake of her head. "Is it OK if I go to my room and read for a bit? I can set the table and then help with dishes after?" She desperately wanted to get out of the patchouli-smelling kitchen and away from this conversation.

An almost proud-looking smile spread over Aunt Carol's lined face at Zoey's words. "That would be a lot of help, thank you."

"It's just dishes," mumbled Zoey.

"I know, but you didn't have to offer," replied Aunt Carol, resuming her gathering of crystals. "You really are a good kid, Zoey."

CHAPTER SIX

Shatter

T he smell of baked salmon that hung throughout her bedroom made Zoey's stomach rumble. The tantalizing scent had grown steadily stronger over the last twenty minutes and told her it was time to make good on her promise.

She set down the copy of *The Healing Power of Mother Earth* that she'd been reading, struggling not to roll her eyes. Since the failed séance with Aunt Carol, Zoey had been flipping through the small array of new age volumes. She'd hoped that maybe they'd help her understand her aunt's strange beliefs better. All they'd wound up doing so far, was help cement in her mind how silly some of this new age stuff could be. The author of this particular volume felt especially ridiculous to Zoey. Whether it be crystals, herbal tinctures, or just spending time out in nature, he believed that every problem man might face could be solved by Mother Earth, regardless of what science had to say on the subject.

She was a little disappointed to see Uncle Will sitting in his office when she reached downstairs. He was poring over a small stack of papers, a frustrated look fixed firmly on his well-lined face. Not pausing long enough for any kind of greeting, Zoey made her way into the kitchen. Her nose wrinkled at the faint trace of patchouli that still hung in the air amid the delicious scents of fish and browned butter.

She began collecting plates from a cupboard indicated by Aunt Carol but paused when she turned to face the kitchen table.

"Are we eating in here or in the dining room?" asked Zoey, unsure.

"We usually eat in here, but your uncle said he wanted to have dinner in the dining room tonight," replied Aunt Carol as she tossed a pan of buttered asparagus.

Unsure whether that boded well for her, Zoey entered the dining room and started place-setting. She had to resist the urge to set her plate on the opposite end from her uncle. Instead, she set one at the head of the table with another on either side. She had only just finished arranging the silverware when Aunt Carol's chipper voice informed her that dinner was ready. Zoey hitched the most natural-looking smile she could on her face. She hoped the upcoming encounter with her uncle would be less charged than last night's

Like the other meals she'd had in the house so far, dinner was several levels of fancy above what she'd become accustomed to over the last two years. She and Aunt Carol set the table with a still sizzling pan of herb-crusted salmon. Soon to join were sides of buttery asparagus and creamy mashed potatoes. Unsure of herself, Zoey sat down and fiddled with her fork. She hoped this setup wouldn't be standard going forward. While the food looked and smelled delicious, it all felt so formal. She couldn't shake the impression that she was sitting in a bright spotlight, awaiting the appraisal and approval of her more rigid relation.

"Will, dinner's ready," called Aunt Carol again, taking the chair at the head of the table before beginning to fill her plate. Perhaps noting her nervous expression, her aunt selected a piece of fish and slid it onto Zoey's plate.

Zoey managed to blurt out a hasty thank you before her uncle took his place opposite her. He looked much as he had the night before, sporting a pair of crisp, black dress pants, a pin-striped button-up, and a patterned blue tie. His hair was so rigidly gelled into its perfect side-part that Zoey wondered if he didn't apply a fresh coat of lacquer to it at the start of each week and called it a day.

She waited for Uncle Will to take his first bite of food before starting in on her own. Like everything else Aunt Carol made, it was incredible. She barely had time to enjoy her first couple of mouthfuls, however, before her uncle's measured voice rose over the sound of clinking cutlery.

"So, what did everyone get up to today? Anything productive?"

"Well, I gave the garden a little bit of a misting, then had a lovely lunch with Zoey. Then I had Andrew and Olivia's lessons to do. How about you? Anything exciting happen at the office today?" replied Aunt Carol.

"Williams case is still a mess, should have never let Jacobs head it."

Zoey pushed her asparagus around on her plate. She'd clocked her uncle's query about being productive as aimed at her. She was, therefore, unsurprised by his next question.

"How about you, Zoey? What did your day look like?"

"I watched a bit of TV after I got up, then had lunch like Aunt Carol said. Then I got my room set up and spent the day reading."

"So you slept until nearly noon? Do you think that's a good use of your time here?"

"Will—" began Aunt Carol warningly.

"Since the three of us are all together, I think it's a perfect time to get on the same page about the situation."

Zoey's cheeks flushed. Privately, she thought that this was something her aunt and uncle should have gotten "on the same page about" before she'd moved in. She knew better than to say something like that out loud, however. She raised her gaze to her uncle and shrugged.

"I'm OK with following the rules. I just need to know what they *actually* are," replied Zoey, laying as much emphasis on actually as she dared.

"Will, we talked about this," said Aunt Carol, a look of annoyance fixed firmly on her face.

"We did, but leaving things vague isn't going to do anyone any favors. With that in mind, I drew up a little something at work, so there's no confusion. We don't want history repeating on us."

Uncle Will got up from the table and headed off toward his study. He returned holding a thin blue folder, not unlike the kind that Zoey used to organize her subjects at school. He resumed his seat across from Zoey and opened the folder, smoothing out the single white page that lay inside.

"Obviously, these are just my ideas, but I think they're all reasonable."

"Will, you needed to bring this to me first. We need to decide what's best for Zoey together."

A high-pitched ringing filled Zoey's ears amid the sound of her own hammering heart. Here it was again. Adults discussing her like she wasn't in the room. Deciding what was best for her without so much as asking if she had any input on the subject.

"There's nothing in here that's unreasonable, considering I'm putting a roof over her head."

When Aunt Carol next spoke, her voice was low but perfectly clear. "If we're just making sure everyone's on the same page, I feel like I should point out that it's technically *my* roof that's being put over her."

The tension in the room, already so palpable, solidified like ice. The expression on Uncle Will's face, so measured and self-assured only seconds ago, was a strange mixture of outrage and, unless Zoey was imagining it, shame. He looked like a toddler who'd been caught with his hand in the cookie jar but was determined to deny it.

Uncle Will took a deep, steadying breath before replying. "I didn't mean to—I know it's *our* house."

"Well, you're not acting like it," snapped Aunt Carol, spearing an asparagus on her fork.

"I didn't do this to start a fight. I'm only trying to set the rules from the get-go so there's no confusion going forward."

"It's certainly going to be confusing if you keep making rules without so much as talking to me about them."

Wishing she could fall right through the floor and out of sight, Zoey did her best to make herself small. She resumed taking small bites of her meal in the hope that by acting like nothing was happening, nothing more would.

"If you'll just read the list, Carol, I can't see you having a problem with any of them. You know I'm not a cruel man, but we can't let her do whatever she wants. That's how she got into this mess in the first place."

"Last I checked, she came to us so she could have a normal life while her mom worked on herself. I think Zoey deserves some freedom and grace."

"She'll have to prove she deserves that grace."

"She already has," retorted Aunt Carol, her voice rising.

"*She* is sitting right here!" shouted Zoey, slamming down the glass of water in her hand so hard it shattered. "This is what it was like back home. People talking about me like I can't hear them, or like I'm too stupid to weigh in on my own goddamn life. I'm sick of it!"

Not caring about the look of hurt on Aunt Carol's face or about the fact that she'd proven Uncle Will right, Zoey kicked her chair away from the table and stormed out of the room. She managed to make it to her bed before the tears started. Once they did, they couldn't be stopped. She buried her face into her goose-down pillow and let out a long, muffled scream.

In the raging tempest of her mind, she couldn't tell who she was more upset with. A tiny part of her had begun to wonder if maybe things would be different here. After all, wasn't that supposed to have been the entire point of shipping her away from everything and everyone she'd ever known? She hadn't even been here a full twenty-four hours before the same song and dance had reared its ugly head.

Worse than her aunt and uncle's spat was how she had reacted to it. Did it really only take one fight, one bit of unpleasantness, for her to lose her temper? She'd spent so long telling herself that she was better than how people saw her, that she was a victim of her circumstances. But here she was, removed from said circumstances and still blowing up at people who were only trying to help her. Maybe everyone was right. Maybe she really was some messed-up kid who couldn't control her temper. Maybe she secretly loved the drama that she herself had helped create.

Numbly, she brought her hand to wipe her face and was shocked to see it streaked with red. An angry gash ran from the base of her ring finger down to the center of her palm. Small beads of blood were bubbling up along the uneven cut. It must have happened when she'd smashed the glass, but she hadn't felt a thing. She brushed one of the droplets away with her thumb, wincing at the sharp twinge of pain that followed. It didn't look too serious, but she'd need to get a bandage on it, at the very least.

With her palm facing upright, she left her bedroom, taking care to not let any droplets fall to the floor. She headed to the bathroom at the end of the hall and ran the cut under the sink. She watched the dots of crimson swirl with the chilly water in her hand before disappearing down the drain in pale pink ribbons. She gathered the bottom of her shirt with her left hand and gripped it against her right. Bleeding all over Aunt Carol's towels didn't seem like a good move.

Zoey turned off the sink and forced herself to take a deep breath. She could hear muffled voices coming from downstairs. Although she couldn't make out what was being said, she knew exactly what they were talking about. She was on thin ice. She'd known that from the moment her aunt and uncle picked her up. Best behavior was required, and her little glass-smashing tantrum was about as far from "best" as it was possible to get. If she were lucky, they were discussing the terms of her one last chance to behave. If not . . . well, she was sure that Uncle Will had the number of the nearest group home on speed dial.

When Zoey removed the pressure from her hand, only a faint trace of red bubbled up. Her first impression had been right, it was shallow. She couldn't imagine how uncomfortable it would have been to ask to be driven to the hospital because she'd sliced up her hand so badly that it needed stitches. She dug through a couple of drawers before finding a wicker basket filled with first aid supplies.

It was hard not to roll her eyes at the chunk of what looked like rose quartz among the other supplies. Aunt Carol wasn't so far gone as to believe that crystals fixed everything, however, and Zoey began wrapping her hand in a layer of gauze. Wincing at the sharp sting beneath the fresh bandage, she dug around in search of something for pain. There was no Tylenol to speak of, but she found something labeled Arnica. She'd never heard of the herb before, but the bottle promised all-natural pain relief with just two pills. She popped one of the light brown capsules into her mouth and swallowed it with a gulp of water from the sink. Hippy herbs on an empty stomach felt best attempted in small doses.

Noting the silence that had replaced her aunt and uncle's muffled voices, Zoey crept back to her room and flopped down on the bed. She didn't want to think about what was sure to come next. She flipped on some music and lost herself in her book. Her hand complained at every turn of the page. She had only finished two chapters when there was a gentle knock at her door. She sat up a little straighter and took a deep breath.

"Yes?"

Having expected Aunt Carol's delicate tones, Zoey was surprised when, instead, Uncle Will's deeper voice replied.

"Your aunt and I wanted to let you know, we think we all handled that poorly. We can talk about it more in the morning. Your dinner's wrapped up in the oven if you still want it."

Her uncle's words were still as measured as ever, but his tone was softer than she'd yet heard it.

The knot of dread in her stomach loosened as she took in her uncle's words: "We *all* handled that poorly." She hadn't considered the possibility of her aunt and uncle accepting a share of the blame for what had happened. An adult admitting to some level of fault against her, that was something of an unprecedented experience. Maybe she wasn't in as much hot water as she'd led herself to believe.

Dreamy strings of piano floated up from downstairs after Uncle Will's surprising announcement. Whatever song Aunt Carol was playing was more cheerful than "Clair De Lune." This filled Zoey with even more hope that she hadn't ruined everything with her outburst. As she'd only managed a few mouthfuls of dinner, Zoey heeded her stomach's call for food after Aunt Carol started playing her third piece. Her dinner was wrapped in tinfoil inside the still-warm oven. On the counter next to it were two sugar cookies and a slice of melon atop a fine china plate. A note folded into a neat triangle sat next to them:

Cookies nine and eight as a little apology for how dinner went.
Take all the time you need, but there's no reason to be embarrassed.
We all let our feelings get the better of us sometimes, and your uncle
and I should have never put you in that position, to begin with.
-Aunt Carol

Zoey folded the note back up and put it in her pocket, then balancing the cookies atop her dinner, made her way back to her room.

CHAPTER SEVEN

Visitor

Zoey drifted through a hazy sea of gray. Though she could register the sensation of her bed beneath her, she couldn't bring her mind to form any intelligible thoughts. Caught in the veil between the dreaming and waking worlds, her body turned on its side. Her foot brushed up against a solid lump at the end of her bed, nudging her mind toward wakefulness. Charlie had no doubt crawled onto her bed after she'd fallen asleep and nestled down for the night. This comforting thought floated through the sea of staticky gray for a moment before it jostled loose a chilling truth. Charlie was back in Ohio.

Zoey's eyes flew open as the thought broke through her sleep-addled mind. She sat bolt upright, wiping away as much of the blurriness from her eyes as she could. As much as her bleary eyes were struggling to make out anything in the darkened room, she was sure of one thing—there was nothing at the foot of her bed. Yet she felt something at the foot of her bed.

Breath caught in her throat, Zoey pressed her foot against the solid mass. Her mind had only begun to register the gentle warmth that radiated from the phantom object when that became the least of her concerns. It moved, shuffling to the side as if to give her foot more room. Unbidden, a long, piercing scream rose out of Zoey's throat, shattering the tranquility of the night.

Zoey twisted out of bed like a drunken crab. She fell to the floor with a loud, room-shaking thud. Her mind was working faster than her body would permit. She needed to get up. She couldn't get up. All she could manage was to scramble away from her bed until her back slammed into something solid. There was a clattering from overhead. Footsteps hammered down a flight of stairs. Was she imagining it among the din? Or did she hear another set of footsteps, scampering away from her bed, toward the opposite end of the room?

"Zoey?!"

The door handle turned, rattling as someone tried in vain to open it. It took the door slamming into her back three times before Zoey had the good sense to get out of the way. She shielded her eyes against the room's lights being flipped on as her aunt and uncle, dressed in their nightclothes, came bursting in.

Zoey received her second scare of the night to see that Uncle Will was holding a handgun.

"Zoey? What's wrong?" demanded Aunt Carol, her face ashen.

"S-something in my bed. R-ran away," replied Zoey, her words coming out in uneven bursts.

Disoriented as she was, she realized the absurdity of that statement. If there had indeed been something on the bed, where would it have gone? The bay window didn't open, so the only way in or out of her room was the door that she herself had only moments ago been blocking. The only option left would have been her closet, which was, of course, a dead end.

Without uttering a word, Uncle Will marched across the room and kicked open the closet door, which had been hanging half open to begin with. Hadn't it been closed when she went to bed? Zoey couldn't remember. He pointed the gun toward the back of the closet and took a step inside. There was a soft click and a light flickered on within. He emerged a moment later and shook his head.

"There's nothing in here."

"N-no, t-there was something sitting on my bed. It was warm! I felt it!"

"Zoey dear, I think you must have—" soothed Aunt Carol.

"It wasn't a dream!" cried Zoey, though as logic caught up with her, she couldn't see what else it could have been.

"Zoey, there's no one else here, just your Uncle Will—" a look of dawning realization spread across Aunt Carol's face. Her eyes grew wider by the second. Paired with her wrinkled nightgown and disheveled gray hair, the expression made her look a little frightening. "Zoey, I think it might have been the spirit paying you a visit."

Zoey was saved the necessity of responding to this bold pronouncement by Uncle Will, who, pointing the gun toward the floor, let out a grunt of frustration. "Carol, not this spirit business again. She had a nightmare. That's all."

"She had a nightmare the very night after we tried making contact with the spirit?" asked Aunt Carol, her voice raised but steady.

"Tried to make contact? Don't tell me you got Zoey roped into that nonsense? You know she has nightmares."

"Her nightmares don't have anything to do with the spirit, Will."

"There is no spirit, Carol. No force, no presence, no mystical mumbo jumbo. My god, you keep talking about how you only want what's best for her. Do you really think filling her head with this nonsense is doing her any good?"

Still too full of adrenaline to give much thought to the fact that her aunt and uncle were, once again, talking about her like she wasn't in the room, Zoey stumbled to her feet. She walked past the arguing pair and peeked into the dimly lit closet. She had been sure she'd heard footsteps running toward this side of the room. As Uncle Will had said, however, there was nothing in there but her now empty suitcases and a small collection of her winter clothes.

"Zoey dear, please tell your uncle about your other experiences since moving in," said Aunt Carol, a note of pleading in her voice.

"You mean the TV and stuff? I don't think that's . . ."

Zoey found she couldn't finish her sentence in good conscience. A malfunctioning TV and a couple of creaks were one thing, not a cause for concern, and certainly not proof of anything paranormal. But what she'd experienced here? She couldn't think of any logical explanation. She had been drifting, not asleep, and was sure it hadn't been a dream.

"Listen, you two," said Uncle Will. "There is no such thing as ghosts or spirits, and there's no boogeyman in the closet." He took a moment to push the door closed. "Zoey had a nightmare, that's all there is to it."

"I'm telling you, Will, there's more to it than that. And would you please put that thing away? You know I don't even like that you have it in the house," replied Aunt Carol, nodding to the gun held at her husband's side.

Uncle Will gave an exasperated sigh before stalking out of the room, an ill-tempered look still plastered across his face. Zoey barely had time to take a breath when a bony hand clamped down on her upper arm.

"Zoey, you need to tell me exactly what happened. I know it wasn't just a dream."

Feeling nettled, Zoey pulled her arm away before recounting the encounter in as much detail as she could.

"You said it felt warm? Spiritual activity is usually associated with the cold. Like all the warmth's been sucked from the area they're inhabiting," said Aunt Carol, sounding uncharacteristically erudite.

"Like cold spots and drafts? Yeah, that's what's in all the movies I've seen," replied Zoey, wrapping her arms around herself. "It was definitely warm, though. I thought it was Charlie before I realized where I was."

"It's all a little strange. I never felt the presence strongly at night, but this is beyond anything it's done during the daytime. Maybe it's particularly attached to this room."

A shiver traveled through Zoey. She didn't know if her aunt was actively trying to make her feel more frightened, but she was doing a fantastic job of it.

"Alright, we need to put this to bed so we can all get back to sleep," said Uncle Will, returning from upstairs. "There is no spirit or ghost. Zoey had a nightmare. That's all there is to it." He turned to face Zoey, a look that was not unkind on his face. "Zoey, you're fine, right?"

Zoey gave a movement that was somewhere between a shudder and a shrug. "I'm not hurt or anything, but I don't want to go back to sleep."

"It's three in the morning, you need to get back to sleep," replied Uncle Will.

Zoey thought about getting back into bed and trying to fall asleep. The idea sent a shiver up her spine. "It doesn't matter. I'm not going to be able to fall back asleep."

"You need to at least try."

"Will, just look at her. The poor thing's white as a sheet. I'll make her some tea, at the very least."

"Carol, you'll get to talking about all this spirit nonsense and keep her riled up. I'm putting my foot down here."

Aunt Carol turned to Zoey, her face filled with concern. "Do you think you could get some sleep if it was in a different room?"

The thought didn't seem as unpleasant to Zoey. "I could try."

"Alright then, we'll get you settled down in the guest room and, hopefully, you can get some more sleep. Will, why don't you go back up to bed? I'll be there in a little bit."

"Just leave the ghost talk for another time, Carol, for her sake," said Uncle Will before walking out of the room.

Aunt Carol let out a long sigh, which told Zoey that she was going to heed her husband's request, even if she didn't agree with it. Zoey couldn't tell if she was grateful for her uncle's intervention or not. Part of her wanted to talk more with Aunt Carol about what had happened. The other part wanted to rationalize away the whole thing, and that would be much harder to do amid another cloud of incense and throaty humming.

"The guest bedroom is just down the hall," said Aunt Carol, her voice low and soothing. "We'll get you settled in there and then I could bring you up some tea if you'd like."

Zoey ran her unbandaged hand along the gooseflesh that had broken out across her arm. "That sounds OK,"

The guest room was much smaller than her bedroom. It contained a queen bed covered with a thick comforter and a large wooden bureau. A TV that was the twin of the one that Zoey had watched cartoons on this morning sat atop the bureau. These objects took up most of the space in the room. Zoey couldn't decide if it was claustrophobic or cozy. Given the alternative, she wasn't about to complain.

"Is it OK if I watch TV for a bit?" asked Zoey, grateful for the idea of something to help occupy her mind.

"Just keep the volume down low. And no horror, ok?"

Zoey let out an involuntary snort. She wasn't sure if Aunt Carol was trying to be funny or not, but putting on a horror movie was the furthest thing from her mind. She climbed into the unfamiliar bed. It had a certain musty smell to it that the one in her room lacked, but was still plenty comfortable. She was glad of the heavy comforter despite it being summer. The AC kept the house chilly, and the blanket's weight and warmth were comforting. She flipped on the TV amid the creaks of Aunt Carol heading down to make her tea and did her best to focus.

There was an exuberant man showing the wonders of his never-dull kitchen knives to his manically impressed friends. Try as she might, the cries of amazement coming from the TV weren't enough to keep her mind from wandering. For all her love of reading about the eldritch and the unknown, she'd never actually believed in any of it. Now that the luxury of supernatural agnosticism had been stripped away from her, she didn't know how to feel. Whatever Uncle Will had said about it having just been a dream, Zoey was certain that something had been in the room with her.

Aunt Carol returned a few minutes later, a steaming mug of tea resting on a plate, along with another sugar cookie. With the thought of Aunt Carol's missing cookies and the fresh memory of the presence at the foot of her bed, the sparkling confection didn't look all that appetizing.

"Oh, those things are great. I've got a set of them downstairs," said Aunt Carol, with a nod toward the TV.

Zoey could tell her aunt was doing her best to keep her comments as far from the supernatural as possible, and she was glad for it.

"Yeah, you never know when you might need to cut through an empty Coke can," replied Zoey, taking hold of her tea. The warmth burned some steadiness back into her.

Zoey could tell in the silence that followed that her Aunt Carol wanted to say more on the subject of their nighttime visitor.

"That's actually the first thing I tried when I got my set," she said, in a tone of forced airiness. Then, after another substantial pause, "Well, I hope you're able to get some more sleep. Don't worry about sleeping in or anything like that. I'm sure even your uncle will agree that this is a special circumstance."

Zoey gave a grunt of ascent, eyes focused on the phone number now flashing across the screen. Her uncle's approval was the last thing on her mind. Aunt Carol left the room a few moments later, closing the door behind her with a click. The wonders of the never-dull knives weren't enough to keep the scene flickering through her mind like an old filmstrip. She suppressed a shudder and took a sip from the mug clasped between her hands. There had been something in her bed. It hadn't been a dream, and it wasn't her imagination. That left her with an important question to answer: What had it been?

CHAPTER EIGHT

Mist

It had taken the rest of the knife infomercial and most of a program expounding the wonders of the Miracle Power Juicer for sleep to find Zoey. By the time she woke up, sunlight was spilling out around the edges of the curtains framing the room's solitary window. She gave her head an experimental shake in an attempt to clear the weighty sensation that always accompanied a night of broken sleep.

She took a sip of what remained of her tea, leaving her sugar cookie untouched. The chill liquid ran down the back of her throat, cloyingly sweet from the honey that had settled among the dregs. The idea of leaving the warm solitude of her bed was not a pleasant one. Convinced as she was that what she'd experienced in her bedroom had been real, talking about it with her aunt and uncle still felt silly in the light of day.

She didn't know either of them all that well yet, but she felt she knew how they'd react. She wasn't nearly awake enough to deal with her uncle's huffy grunts, nor her aunt's wide eyed excitement. If this wasn't a case for killing some time, Zoey didn't know what was.

A shower seemed in order. Maybe the warm water would burn away some of the anxiety that still sat heavy in the pit of her stomach. She walked into the bathroom but stopped short of peeling out of her clothes. She'd first need to pick something out to replace them, and for that, she'd have to go into her room. There was no getting around it. She couldn't avoid the place forever. She forced her feet forward. The idea of being alone in there wasn't any fun, but she'd rather go it alone if the alternative included crystals and incense.

Her hand trembled as she grasped the cool brass of the door handle.

It's just a room, brainless. This isn't a movie, and you're not Regan MacNiel.

Holding her breath, she pushed the door open and hurried inside. It looked just as it had the day before, with bright sunlight pouring through the bay window and her possessions standing out against the otherwise classic appearance of the room. The sight of her bed, unmade and disheveled, pulled at her. As if to erase the events of last night, Zoey took a moment to rearrange the blankets, smoothing out the edges and creases until it looked hotel-ready.

She dug around in the dresser drawers, eager to get out of there as quickly as possible. Pinpricks rippled across the back of her neck. Something was off about the room. She just didn't know what. It didn't matter. She wouldn't be staying long. She just needed to grab an outfit, any outfit, and then she could leave. With fresh clothing in hand, she had all but made it out to the hall when the realization froze her in her tracks. The closet door was open.

Uncle Will had closed it last night, she was sure of it.

Get a grip, it's just a closet. You're not five. There's no boogeyman hiding in there.

But if that was true, then why was looking at the open closet making her heart beat faster? Why had her legs tensed, itching to bolt from the room? Had this been what Aunt Carol had meant when she had mentioned feeling as though she were being watched?

Zoey set her jeans down on top of the dresser and crept toward the closet. If this were a horror movie, she'd be rolling her eyes at the idiot walking towards her unfortunate end. As this wasn't a movie she could only think how stupid she must look, inching her way across the room as though she were approaching a sleeping lion.

"Is someone there?" whispered Zoey.

There was no reply.

Reassured by that fact, Zoey relaxed her posture and approached the door with a more confident stride. Peering inside from the relative comfort of her bedroom, she saw the same thing as she had the night before. An empty closet containing little more than the small number of winter clothes she'd had the foresight to bring with her.

Shaking her head in an attempt to rid herself of the tight knot of anxiety that persisted in her stomach, Zoey stepped into the closet. She hadn't known exactly what she expected to happen. A ghostly wail, a sudden drop in temperature, or, based on last night, the unnerving presence of some invisible but solid force. The only thing that happened was she found herself standing in her closet, feeling silly in the letdown of her grandiose expectations.

"It's literally just a closet," she said to herself, shaking her head out of annoyance with herself this time. "Get a grip."

She pulled the beaded chain above her, illuminating the closet in the feeble glow of a single incandescent light bulb. Its light was dim enough that she could see every coil of the glowing orange filament. The closet itself wasn't quite wide enough for her to extend her arms at her sides, but it was at least six feet deep. Unlike her bedroom proper, it had panel molding around its lower half.

Whatever had been on her bed last night had run in this direction, she was sure of that. But why run to the closet? There was no place to go from here. That was, of course, coming from the perspective of someone who was impeded by walls. But if solid objects meant nothing to the spirit, or whatever it was, then why did it bother with opening doors in the first place? For that matter, why didn't it float down through her bed when she'd woken up? Why had it run, and more specifically, why to here?

She clicked the light off and turned to leave. A shiver ran up her spine. Something was telling her not to go, that she was close to something. Something she needed to see. It felt akin to instinct, though that wasn't quite the right word for it. Whatever it was, it filled her up like drink.

She pulled the silver chain again, determined to take one more good look at the tiny room. She walked to the back of the closet and placed her hand against the gray wall that marked its end. She had expected the smooth surface beneath her hand to be cool to the touch, chilled by the AC circulating throughout the house. Zoey took in a deep breath. It wasn't cold. It radiated a gentle heat, as though it had been basking in the first rays of the early morning sun. The smooth panel beneath her hand pulsed as if it were taking slow, tiny breaths. It should have terrified Zoey, repulsed her even. Instead, the sensation sent a wave of contentment through her body, as though she were sinking into a warm bath.

Her body moved without conscious thought. She crouched down and pushed against the panel. A sound of rushing air hissed around the edges before it fell inward with a dull thud. A chill breeze wafted out of the dark square she'd created. It carried with it a strange scent, like the air before a thunderstorm and something vaguely sweet that she couldn't quite place. Waves of opaque, silver-gray gas lapped up against the space where the panel had been moments before. It didn't look like anything Zoey had ever seen before. It wasn't thick enough to be smoke or fog, but it was more substantial than something like steam. The word "mist" fit best in Zoey's mind, though that didn't quite capture it either. Tendrils of the silver-gray substance flowed across the empty space as though a sheet of glass had replaced the missing panel.

The sensation that had brought her to press against the panel in the first place urged her forward, flying in direct defiance of her common sense. Even with the supernatural taken out of the equation, there could have been any number of unpleasant things in there. For all she knew, she'd opened up some kind of maintenance panel. There was every chance that all she'd find inside was itchy insulation, frayed wires, and, perhaps, a dead mouse or two. Then there was the mist. It didn't look like smoke, and it certainly wasn't behaving like it either. Still, she couldn't shake the memories of countless fire safety days in elementary school. Where there was smoke, there was fire. If that was true, she needed to move away, not toward it.

A dreamy smile spread across Zoey's face. Everything would be fine. She reached her hand into the billowing mist, slipping past whatever invisible force held it contained. A pleasant warmth traveled up her arm before spreading out. It radiated through the core of her being. Her muscles relaxed, her troubled thoughts quieted. A dreamy sigh escaped her lips. She needed to go forward. It was the right thing to do.

She crawled through the panel.

Zoey got to her feet on the other side and looked around. There was nothing but a sea of swirling mist as far as the eye could see, which was a substantial distance, considering she should have been in a crawlspace. She turned to face where she'd come in, and her heart jumped. Where there should have been a wall, there was only swirling silver. The passage back to her bedroom remained, however, floating unsupported in the sea of mist that rose all around her.

She reached her hand out in search of something solid and found nothing. She moved forward with tiny, cautious steps. Each foot searched for the continued solidness of the floor beneath her before putting down any pressure. Although she had taken several overwary steps, the space in front of her, searched by her outstretched hands, remained empty.

Zoey walked around the floating square in a tight circle, still taking the same measured steps. Though her position changed, her view of the passage didn't alter in the slightest. There was no looking at it from the side, or coming up behind it. It remained fixed in place. An absolute point in the sea of boundless nothing. She had only come to that conclusion when, with the rapidity of a lightbulb blowing, the square popped out of existence.

The sense of well-being that had been holding her spellbound evaporated along with the door. She spun around, her heart pounding. Her eyes darted wildly in their search for the way out. All was endless, swirling mist. She let out a cry that traveled out in all directions. It sounded as though she were yelling in an open field rather than what should have been a cramped crawlspace. Before she could begin to work out what any of that meant, the floor dropped out from under her.

There was the sensation of weightlessness, then gravity. Her screams reached a new pitch. Air rushed past her ears. Her hair whipped across her face. All the while accompanied by a horrible plunging in the pit of her stomach. She plummeted onward. Her voice was threatening to break. Was she going to fall forever through endless silver? No, she was reaching the end. She could feel it coming. Ground was rushing up beneath her. She closed her eyes and braced for impact.

Where there should have been a splat, there was only the familiar lurch of missing a step going down a flight of stairs. She floated, suspended in the void before, with a muffled thud, her feet found solid ground once more.

With everything silent, Zoey had no problem hearing the muffled sliding of the panel opening back up. She whipped around and made a mad, scrambling dash toward the dim square of light.

With a thud and much gasping for air, she landed sprawled on the cool hardwood of the closet floor. The relief at the ability to see anything but silver surrounding her flickered out in almost the same instant that it roared to life. She was back in a closet alright, it just wasn't the one she'd come in through.

CHAPTER NINE

Nicole

Zoey's breath was coming in sharp, short bursts. The terrifying experience of falling through nothingness had been bad enough. Now, on top of that, she faced the undeniable reality that wherever she was, it wasn't the closet in her bedroom. It was the same size and shape as the one that she'd come through, but that was where the similarities ended.

The feeble iridescent light bulb had been replaced with a duo of humming fluorescents that bathed the closet in a harsh, blue-white glow. The closet was filled with an array of objects that Zoey was sure didn't belong to her aunt or uncle. An army of stuffed animals in varying conditions lined the perimeter of the small rectangular room. There were coloring books, some open to pages of half-finished creations. Crayons with the wrappers missing or half peeled off. Jump ropes tied up in knots or curled in lazy loops. Board games, rubber balls, an assortment of gaudy costume jewelry, and colorful dress-up supplies. All of this and more lie scattered throughout the closet, with only a narrow path down the center leading to the partly opened closet door.

A delicate silver haze hung in the air. It wasn't enough to obscure Zoey's vision. If she relaxed her eyes, it disappeared from her view entirely. With each breath, she could smell the strange combination of scents that had suffused the mist-filled room that she'd fallen through to get here. Whether she saw it or not, she knew it was there, tendrils rolling across every surface of the closet. She ran through the scant number of logical explanations she'd managed to cobble together.

You're dreaming.

That was ruled out by the dull throb coming from the cut on her right hand. It was not at all happy about the way she'd used it to push herself up from her prone position.

The crawl space led to another part of the house

.But why would her aunt and uncle have a closet filled with things that looked like they belonged to an eight-year-old girl? And what about the endless expanse that she'd fallen through to get here? Whatever that place had been, it wasn't a crawlspace.

Impossible as it seemed, she had to accept the fact that she was crouched in a closet that belonged to someone else. If she accepted, she had two options as far as she could see. She could head back through the crawl space and hope it lobbed her back out where she'd come from. As illogically logical as that thought was, Zoey couldn't bear the idea of rushing through the empty void again. What if it didn't take her back the way she'd come? What if, when she fell, she kept falling forever? No, going back wasn't an option. That left her with only one course of action.

Careful not to disturb the colorful horde on either side of her, Zoey inched toward the partly opened door. Her ears worked furiously, searching for any sound coming from the other side to indicate what she might be making her way toward. All she managed to hear was her own distressed breathing. She forced herself to take a deep, steadying breath. Panicking would only make the situation worse. Some of the tension left her chest.

Zoey placed both hands on the door, and, ignoring the dull throb of protest from her right hand, pushed it open. At least she tried to push it open. Despite hanging ajar by a couple of inches, it felt to Zoey as though the door had been welded firmly in place.

Whatever sense of calm she'd managed to grab hold of was threatening to deteriorate. She refused to go back, and it looked like she couldn't go forward. If both those things were true, then that meant she was trapped. That couldn't be true. She wouldn't let it be. Zoey summoned all the strength she possessed and pressed her weight against the door. Her sock-clad feet slid back from the force she was exerting while the door stayed stubbornly shut.

"Let me out!"

Zoey accompanied her cry for help by throwing herself against the door. This accomplished little more than sending a shock of pain through her shoulder. She was rearing back for another attempt when a voice from the other side cried out.

"You came! I knew you'd come!"

Without warning, the door was flung open from the other side to reveal a young girl. A wide, excited grin plastered over her freckled face. She looked as though nothing could have made her happier than opening her closet door and finding a disheveled fourteen-year-old girl. A million questions swirled through Zoey's mind as the unknown girl stared up at her with wide, excited eyes.

"What the hell is going on?"

The girl, who looked like she couldn't be any older than ten, gasped. She looked reproachful before giving an excited jump, the smile reappearing on her face.

"You said a swear word," she said, sounding more impressed than offended. "It's OK, my brother swears all the time."

"Seriously, what's going on? Who are you?" demanded Zoey, still standing in the door frame.

"My name's Nicole. Your name's Zoey, right? That's what I heard your auntie call you."

"How did you . . . ?" She let her sentence trail off. Things were falling into place in her mind. The missing cookies. The TV being tuned to a kid's channel. The warm presence at the end of her bed. "Are you the ghost?"

Nicole's excited expression faded, her bubbly air going with it. "What?! I'm not a ghost. That's really mean!"

"If you're not a ghost, then wh—"

"You have to be dead to be a ghost, and I'm not dead!" said Nicole, her voice rising as a sheen of tears filled her eyes.

Zoey took a step toward Nicole as she sniffled, but caught herself before reaching out a hand to comfort her. She might look like a teary-eyed little girl, with her rosy cheeks and long, dirty blonde hair, but that didn't mean that she wasn't something else, maybe even something dangerous.

"OK, OK, I'm sorry. You're not a ghost. But what are you? Was that you in my room last night?"

Nicole looked up at Zoey through watering eyes, a look of innocent confusion on her face. She took a second to wipe her eyes with the back of her hand before replying.

"I'm just a kid," then with a pang of guilt to her words, "I'm sorry I scared you. I was just curious. I never saw anyone sleeping in that room before. I wanted to look at you for a little bit."

Zoey repressed a shiver. Her head was spinning. The way this little girl talked, it sounded like she frequently went wandering around Aunt Carol's house in the dead of night and thought nothing of it. She would have pinched herself if it wasn't for the dull ache spreading across her head.

"OK, so you're a kid and your name is Nicole. Can you explain what's going on, please?" asked Zoey, rubbing her thumb against her temple.

"Oh! Right," said Nicole, as if she'd forgotten something important. "I was really scared the first time I went into the back of the closet, too."

Without another word, Nicole pranced over to a twin bed covered with a comforter that was a violently bright shade of bubblegum pink. She sat cross-legged on top of it and rocked back and forth in a way that reminded Zoey forcibly of her friends who struggled to sit still back when she was younger. Not seeing what else she could do other than to submit to the impromptu story time, Zoey crossed to the bed but stopped at the point of sitting down.

For what felt like the hundredth time that day, a shiver traveled throughout Zoey's body. As focused as she'd been on Nicole, Zoey wasn't sure how it had taken her this long to notice. Much like the closet, the room she was standing in was identical to hers in structure, though strikingly different in detail. Whereas the walls of her room were a restrained shade of gray, Nicole's walls burst with color. Vivid greens rose out of the baseboards, stopping halfway up the wall. From there, large swirls of bright colors took the form of a multitude of large, blooming flowers. The entire rainbow was represented in full force in the colorful blossoms, though it did look like pink got more than its fair share of representation.

Nicole, who hadn't missed Zoey's examination of the walls, sat up a little straighter, beaming.

"Do you think it's pretty? My mom did it. She's an artist. I wanna be an artist when I grow up."

"Yeah, it's really pretty. Your mom must be talented," replied Zoey.

Despite her best efforts to stay on her guard, Zoey relaxed a little at the smile that spread across Nicole's face at the compliment. She knew she should have been more weary of the girl, but something in her couldn't help but trust that Nicole was, as she'd said, just a kid.

"Do you like to draw? I didn't see any drawings in your room. It would be really fun to have someone to draw with," said Nicole, still rocking back and forth as she looked up at Zoey with wide eyes.

"I'm not very good at drawing . . . but hey, weren't we going to talk about how I wound up here?"

Realization bloomed on the younger girl's face, as though she was only now remembering the impossible circumstances that had led Zoey to be in her room. She stopped her excited rocking and sat up a little straighter.

"I don't know how it works, but the little door in the back of my closet leads to your bedroom," said Nicole, as though that explained it all.

"Yeah, I figured that part out myself," replied Zoey. "But how does it lead here? And where is here?"

"It must be magic. And this is my bedroom."

If Nicole were any older, Zoey would have cussed her out. She knew she wasn't being purposefully unhelpful, but she couldn't help feeling annoyed.

"OK, how about this? Do you know your address?"

"I'm not supposed to tell strangers where I live . . ." replied Nicole warily. "But you're not really a stranger, right?"

Zoey had to think about that for a second. Looking at things plainly, she was, in fact, a stranger. One who'd snuck into a little kid's bedroom at that. The circumstances causing that statement to be true, however, were so bizarre, and with Nicole being linked to them, Zoey couldn't help but feel like the two of them were together in this somehow.

"I mean, I am kind of a stranger. But I guess we sort of share a room."

Zoey winced at the thought. She was making things creepier rather than less.

Nicole grinned more widely than ever at this.

"We do. I always wanted a sister to share my room with." Began Nicole, rocking back and forth again, "we know each other's names too, so we're not really strangers. My address is twelve fifteen Maple Drive."

"That's my address, too."

"That's really cool. Our houses are kind of the same, but I didn't know our addresses were. Isn't every house supposed to have a different address?"

"They do, normally," replied Zoey, painfully aware of how far from normal the entire situation was. "You said you were going to explain what's going on?"

"Oh, right! I don't reallllly know how it works. But when I go into the little door at the back of my closet, I come out in that other lady's house."

"And you can get back to your house by going back through the little door?"

"Yup! It was scary the first time, but kind of fun, too."

"You think it's fun?" asked Zoey, even now dreading the thought of having to experience the plummeting, whirling darkness to get back home.

"I like the big rides at the fair that make you go upside down and spin around," said Nicole.

The delighted way that Nicole was talking about the experience forced a chuckle out of Zoey. Thinking back, she remembered feeling like that when she was younger. When anything could be an adventure, and, more frighteningly so, when she lacked the capacity to gauge how dangerous something was, so long as it was fun.

"So you come over through the, uh, closet ride just to wander around and sneak cookies?"

"It's really fun," insisted Nicole, "like having my own bigggg fort."

Zoey suppressed another chuckle. She had to admit, the idea of having a giant fort stocked with cookies would have been on her own wishlist back when she was Nicole's age. Even at fourteen, it was a pretty cool idea, so long as you stripped away the headache that came with the impossibility of the situation.

"How long have you been coming over?"

"A little bit before summer break started," said Nicole, a frustrated look creeping across her face. I told my friends about it, but they didn't believe me. Then I tried to show Kaitlyn C., but the door wouldn't come out when she was over. She told everyone I was making it up." She paused for a moment, looking still more upset. "No one believes me, not even my mom."

"It'd be pretty hard to believe unless you saw it yourself," replied Zoey, thinking of how she'd feel if someone tried convincing her of it. "When you come over to my aunt's house, none of us can see you?"

"No, they can't hear me either. I tried talking to your auntie the first time I came over, but she acted like I wasn't there. She makes really good cookies, though," said Nicole, as if Aunt Carol's talent in the kitchen made up for her inability to perceive her otherworldly guest.

Zoey lined the facts up in her head: There was a crawlspace in the back of her closet. It acted as a link between her and Nicole's rooms. It didn't work when Nicole tried to show her friends. When Nicole came over to her world, no one in Zoey's world could see or hear her. None of it made sense, but it was all somehow true.

Zoey shifted her weight from one foot to the other. "Were you watching TV in my world yesterday morning?"

"That was a lot of fun. I knew you couldn't see me, but it was like we were watching together."

Privately, Zoey thought the experience was leaning more toward creepy than fun, but decided not to contradict Nicole.

"Why over at Aunt Carol's, though? Do you guys not have a TV?"

"We do, but all the shows are different on yours. I realllly like Sparkle Squad Five, but it's never on over here."

"That was my favorite when I was your age."

"Don't you like it anymore? You watched it with me yesterday," replied Nicole, sounding a little disappointed.

"I guess I grew out of it. It was fun, sort of nostalgic."

"Nostalgic?"

"Oh, I guess it means, like going back to a happier time for a little bit."

"Aren't you happy now?" asked Nicole, sounding confused at the idea.

Oof, that's a loaded question, thought Zoey. "Maybe not as happy as I was back when I was your age." Before Nicole could delve deeper into these uncomfortable waters, Zoey interjected with a question of her own. "Do you think you could show me around your house? I'm curious how the rest of it looks compared to my aunt's."

"Sure!" said Nicole, hopping off the bed. "I can't show you my parent's room, though. I'm not supposed to go up there without asking."

"That's alright, good job listening to your parents."

Nicole smiled toothily and led Zoey out of her room and into a hall that was a mirror image of the one outside her own bedroom. The only differences were in terms of decor. A potted plant with large green and white striped leaves sat in repose at the end of the hall. Various framed pictures lined the walls. There was one of a bowl of fruit in oils. Another showed frothing turquoise waves rolling along a sandy and pebbled beach.

"Did your mom do these?" asked Zoey.

"Yup! They're really pretty, aren't they? Ohhh! Can I show you my favorite?" Without waiting for a reply, Nicole grabbed Zoey's hand and pulled her toward the opposite end of the hall. They stood in front of the door that led to the room where Zoey had spent the previous night watching infomercials. "I'm allowed to come in here and look, but we can't touch anything, OK?"

Looking back down at Nicole's surprisingly firm expression, Zoey nodded.

"Alright, I won't touch anything. I promise."

Nicole's excited grin returned in full force. She pushed open the door and led Zoey inside. The sharp smell of paint hit Zoey on her first breath. Just as it was at Aunt Carol's, the space inside was somewhat cramped. Instead of a bed and TV, however, the room was filled to the brim with art supplies. Paints of all kinds sat on shelves, grouped by color in neat rows. Easels, stencils, and canvas lay stacked along the walls. Some were blank, while others bore large, surreal swirls of colors or depictions of everyday objects with artistic embellishments. Zoey hadn't expected the room to be so organized. She'd always thought an artist's studio would look a little more chaotic. But what did she know? Her own artistic prowess didn't extend much further than stick figures.

"This one's my favorite," said Nicole from somewhere off to Zoey's left.

She was pointing to the only painting that was hung up properly. It depicted a field of flowers at sunrise. The myriad of blossoms stretched out into the distance, while in the foreground, a woman in a gossamer dress lay among the flowers, staring up into the early morning sky as she cradled something in her arms. The scene was bathed with a soft, rosy light that gave everything a blurred, ethereal quality. Though the picture was quite still, Zoey thought she could see the flowers swaying in a breeze, captured by Nicole's mom.

"I can see why you like it," said Zoey, thinking of the pink blooms that adorned Nicole's bedroom. It was more than that, though. Zoey didn't claim to be any sort of art authority, but the painting had a hopeful, almost magical quality to it. She knew even less about Nicole, but from what she did, it suited her.

Nicole beamed still more widely, but before she could reply, a voice rang out behind them.

"Hey, pipsqueak, I don't think you're supposed to be in here."

Standing in the doorway was a boy who looked like he was at least a couple of years older than Zoey. His dark brown hair was styled up into an oily faux-hawk above a face that was sporting more than a couple of angry red zits.

Zoey froze, aware of how inappropriate the situation would look from his point of view. Her heart hammered as his eyes fell on her and Nicole. From the banal, slightly annoyed expression on his face, however, he could only see Nicole.

"Mom said I'm allowed in here as long as I don't touch anything," replied Nicole, sounding defensive. "I wanted to show Zoey."

"Who's Zoey?"

"She's my new friend. She's standing right here."

"So, she's imaginary? Aren't you a little old for that?" asked Tyler, raising an eyebrow.

"She's not imaginary! She just moved into that other house and she's really nice."

"Didn't Dad tell you to cut it out with that other house stuff? Stop acting like a baby."

Dislike welled up in Zoey as a red flush crept over Nicole's freckled face. Even if Nicole was making it all up, Zoey couldn't see where he got off talking to her like that. Nicole couldn't have been more than ten. What was wrong with a ten-year-old having an imagination?

"Ty-ler!" whined Nicole, clearly offended by what he'd said.

"Nic-ky," replied Tyler, in mocking imitation.

Several long seconds passed with the two siblings staring each other down. Nicole's face was caught burning somewhere between defiance and hurt, while Tyler stared on with a look of vague annoyance. Nicole won the silent war they were waging, however, when Tyler rolled his eyes.

"Alright, I'm sorry I called you a baby," said Tyler. His voice sounded as though it couldn't decide if it wanted to come out as tenor or baritone. "Look, Dad just texted and said he's busy so I've got to take you over to visit your mom. So tell Zoey that she has to go home and let's go. I've got other stuff I wanna do today."

"But Dad said we were going to visit together. He said he'd let me pick out a snack to bring, too," replied Nicole, childish disappointment audible in every word.

"I just told you, he's busy, and I don't have time to drive around finding you something to eat."

"It's not for me. Mom says she misses real food."

"She can text Dad to bring her something next time he visits then. Come on, get moving or I'm not going to take you at all."

Nicole looked as if she wanted to argue the point, but nodded and followed her brother out of the room.

"Can I go get my art stuff? Mom promised we could draw together last time."

"Whatever, just hurry up."

With that, Tyler stalked off down the hall, the sound of creaking stairs following shortly after.

"I'm guessing that's your brother?" asked Zoey as they walked back to Nicole's room.

"He's got a different mom than me, but Dad says that doesn't mean he's not my real brother," replied Nicole, sounding a little bitter. "Hey, do you want to come to visit my mom with me?" she added, more cheerfully.

Wandering around the house with Nicole was one thing. Zoey was curious to see how things in this other world differed from her own, but that didn't mean she was ready to go on a day trip.

"I don't think so . . . Is it OK if I just look around some more? Then I think I need to go home."

"Oh . . . OK," said Nicole, her face falling again. "But you'll come back to visit tomorrow? Or I can come over and see you when I get back?"

Zoey didn't know what to say to that. She still had about a thousand questions she wanted to ask, but didn't think Nicole would have answers to most of them. She didn't know if there was anyone who could explain the whys and hows of the situation, but she was certain that they were well beyond any ten-year-old's grasp. With their bedrooms linked and Nicole's apparent immunity to fear, one thing was certain—they were going to be seeing more of each other.

"Maybe tomorrow? You don't have school, right?"

"Nope, it's summer break."

"Alright, I'll come back tomorrow then."

"OK! I'll think of something really fun to do," replied Nicole as she gathered up some of the art supplies from her bedroom floor. Then, as if an important thought had occurred to her, she piped up, "Oh! If you want to open up doors or pick stuff up here, you probably have to say it out loud."

"What?" asked Zoey, caught off guard by the nonsensical string of words.

"The first time I went to your auntie's house, I couldn't move things. I was trying to open up the door to the hall, and it felt really, really heavy. Then I just said, 'Open up!' really loud. Then it got light and opened up. I think it's magic."

Zoey was about to question the odd set of instructions when she remembered trying to open the closet door. It hadn't budged for her, but Nicole had opened it easily. She didn't know if it was actually magic, but if Nicole said that's what she needed to do, then she was probably right.

"So if I wanted to open up a cookie jar, I'd have to say 'Open up, cookie jar'?" asked Zoey, with a touch of humor.

"Just 'Open up.' But we don't have a cookie jar here."

"Hey, Pipsqueak! Get your butt down here," called Tyler from downstairs, his voice cracking as he shouted.

"OK, I gotta go. But you promise you'll come back tomorrow, right?"

"I promise."

Nicole gave an excited trill as she scooped up what was apparently the last piece of paper she needed for her visit. With a hop and a slightly manic expression on her face, she tore out of the room at a sprint. Zoey could tell by the sound of skidding socks that she'd overshot and had to double back before taking the stairs at what sounded like two at a time.

Zoey let out a sigh and plopped down on the edge of Nicole's bed. She couldn't shake the feeling that she'd landed herself a job as an unpaid babysitter for the rest of the summer. Well, it wasn't like she had anything else going on in her life. She couldn't exactly ignore the other world now that she knew it existed, and Nicole was the only person she could talk to about it.

She listened from the second floor until she heard the front door open and close. With the image of Nicole wandering through Aunt Carol's house fresh in her mind, a smile spread across Zoey's face. Now it was her turn to do some haunting.

CHAPTER TEN

Barrier

As much as Zoey felt justified in wandering through Nicole's house in search of answers, a twinge of guilt nagged at her as she thought of where to start. Regardless of how similar the house looked to Aunt Carol's, they weren't the same. This one belonged to Nicole and her family. Although Nicole seemed to think that they had become fast friends, Zoey was a complete stranger to these people. She'd never go digging through someone else's house under ordinary circumstances and though this situation was a lot of things, ordinary was not among them.

Zoey crossed the hall to the door that led to the TV room at Aunt Carol's house. She grabbed the brass handle and pressed down. It refused to budge. With a grunt of frustration, she pressed with as much force as she could manage. Still, the handle remained stubbornly in place. She jiggled the handle. It didn't budge. There, that was something, a solid fact. If the door were simply locked, then there would at least be some give. The handle should have been able to rattle up and down while still barring her way into the room. This was something else.

She remembered what Nicole had said, about having to ask things to open when she was over at Aunt Carol's. It sounded childish, impossible even, but maybe Nicole was right.

"Open up," said Zoey. Nothing happened. She squared her shoulders and dug into her own memories of childhood magic. "Open, Sesame." Still nothing happened. An embarrassed prickling spread across her cheeks.

Abandoning the door, Zoey crossed back into Nicole's room. She selected one of the colored pencils on the floor and tapped it with her fingers. It gave a familiar 'tick' as her nail tapped the smooth surface of the sky-blue cylinder. Encouraged by this, she grasped it between three fingers and made to pick it up. As though it were in cahoots with the door handle, the colored pencil refused to be picked up.

"What the hell!"

The dull prickling in her cheeks bloomed into a full flush of frustration. None of this made sense. Nicole could move through Aunt Carol's house. She could open doors and turn on televisions and sneak cookies from the kitchen. This was stupid. She was sure that if Nicole could do it, she, Zoey, could do it, too. She grabbed hold of the colored pencil once more and tugged. It was a tiny stick of wood. She'd been using them since she was in kindergarten. It was effortless. It wasn't supposed to be hard. She should have been able to grip it between her fingers and pick it up.

Zoey's hand flew upward so fast that she almost smacked herself in the face. She gawked at it for a full five seconds. Swirling silvery mist had condensed around her fingers, enveloping both it and the colored pencil in wispy tendrils. She let the stick drop, expecting it to land with a heavy crash. Instead, it hit the floor with a series of light ticks before coming to a stop.

She checked her hand. The tendrils of mist had faded back into the general, almost imperceptible haze that floated throughout this world. Zoey picked the pencil back up. The mist swirled around her fingers once more. She let it fall back to the floor before snatching up the pencil's pink counterpart. The mist condensed, the pencil obeyed.

Something had changed since her first couple attempts at lifting the pencils, but what was it? She searched her brain. She had been frustrated, straining her fingers in the attempt to lift the pencil up. It clicked. The last thing she'd thought before nearly concussing herself in the face had been how easy the task should have been. No, not quite that. She had remembered herself using colored pencils in her past, pictured it in her mind's eye.

Zoey sprang upright and bounded back toward the stubbornly sealed door. She conjured up an image of opening the same door at Aunt Carol's house. It was effortless. It was simple. It was so easy she didn't have to think about it. This time, she watched the mist as it took form. The surrounding haze pushed together, condensing into a transparent silvery cloud that enveloped both her hand and the piece of metal clenched within. She took a steadying breath and pushed down. The latch gave a satisfying click.

Heart light with her triumph, Zoey pushed the door open and peered inside. Her nose wrinkled before she'd even finished opening the door. It smelled of sweat and unwashed clothes, mingled with some unholy mixture of cheap cologne, hair gel, and body spray. The inside matched the pungent aroma that invaded Zoey's nose. A twin bed sat against one wall, the covers cast in a tangle at its side. Scattered across the floor were any number of crumpled clothes. From t-shirts and polos to faded jeans, and, Zoey blushed, a great deal of underwear that looked as though they'd seen better days.

Nothing good in here.

She made to shut the door but found it stuck in place. Grumbling, she drew her thoughts away from the disaster of a room before her. She pictured the door following the pull of her hand, an action she'd done countless times. She willed it to happen, to be easy. The mist condensed and the door heeded her command, locking the funk of teen spirit behind it.

Feeling as though she had something resembling a handle on interacting with the world around her, Zoey headed downstairs. Though she was itching to explore the house for the sake of seeing how it differed from Aunt Carol's, she had a goal in mind. She poked her head into what she knew as the piano room. Instead, she found a family room. A four-person sofa, a love seat, and a battered old recliner sat at three points around an expensive-looking TV. Nothing remarkable. Not what she was looking for.

A knot of anxiety took root in her chest as she walked toward what she knew as Uncle Will's office. If her quarry wasn't behind this door, then she'd be nearly out of options. Careful to keep the image of it swinging open fixed in her mind, Zoey pushed open the door. Her heart leaped. The room held a couple of tall bookshelves, a large wooden desk, and, most important of all, a desktop computer. Zoey strode toward the beautiful machine and sat herself down in front of it.

She pictured all the times she'd used computers in her life, watching the mist condense around the mouse beneath her hand. She jiggled the mouse and, heart leaping, was treated to the sight of the default desktop wallpaper. Thankful that Nicole's parents didn't use child locks, Zoey searched the icons for what she was looking for. She didn't recognize any of the options before her but was able to summon the internet after only one failed attempt. IcyLynx was a strange name for a browser, but beggars couldn't be choosers.

Determined to start small and work her way up, Zoey typed in, "Who is the president of the United States?" The unfamiliar search engine worked just as well as the ones she knew and brought up a middle-aged white man that she'd never seen before. Despite the fact that it wasn't what she was here for, Zoey couldn't help but skim a couple of articles about this universe's leader of the free world.

Scandals weren't unique to the America she knew. Apparently, a former classmate of James Arthur Scott had come forward with a series of unflattering photographs from the president's college years. The response? The photos were taken out of context, relics of a single night in the president's life, not a depiction of who he was as a person. Besides, everyone went a little wild in college. It was as American as apple pie.

"I guess some things are constants . . ." mumbled Zoey, clearing the search bar.

She knew what she wanted to look up next, so why were her fingers refusing to cooperate? Her heart pounded in her head. This is what she wanted, no, what she needed to know . . . But then what? How could it help her? Wouldn't it just add a whole new layer of hurt for her to deal with?

Zoey's stomach churned. Once she did this, there'd be no going back. She let out a long, steadying breath before typing "Jared Michael Thompson" and hitting enter. Her heart leaped and lurched in equal measure as the search engine returned page upon page of results.

She was able to rule out most of them at a glance. Her father wasn't likely to be the all-state basketball star who scored the winning basket, or the beloved grandfather of ten who had passed away in March of last year. Every time she found a heading that could fit her father's description, her heart gave a hopeful leap. This made the accompanying disappointment that followed all the more painful. None of them were her dad. She widened her search. She looked for her mom, for her grandma, for her friends, she looked up herself.

Hot tears threatened to spill out as she struggled to accept the truth. That this world was, for better or worse, not an alternate version of her own. There would be no tearful reunion between her and her father. He had left the world they had shared, and neither of them existed in this one. Zoey wiped her eyes with the back of her hand. She had been stupid to even look this up. Her heart was aching in a way that it hadn't since the early days following her dad's death.

Worse yet, the thought of what would have happened if she had found her dad's doppelgänger bubbled up in her mind. What would that have accomplished? She wasn't from this world and no one but Nicole could see her. Even if he existed here, would finding a version of her father who could neither see nor hear her really make her feel any better? A version of her dad roaming through the world, without a single thought of her in his head. . .That would have been worse than him being dead.

Furious with herself, Zoey pushed away from the computer. She needed to move, to get away from the terrible sensation in her chest that her own foolish actions had awoken. Explore, she needed to explore. The fact that this was a separate world wasn't to be mourned. She forced herself to pull away from her self-inflicted grief. The mist swirled around her hand as she grabbed hold of the front door handle.

The summer day on the other side greeted Zoey in a symphony of sensations. The wind rustled through the trees above. It carried with it the smells of grass and summer flowers. All around her came the persistent cries of cicadas. She let the glorious sunlight wash over her, extending her arms to catch more of its warming embrace. She let herself relax, willing the summer sun to burn away the tight knot of dread that still gripped her heart.

Her feet began walking of their own accord. The front yard was different from the one she'd sat reading in the day before. Hedges that looked in need of a good trim stood in place of Aunt Carol's manicured rose bushes. A pink bicycle with a large white tuft of stuffing sticking out of the seat lay abandoned in the grass. Zoey hopped over the low gate that connected the two lengths of peeling white picket fence surrounding the house and made her way down the street.

Everything was new to her this time, with no familiar framework to vary from. The street now looked as bright and cheerful as it had dark and mysterious when Zoey had first seen it from inside Uncle Will's car. The lawns were manicured and lush, the flowers in bloom. A sense of overwhelming cheer washed over Zoey. It was that ineffable sense of true freedom that she'd had always associated with being outside during summer break.

She walked in long, lazy strides with no real plan of where she was going. She turned her head this way and that to take in everything about the summer's day around her. In broad strokes, it was all the same: Warm sun, bright colors, fresh scents, but it was all landing differently. Though the sun shone brightly above, she couldn't help but think about roaming her house in the dead of night. The feeling of tranquility, of solitude in a way that brought comfort rather than loneliness. Like the late hours of the night, this world felt as if it belonged to her and her alone.

She rounded the corner, the back of her hand trailing against the rough surface of an old painted fence. A vague plan had formed in her mind. One large loop around the neighborhood. She didn't even want to think about what getting lost in a world where no one could see her might mean. She could go on for a while, though. As long as she turned right two more times, she'd travel in a circle, and there was always doubling back.

She had begun to wonder if she had to worry about getting sunburned in this world when it happened. A tingle broke out across her entire body. Her stride slowed as she contemplated the sensation. It felt almost like it did after her emotions had reached their limits. After hours of sobbing over the loss of her father, or a prolonged screaming match with her mother. It was numb and empty.

The warmth left the day, replaced not with cold, but with a dull, flat nothing. Zoey looked up to see if the sun had moved behind the clouds. It was shining as resolutely as it had been before. A concerning fact clicked into place. She was looking at the sun, but its light didn't hurt her eyes. She stopped walking, continuing to stare into the blazing disk in confusion.

As she watched, it flickered like an old TV that was on the fritz. She pulled her gaze away from the glowing sphere. It wasn't only the sun. The world surrounding her had begun to flicker and falter. One second all was bright, vivid, and solid, the next it was black and empty, as if it were beating out an uneven string of morse code.

A wave of nausea overtook Zoey. Her muscles ached. Her head throbbed as though it might split down the middle at any second. She fell to her knees, her breaths were coming in short, ragged gasps. Her lungs screamed for air. Was she dying? Was this what it had been like for her dad as the life trickled out of him after the impact? Trembling, Zoey forced herself to stand. The blinking landscape did nothing to help her calm down. She started walking in clumsy, staggering steps back the way she'd come. She needed to get help.

Her body protested every step she took, willing her to collapse to the ground. But to do that in a world where she was unseen would be certain death. She didn't know if she could make it back to her world, but she had to try. Time blurred as she staggered forward. How many steps had she taken? It felt like a thousand, but she hadn't even made it to the corner, if she was going in the right direction at all.

It was no use. Each step was costing her an incredible amount, as though she was dragging herself through quicksand. Her legs spasmed. She lost her balance and tumbled forward. She braced for an impact, but there was only a soft pressure on her chest. Like floating in a pool of tepid water. Her breathing relaxed. Air filled her lungs more easily. But her body was spent. She made to trace her fingers along the rough pavement beneath her. Her hand felt fuzzy and fat, almost as though it had fallen asleep.

If this was dying, it wasn't so bad. Her body was tired, but the pain had stopped. The world was still flickering, but, if she closed her eyes, she could convince herself that she was relaxed. She wondered what dying as a visitor to this world might mean. Was there an afterlife? She'd never been sure of that in her world, but maybe it was a known fact here. If there was, would she be welcomed with open arms? Or maybe she'd be cast out, left to wander this strange, mist-filled world forever.

Zoey's eyes flew open. The mist! Squinting at the still-flicking world, she saw nothing hanging in the air around her. It was clean and clear, just as the air looked back in her world. She forced her head off the sidewalk. Her heart leaped. There, only a few feet away was the faint haze of mist that she had assumed permeated this entire world. Like the denser swirls within the closet, the faint traces were pushing up against some invisible force.

Summoning all the strength she possessed, Zoey pulled herself to her hands and knees. Her body shook so badly she was surprised her bones didn't rattle right out of her. Every inch cost her a tremendous deal, but slowly, torturously, she pulled her way toward the beckoning silver. She just needed to make it back into the mist, and she'd be fine. With a last burst of strength and a guttural cry, she plunged her hand past the invisible barrier. A jolt of energy surged through her body. The flickering world solidified back into steady summer colors.

Zoey allowed herself to lie there for a moment, taking in deep lungfuls of rich, life-sustaining air. Her strength was returning at an almost alarming rate. She pulled the rest of her body across the invisible barrier with a triumphant cry. The pain that racked her body faded all at once. She pulled herself up into a sitting position and stared back at the mundane stretch of sidewalk. Her mind was reeling with her recent brush with . . . what exactly? Death? Fading from existence? Whatever it had been, it would have been final, and she had barely managed to escape.

She got to her feet again, her legs shaking out of nerves rather than the agonizing sensation that, only moments ago, rendered them all but useless. In complete defiance of common sense, Zoey reached toward the shimmering wall of mist. She pushed the tips of her fingers through. After several moments, they tingled as if falling asleep. Zoey ripped her hand away from the barrier, unwilling to risk exposing it to the other side for another moment.

That confirmed it. She was safe as long as she stayed where she could see traces of the mist that had brought her to this world. But, why did the mist end here, and what would have happened if she hadn't been able to claw her way back into it? She shuddered at the thought. It was possible that Nicole might shed some light on what had just happened. Zoey dismissed the idea. She couldn't see Nicole being as bubbly and excited about crossing between the two worlds if she'd experienced what wandering outside of the mist entailed. Though she was fine on this side of the barrier, something had shifted in Zoey's mind. This world wasn't just mysterious, it was dangerous, too.

She turned her back on the site of her collapse and wobbled toward Nicole's house. She'd had enough of this place, at least for today. Her protesting muscles told her that her brush with the other side of the barrier hadn't been without consequence. Her feet dragged with each step she took, her head cloudy and muddled. There was no stopping to rest here, though. She was determined to keep well upright until she got back to her world.

Her eyes worked overtime as she walked, on the lookout for any sign of another spot where the mist didn't reside. Her vigilance proved unnecessary. She didn't spot a single patch of mist-free space on her way back to the house. Was there some giant bubble surrounding the mist? One that held it contained in the area surrounding Nicole's house? The mist that was, for whatever reason, something she needed for her survival in this world. What if the bubble popped, and the mist spread out, too thin to do any good? Zoey didn't want to think about it.

She made her way back inside and marched upstairs. She stopped to stare at the square of churning mist in Nicole's closet. Despite it being the thing that saved her on her walk, she couldn't help but be wary. Whatever force had first drawn her through the crawlspace wasn't returning. Zoey thought it likely to have evaporated forever as she lay gasping for air on the sunbaked sidewalk. Staying in Nicole's world forever wasn't an option, though.

Zoey paused at the point of crawling through to the other side. She hadn't noticed the last time, panicked as she'd been, but unlike her side of reality, there was no barrier keeping the mist in. It poured in a steady stream out of the empty space where the panel had been.

Why was there a barrier on her end of the passage, but not here? Another question she didn't have an answer to. She could stand there thinking about it for the rest of her life and never come up with an answer. Not only would it be a waste of time, it wasn't a priority. She needed to get home, even if the thought of crawling back into the mist's source made her stomach churn. Resigned to her fate, Zoey moved into the mist and let the silver gray become her entire world once more.

CHAPTER ELEVEN

Lies

By the time Zoey walked out of the closet at Aunt Carol's house, she was dragging worse than ever. Despite the bright sunlight spilling through the bay window, Zoey wanted nothing more than to crawl into bed and pull the covers over her head. Her journey to the other side of reality hadn't pushed the events of the previous night out of her mind, however. She knew she was due for a discussion with her aunt and uncle.

She checked the clock on her phone and received a shock. It was already well past one. She'd spent almost two hours in the other world. If she was lucky, her aunt and uncle would have thought she was sleeping in after her nightmare, but if not . . . Zoey crept toward the stairs, listening for any trace of her aunt and uncle. She didn't have to listen very hard.

"I'm sure she's not up to anything awful, Will."

Despite the reassuring words, Aunt Carol's tone was peppered with doubt. Zoey's heart stopped. They'd noticed she'd left. She needed to work fast.

"She snuck out of the house. No note, didn't say a word to either of us. Does that sound like the kind of thing someone would do unless they were up to something?"

All thoughts of returning to bed obliterated from her mind, Zoey snuck back to her room as quickly as she could manage. She stripped out of her nightclothes, wadded them up, and tossed them toward the back of her closet. She dawned a fresh pair of jeans and a comfortable shirt before grabbing the keys from her bedside table. If her aunt or uncle had snooped and found her keys, then her lie was only going to make things worse. But since she couldn't tell them the truth of what happened, that was a risk she needed to take.

She made it out to the hallway before she'd noticed it. Just like the house on the other side, silvery tendrils of mist were everywhere. Did it follow her over? Had her crossing the barrier changed things somehow? What if the mist stopped outside Aunt Carol's house like it did Nicole's? What if she was trapped inside a transparent bubble that had formed to mirror the one in the other world?

A shining fact broke through the surface of Zoey's panic. She had dressed herself and picked up her keys with no conscious thought behind it. She grabbed hold of the nearby door handle and pressed down. It moved effortlessly, with no change to how the mist flowed around her hand. The rules weren't the same. She wasn't trapped . . .

Demanding as her new train of thought was, she needed to push it out of her mind. One crisis at a time. The mysteries of the mist could wait. Dealing with her aunt and uncle couldn't. Holding her breath, she crept down downstairs, taking care to avoid the fourth step. She stopped at the first landing and listened.

"I'm just asking you to look at the facts, Carol. The girl's barely been here two days, and she's already lost her temper so badly that she smashed a glass, and now she's snuck out to do only God knows what."

Uncle Will's muffled words were coming from the direction of the kitchen. It seemed like luck might be on her side after all.

"Of course it sounds horrible when you say it like that. But really, Will, we both agreed that her outburst was just as much our fault."

"And this little 'walk' of hers?"

"I'm sure that's all it is . . ."

Zoey's heart gave a guilty lurch. She didn't know whether Aunt Carol's trust in her was unique, or something she gave to everyone. Either way, it was about to be betrayed. She crept the rest of the way down the stairs and made for the front door. There was no use delaying it. Zoey rattled the lock and jiggled the handle. After a beat, she opened the door as loudly as she could and pushed it closed, jangling her keys for good measure.

"Aunt Carol? Uncle Will?"

Her aunt and uncle rushed from the kitchen. Aunt Carol's expression was somewhere between relieved and worried. Uncle Will, on the other hand, had narrowed his eyes in suspicion.

"Zoey, where have you been?" asked Aunt Carol.

"All over the place I guess," replied Zoey, delivering the words with what she hoped was a convincingly exasperated sigh. The expression on her uncle's face, however, told her that wasn't anything resembling an acceptable explanation. "I went out for a walk and got a little bit lost. Everything around here looks kind of the same to me."

It was a weak lie, Zoey knew it, but it was the only one she had.

"Without telling anyone?" asked Uncle Will, clearly not buying it.

"I didn't think I'd be gone long. I'm sorry if I made you guys worry."

She blinked rapidly in an effort to rid the mist from her vision. She was finding it hard to keep herself in the conversation while watching the silvery substance billowing about.

"And you decided to take this little walk without your shoes?"

Crap. How could she have forgotten something so obvious? She'd left her shoes at the back door the night she arrived. Hoping her uncle couldn't hear her hammering heart, Zoey racked her brain.

"Grounding!" The word slipped out of her too forcefully, but she barreled onward anyway. "I was reading one of Aunt Carol's books last night, and it was talking about how walking outside without shoes could help with all kinds of things."

"Oh, Zoey, it really can," replied Aunt Carol, the look of anxiety on her face evaporating in an instant.

"Yeah, that's what the book said. I thought it might help me relax a bit. I'm still kind of shaken up from last night."

She considered throwing an apologetic look at her uncle with her last comment but thought that might be pushing it. Uncle Will stared at Zoey with a level of intensity that felt almost indecent. His eyes darted toward Aunt Carol before focusing back on Zoey.

"Zoey, let me smell your breath."

Zoey wanted to be outraged, but couldn't bring herself to do it. Her story was flimsy at best, and, if she looked as tired as she felt since her encounter beyond the mist, she must have looked terrible. She turned to her aunt for help. Was she imagining it, or did she suddenly look as concerned as Uncle Will?

Relenting, she took a step toward her uncle and exhaled. His nose twitched. He and Aunt Carol shared a look in which he shook his head. For good measure, Zoey turned out her pockets, feeling a sense of vindictive satisfaction in knowing they were empty.

"See? No drugs, nothing fishy. I just got lost."

"Watch the attitude, please," replied her uncle in a clipped tone.

Zoey's cheeks flushed. Here she was, stuck dealing with the aftermath of learning that the immutable laws of the universe weren't at all what she'd thought, and her uncle's biggest concern was that she'd been out drinking. She longed to hurl the truth at her uncle, that she wished that was what she'd actually been up to. Maybe being nice and drunk would have made the impossible situation easier to swallow. Biting back the vicious diatribe that pressed against her lips, however, Zoey nodded.

"I'm sorry, but I wasn't out drinking or anything like that. I know I probably look terrible, but I'm just tired, I promise. "

Her uncle considered her words for a few moments. His expression of icy disapproval wavered.

"This is exactly why I wanted to set some rules last night. If you would have told one of us you were going on a walk, this wouldn't have been a problem."

"I'm all for some rules, I just need to know what they are," replied Zoey, mirroring her sentiment from the night before.

"Your uncle and I were just discussing them. How about we talk about them over lunch?"

After agreeing to what she felt likely to be another awkward meal, Zoey dragged herself upstairs. Aunt Carol had informed her she had at least twenty minutes to kill before the meal was ready. Zoey breathed a sigh of relief. She needed to clear her head. A shower seemed warranted.

She stood under the jet of steaming water with her eyes closed, willing it to wash the muddled cacophony from her mind. An unexpected benefit of the hot water turned out to be the fact that the steam obscured the faint, ever-present mist from Zoey's vision. It did little to clear it from her thoughts, however. She tried to organize the events of the morning into objective facts. Every time she started, it seemed laughable. Otherworldly ten-year-olds and a closet full of magical mist didn't gel well with rational thought processes.

She had been apprehensive about promising to visit Nicole tomorrow at the moment, but now the idea held a great deal of appeal. Zoey didn't expect her to have any answers to the questions swirling in her head, but at least they could talk about the situation openly. A ten-year-old confidant was better than none after all.

Fluffy white suds slid off her body and spiraled down the drain. She couldn't help but think again of the giant bubble over Nicole's house. She'd dismissed the thought of another such sphere over on her side of reality, but did she really believe it? She had half a mind to leap out of the shower and go running down the block to check. The idea that she was trapped here made her skin crawl.

Stepping out of the shower, Zoey wrapped a towel around herself, its fluffy embrace protection against the chill in the pit of her stomach. Her heart fell further when she opened the bathroom door and saw the other side still filled with faint, silvery mist. Why was it over here? And why couldn't her aunt and uncle see it? She needed answers, but how on earth was she supposed to get them?

Zoey crossed her room to the closet and made her way toward the back. In the dim glow of the singular lightbulb, she found what she was looking for. The panel that fell away to reveal the silver-filled world was firmly in place, no trace of what lay behind it. She took a step forward and gasped. It vanished from sight. In its place was the view into the world of mist beyond. There was no invisible barrier holding the churning substance back this time. Silver gray gushed from the empty square, dissipating into the closet surrounding it.

In some perverse parody of the bunny hop, Zoey took a step back, then a step forward, then back again. When she moved close, the panel vanished and the stream of mist appeared. While standing back, the panel stood firmly in view, no source of the ambient mist discernible.

"What did I do . . . ?" mumbled Zoey.

She had to assume that her crossing over had caused this breach. Had she let something in? Something that was supposed to remain locked away? If she had, what did that mean for her, or more troublingly so, for her world at large? Feeling nauseous, Zoey forced herself away from the panel. She dressed in a whirl, not paying attention to what she was putting on. She left the room as if by doing so she could also leave the reality of what she'd unleashed behind her.

She sat at the kitchen table where Uncle Will was already thumbing through the Sunday paper. She nodded in thanks when Aunt Carol set down a shallow bowl and a tall glass of water in front of her. Her aunt joined them and began making small talk that didn't quite make it to Zoey's ears. In an effort to hide her detachment from the situation, Zoey took a bite of salad. It was some kind of quinoa and vegetable concoction, with a sharp dressing and chunks of leftover salmon. The colorful vegetables and the tempting scent of herbs and fish wafting off it told Zoey that it was probably delicious, but it tasted like cardboard in her mouth.

Talk soon turned to the rules that her aunt and uncle had agreed to. Zoey did her best to feign interest in the conversation. She nodded along, and even forced out a smile or two to mirror her aunt and uncle. By the end of lunch, she hadn't said more than a couple of words. Though she had absorbed the new rules that had been laid down.

She was expected to be out of bed no later than ten thirty each morning and in bed by midnight at the very latest. If she found she couldn't sleep, she was allowed to get a snack from the kitchen and to read something so long as it wasn't horror. No TV after lights out. If she had a night where she couldn't sleep, her wake-up time could be pushed back, within reason. She had to keep her bedroom tidy, help with dishes, and, when asked, tend the garden with her aunt. She could leave the house as long as she told her aunt or uncle where she was going and how long she would be gone. If she made any friends, she needed to introduce them to her aunt and uncle.

They were all reasonable rules, and yet, Zoey couldn't help but feel resentful. Why did her helping with the dishes matter in the slightest? How could something as banal as what time she went to bed be discussed when the world was filling with some unknown force that she herself had unleashed upon it?

Zoey thanked her aunt for the meal in robotic tones and pushed away from the table. The newly established rules flickered through her mind. She asked if it was alright if she went on another walk. A quick one this time. A look from Uncle Will, a playful "just don't get lost this time" from Aunt Carol, and Zoey was on her way.

The warmth on her skin told her that the day was as glorious as the one in Nicole's world had been. The sight of the omnipresent haze swirling all throughout the backyard sapped away any joy she might have drawn from the beautiful weather. Since the mist wasn't, as she had feared, contained to the house itself, she had a mission. It was all linked to what happened next. If she wasn't trapped within the mist, then everything would be OK. It wouldn't make any more sense than it now did, but it would at least be OK.

Rounding the corner, Zoey made sure to keep her eyes focused on the shimmering mist around her. She took the same measured steps as her walk through the other world, not keen on another near-death experience. She saw what she had dreaded almost immediately. Partway down the block, she could make out where the fog appeared denser. Fists clenched, she inched toward the rippling anomaly, determined to follow through with her plan.

She checked over her shoulder to make sure no one was watching. Since they couldn't see the mist, she knew what she was about to do would look bizarre to anyone passing by. With the coast clear, Zoey extended a shaky hand toward the barrier. Like before, she dipped the tip of her finger through to where she knew no mist was waiting on the other side.

She stood there with her finger pointed, as if in accusation, at the blank space in front of her. Her body tensed, waiting for the numbness to start. It didn't come. Not daring to believe what that could mean, Zoey took a step forward. Her entire hand now rested on the other side of the barrier. Zoey wiggled her fingers.

Any moment now she was expecting the numbness to set in, to tell her she was trapped, incapable of leaving the embrace of the mist ever again. The numbness still didn't come. With a deep breath and forcing herself to be braver than she really was, Zoey stepped through the barrier.

No lightning bolt ripped through the sky. No sudden surge of pain racked her body. The other side was nothing more than a stretch of suburban mundanity. The sun was shining. Tiny insects buzzed through mist-free air, and most heartening of all, her body felt fine. She let out a breath that she'd been holding since she'd come back to this side of reality. She wasn't trapped, and the world wasn't doomed. Not yet anyway.

There was still so much she didn't understand, but discovering that her situation wasn't as dire as she'd thought was a marvelous tonic. The summer's day surrounding her came to life. The sun warmed her skin, the air smelled fresh and alive with green things. With her panic soothed, her body remembered how tired it was.

She stifled a yawn and turned back towards the house. She didn't care if it meant an increase in huffines from Uncle Will. She'd earned a nice, long nap.

CHAPTER TWELVE

Playdate

A soft sigh escaped Zoey as she turned restlessly to her side. As desperate as she was for a good night's sleep, it wasn't happening. For once, it wasn't because of horrible dreams or her mother's absence. She'd lost track of the number of times she thought she'd quieted her mind. Each time she did, some detail would slide into focus before she could drift off. Her eyes would snap open. Her thoughts would start back up, and the cycle would repeat.

Nicole. The mist. The existence of a separate reality. Her mind refused to table even one of the endless thoughts it conjured up. She tried focusing on other things, which only yesterday had been so important to her. In the light of her recent discoveries, clashes with Uncle Will and thoughts of how school might go in her new setting seemed insignificant.

Her preoccupation hadn't gone unnoticed by her aunt and uncle. She'd managed to sneak in a quick nap after she returned home. After that, Aunt Carol seemed determined that the two of them were to bond. She tried tempting her with some instruction on the piano, which Zoey refused. Not to be discouraged, her aunt had brought up *The Healing Power of Mother Earth*. The conversation that followed was full of short replies, a lack of opinions, and frequent glances toward the door.

When it came time for Zoey to help with dinner, she stood for a full five minutes clutching the silverware as though she'd never set a table in her life. Dinner was some chicken dish that hadn't made any impression on Zoey. From the looks she caught her aunt and uncle exchanging through the meal, she knew they were concerned. Well, Aunt Carol had looked concerned, her uncle had looked suspicious.

Exhaustion overcame her restless mind in the early hours of the morning. She slipped into a dream that, like her waking world, was filled with mist. It was thicker than she'd ever seen in waking. It clung to her body like wet snow, weighing her down as she fought against it. She couldn't breathe the thick saccharine air that invaded her lungs with each shuddering attempt. Somewhere off in the distance, a voice was calling her name.

"Zoey . . ."

She tried to call back to them but found she had no voice. She had no air in her lungs to form sounds.

"Zoey . . ."

There was only mist within her now. Within and without.

"Zoey . . . ?"

She wasn't herself anymore. She was mist.

"Zoey!"

Zoey's mind lurched. The last cry hadn't come from some far-off place like the others. It had been right in front of her. Her eyes snapped open. Blurry shapes formed amid the stars clouding her vision. Nicole was standing beside her bed, green eyes shining, a look of innocent concern on her youthful face. She was clutching a collection of coloring books to her chest with one arm, an enormous box of crayons held at her side by the other.

"Nicole? What are you doing?" Zoey hissed, sitting upright.

Nicole blanched.

"Y-you said you were going to come visit me today. I've been up for a really long time and I thought you forgot."

"What time's it?"

"It's almost lunchtime."

"Look, you can't just come into my room like this . . ." She caught the look of hurt on Nicole's face even through her own exhaustion and let out a sigh. "I mean, just don't wake me up like that, alright?"

"You looked like you were having a bad dream."

"It wasn't so bad. I've had worse anyway."

"You're not mad?" asked Nicole, her voice timid.

"Not mad, just tired. I was going to come and see you like I said."

Zoey reached for her phone and flipped it open. It was ten fifteen.

So much for almost lunchtime . . . thought Zoey indignantly. Before Zoey could get her head around her thoughts, Nicole let out a groan of longing.

"You've got your own phone? That's so cool!"

"Uh, I guess so . . ."

"Everyone else in my family has one, but my dad says I can't until I'm older."

"Well, I got my first phone when I was twelve, so you might have to wait another few years."

"Just two!" interjected Nicole with a petulant stamp of her foot. "I'm ten and a half."

Zoey had to stifle a chuckle. Nicole had reminded her forcibly of how she'd felt at that age. Back then, every single month's worth of age was a precious treasure. One step further on the path toward becoming a grownup.

"Just two then. Or hey, maybe sooner. A bunch of my friends had phones before me."

"Maybe if I get one we can send each other messages!"

A pang of guilt jabbed at Zoey. It was obvious that Nicole felt like she'd found a best friend. While it was true that she'd been looking forward to seeing Nicole, the draw had been more for the sake of letting out the overcrowded thoughts she couldn't share with anyone else.

"Yeah, maybe. I don't know if they'd work, though. You know, because of the mist and everything."

A surprised expression settled on Nicole's face, as though she'd all but forgotten about the fact that they were from different worlds. With her mind working more clearly, Zoey pulled herself out of bed. She wanted to ask Nicole some questions, but here didn't seem like the place to do it. Aunt Carol was a little airy, but she was bound to have questions of her own if she overheard Zoey having a lengthy conversation with herself.

"Wait here for a minute, OK? I need to go see if my Aunt's up."

Nicole looked like she was about to pout, but sat down on the edge of the bed and nodded. It didn't take more than a couple steps into the hall for Zoey to realize that her aunt was already awake. At least, Zoey doubted that the delicious scent wafting up from downstairs was made by her uncle.

When she walked into the kitchen, Aunt Carol was sitting at the table with her nose buried in a book titled *The Not So Distant Beyond*. The table was set for one. A slice of quiche sat untouched next to a steaming mug. Aunt Carol's eyes flicked up at the sound of Zoey's approaching footsteps. A warm smile spread across her face. She set the book to rest beside her plate.

"Zoey dear, I wasn't expecting you to be up for a while. Does this mean you got some good sleep last night?"

"It was alright," lied Zoey. "Where's Uncle Will? At work?"

"In the office every Monday by eight," replied Aunt Carol with a chuckle. "You could set your watch by that man. But, let's not get into that. I wanted to have a little chat with you. About your visitor a couple nights ago."

Zoey suppressed a grimace. She was sure she knew where this was going, and she wasn't looking forward to it. Maybe if she got things rolling herself, then she'd be able to get away more quickly.

"I was thinking about that, too. I think Uncle Will was right, it was just a nightmare."

Aunt Carol's face fell. "Do you really believe that?"

Zoey shifted. She didn't know how she could answer "yes" when she knew full well that she didn't. She was sure, however, that Nicole wasn't a ghost or spirit, which was clearly where Aunt Carol's mind still was. She could at least refute that part while remaining honest.

"I don't think it was a ghost."

Aunt Carol rose from the table without a word. She glided across the kitchen and, after a few moments of clattering, returned holding a plate bearing a thick slice of spinach quiche.

"Would you sit? I think I should tell you why I'm so interested in this."

All too aware that she had an invisible ten-year-old waiting for her upstairs, Zoey's eyes flicked up to the ceiling. There was no doubt that she owed Aunt Carol. Not only for taking her in but for doing her best to treat her like a regular person rather than a troubled teen.

She couldn't see any way to refuse her aunt. She nodded and took a seat. Aunt Carol set down a plate in front of Zoey and resumed her seat. Her eyes fixed at a point somewhere above Zoey's right shoulder.

"Did you happen to notice the hope chest in your bedroom?"

Wherever Zoey had thought the conversation was going, it wasn't there.

"I did, it's beautiful."

Aunt Carol smiled, her eyes still not meeting Zoey's. "My late husband made that for me, the first year after we were married."

Zoey froze midway into bringing a forkful of quiche to her mouth. She tripped over her words before managing to croak out, "I'm sorry . . ."

Aunt Carol smiled. "Thank you, but it's OK. I miss him terribly sometimes, but as they say, life goes on. I've healed. Or at least, I thought I had. You see . . ." Aunt Carol fiddled with one of her bangles. Her eyes unfixed from the spot behind Zoey. The misty gray of her iris blurred as her aunt's gaze turned inward. "I can't help but wonder if this spirit isn't him, trying to reach out to me."

Zoey took a bite of her quiche in an attempt to be spared the requirement of replying. Her aunt seemed intent on hearing her thoughts on the matter, however, and took a sip of her tea to fill the silence. Zoey swallowed her mouthful of quiche, then, with a great effort, forced herself to look at her aunt.

"What makes you think that?"

Aunt Carol ran her thumb along the spine of her book.

"I told you I've felt like I'm being watched sometimes, right? Well, I feel it most often when I'm at the piano. Keith loved to listen to me play. Back then, I'd be playing and catch him standing there, watching me. When I'd ask what he was doing, he'd say that, as my biggest fan, he never wanted to miss one of my shows."

The sheen in Aunt Carol's eyes threatened to spill over as she brought a small bite of quiche to her mouth. Heart aching for her, Zoey reached out a hand in comfort but caught herself. She hated when people did things like that to her. Kind words and lofty platitudes didn't bring loved ones back.

"It sounds like he loved you a lot."

"Oh, he did. We both did. Love each other, I mean," replied Aunt Carol in a clipped, flustered tone. "And I know it must sound crazy, even I think it's a little crazy. I've never heard about a spirit that eats, but Keith absolutely loved my baking. Every year, when I'd ask him what he wanted for his birthday, he'd ask me to bake him something—even though I did that all the time, anyway."

Shame welled up inside Zoey. She'd never known the kind of love Aunt Carol was talking about. If losing it was anything like losing her dad, however, Zoey could see why Aunt Carol was clinging to this small shred of hope. Hadn't looking up her father been the first thing she'd done in the other world? She had been desperate to find anything at all that would allow her to regain that bond. How was Aunt Carol hoping that her husband was trying to communicate to her from the beyond any different?

"Zoey . . . ?"

Zoey jumped about a foot in the air, a cry of surprise catching in her throat. The voice had come from behind her, timid and unsure.

"Zoey dear? Is everything alright?"

"M-muscle cramp," invented Zoey wildly, jumping up from her chair. "Going to walk it off, I'll be right back." With Aunt Carol looking bewildered behind her, Zoey threw a significant look at Nicole and hobbled her way back upstairs in what she hoped was a convincing display. "Nicole!" she hissed when the two of them had made it back to her room. "I told you to wait here."

"Y-you were gone a really long time," replied Nicole, looking somewhere between concerned and defiant. "Why was your auntie crying?"

"Becau—" Zoey faltered yet again. The same way she couldn't tell Aunt Carol the truth about the "spirit," she felt she couldn't tell Nicole the truth about Aunt Carol. How did you tell a ten-year-old that her wandering around the house made someone think they were being haunted by the spirit of their husband? "We were talking about something sad."

"Are you going to make her feel better?"

"I, what?" asked Zoey, thrown by the bluntness of the question.

"When someone's sad, you're supposed to try and make them feel better. That's what my mom says."

"I don't know if I can, it's complicated."

"Oh! We could make her a card! My mom always says she feels better after I make one for her."

"I don't think a card is going to help here," replied Zoey. "Look, maybe you should go back to your room, then I can come by—"

"No! I want to stay here. I'll be quiet, I promise."

Nicole extended her hand toward Zoey, pinky extended and a pleading look on her face.

"Alright, but you need to stay up here, OK?"

"OK, I promise," said Nicole, eyes wide as she nodded her head.

Zoey sighed and met Nicole's pinky with her own. They twisted together, shook up and down, then released. Afterward, Nicole looked so pleased that Zoey couldn't help but smile. She couldn't remember the last time she'd made a pinky promise. It was nice, like stumbling upon an old childhood keepsake.

With the distraction of Nicole out of the way, Zoey's mind turned to what was waiting for her downstairs. Her hasty declaration that she believed Nicole's visit had been a dream felt immoral now that Aunt Carol had shared something so personal. To insist that there was nothing strange going on was downright awful, but feigning a belief that the presence in the house might be Aunt Carol's late husband felt even worse. Telling the truth was out of the question, too.

"Sorry about that," said Zoey, reclaiming her place at the table. "I must have slept on it funny."

Aunt Carol stared at Zoey, her brow furrowed as if she were thinking hard about something. When Zoey met her gaze with an apologetic look, however, her aunt's expression reverted to its usual, affectionate state.

"Wait until you're my age. Turn the wrong way in your sleep and it's with you for the rest of the week."

Zoey didn't know whether or not she was supposed to laugh. She compromised by taking an extra large bite of quiche. She was glad to find that she'd regained the ability to taste since yesterday. It was quite as delicious as everything else Zoey had tasted since moving in. They sat in silence but for the clinking of silverware for several moments.

"Look, Aunt Carol . . . maybe it wasn't just a dream, but I'm not sure it's, uh . . ." Zoey faltered. Even knowing that it wasn't the case, saying outright that the presence wasn't her late husband still felt cruel. "I mean, why would it start happening now if he died so long ago?"

Aunt Carol didn't seem thrown by the question. On the contrary, a wistful smile spread across her face.

"He always wanted children. We did, I should say. It wasn't in the cards, though. This all started happening when your Uncle Will and I were first talking about having you to stay. If Keith is the one visiting us, then I'm sure he's just as thrilled to have you here as I am."

Aunt Carol's words pierced Zoey like a knife. She forced a smile on her face. It only made the guilt sit more heavily in the pit of her stomach.

"That's really nice, especially since all I've done so far is cause problems."

"It's been a little bumpy maybe, but that's life, isn't it?"

"I guess so . . ."

More silence passed between them. Zoey did her best to devote herself to her dwindling slice of quiche while Aunt Carol gazed down at her book.

"I wanted to tell you these things because, well, if strange things keep happening, I don't want you to be afraid. I'm not sure if it's Keith or not, I think it is, but if it isn't, I'm sure it's not anything malevolent. The signs are all wrong for that."

"I don't think it's anything evil either," agreed Zoey, thrilled to be able to tell a bit of the truth.

"That makes me happy to hear," said Aunt Carol, checking her watch. "I've got some errands to run in town today if you'd like to come."

Zoey could tell that her aunt was hoping to continue their conversation. Part of her wanted to keep talking as well, if only in the hopes that she might reveal more bits of the truth to assuage her guilty conscience. But Nicole was waiting upstairs, and the two of them had made a promise. Then there were the questions that she needed to ask Nicole.

"I think I just want to stay here," began Zoey, but seeing her aunt's face fall at her words, she added, "I thought I might try working through some of those piano lessons."

"That sounds like a lovely idea."

Looking more cheerful than she had throughout their conversation, Aunt Carol collected the plates from the table and headed for the sink. Zoey's offer to help was waved away. Aunt Carol slipped the plates into the dishwasher.

Thinking of Nicole, Zoey opened up the cookie jar. Two crumbling sugar cookies sat at the bottom of the smooth ceramic vessel.

"Is it OK if I take the last of these?"

"Of course, dear. I'd actually be a little offended if any of my cookies hung around long enough to go stale," said Aunt Carol, before clapping her hands together. "If you tell me your favorite, I can pick up the ingredients while I'm out. If we have time, I could show you how to make them when I get back."

Zoey repressed a smile. Finally, a request she didn't have to shoot down.

"Oh, sure. That sounds fun. I like all kinds, though, so you don't have to buy anything special."

"Now, Zoey, I asked you for your favorite. It's no trouble at all, really. It all comes from the same store."

"I like chocolate chip," said Zoey, feeling suddenly five years old.

"That's perfect. There's a new brand of chocolate morsels I've been wanting to try out."

Zoey headed back upstairs. Babysitting, learning the piano, a baking lesson with Aunt Carol. None of those things were on her to-do list a week ago. She'd been worried that living at Aunt Carol's was going to be boring. She didn't know what words she'd use to describe her life as of late, but boring certainly wasn't among them.

CHAPTER THIRTEEN

Coloring

By the time Zoey got back to her room, Nicole had made herself at home. She was lying on the floor with crayons scattered around her as she colored. Zoey watched from the doorway as the younger girl worked. She was twiddling a bright blue crayon between her fingers, biting her lower lip as she surveyed the drawing. Zoey hadn't noticed it before, but the mist looked thicker around Nicole. It was as if she were outlined like one of the pictures in her coloring book. Zoey examined her hand. The mist drifted across it but there was no outline.

"Hey, Nicole, you can see the mist over here, right?"

Nicole looked up from her drawing, her face breaking into a grin.

"Yup, it's always been over here. It's pretty."

"And after you came here for the first time, you could see it back at your house?"

Nicole nodded, her face falling. "I asked my dad if he could see it, and he said I might need glasses." Then without missing a beat, added, "Are you done having breakfast with your auntie? Do you want to color?"

Thinking that doing something quiet until Aunt Carol was out of the house was a good idea, Zoey nodded. She closed the door and claimed a patch of floor next to the one Nicole had carved out for herself. Now that she was closer, Zoey could see that Nicole wasn't merely filling in the outlines that the book provided. The page she was working on depicted a shining sun overlooking a meadow, with snow-capped mountains in the background. Nicole had colored the mountains in progressive shades of gray, with added strokes that ignored the lines here and there. The effect created a sense of depth that Zoey was sure hadn't been present in her own work at that age. It was the same with the field. The grass appeared to wave in a phantom breeze, while the rays of the sun shone down in bright orange and yellow whorls.

"That's really good," said Zoey, impressed.

Nicole beamed at the compliment.

"Do you want to do one together?" she asked, turning to the next page.

"I don't think I'd be able to keep up. Seriously, you're great for your age. A lot better than me anyway."

"My mom says it doesn't matter if you're good, as long as you have fun."

Zoey smiled. "Alright, one second."

She opened up the chest at the foot of her bed. Now that she knew it was a relic of Aunt Carol's deceased husband, she felt even stranger about storing her things inside of it. She hadn't thought to ask at the time, but she wondered why it was in her room rather than her aunt's if it was such an important piece.

She eased the lid shut, then popped in the CD that she'd retrieved from within. The music that poured out of the purple boombox was bright and cheerful, a catchy song from one of the movies Zoey had grown up on. As much as her tastes had changed since she'd left elementary school behind, she couldn't deny the soft spot she still harbored for this kind of music.

Zoey reclaimed her spot on the floor. Nicole had chosen an ocean scene. The bright blue crayon that Zoey picked out reminded her of a question she had been sitting on.

"Hey, Nicole, do you have to concentrate to pick these up?"

"No? They're just crayons," replied Nicole, sounding confused.

"When I was over at your house, I couldn't pick up your pencil crayons at first. I had to sort of think about all the times I did it before."

"Ohhh," began Nicole, understanding flashing across her face. "Yeah, sometimes I have to think really hard to get things to move at your house."

"But not things you bring over?"

"Nope," replied Nicole as she shaded in some sand with a dusty purple. "Aren't you going to color?"

"I guess I don't know where to start."

"You can do the little fish there," said Nicole, indicating a cluster near the corner of the page. "I'll color the water over here."

"Alright, but don't blame me if they look more like underwater potatoes than fish when I'm done with them."

Nicole let out a loud giggle at the lame joke, coaxing a smile out of Zoey. The two of them got to work. As bizarre as the situation was, Zoey got into a bit of a groove. By the time she'd finished her last fish, which, to her relief, didn't resemble any sort of tuber, the simple pleasure of the activity had carried some of her anxiety away. It wasn't as if it were a new experience. She had memories of coloring with her friends that stretched all the way back to preschool. She couldn't remember the last time she'd done it, though. The realization pulled at her heart. She hadn't realized that the last time she'd colored with her friends had been the last time. She pushed the thought away.

"Doesn't your family notice you're gone when you come over here?" she asked, thinking of how she'd already had to lie to cover up her solitary venture into Nicole's world.

"My dad's really busy. He says Tyler's supposed to watch me."

"I'm guessing he doesn't do a very good job?"

"Not really . . ." said Nicole, pausing to finish shading in a starfish. "He used to play with me a lot when I was little. Now, he says he's busy and to leave him alone."

"That's not very nice."

"It's OK. I like playing by myself sometimes."

"What about your mom? He took you to visit her yesterday, right? Are your parents divorced?"

"What? No!" replied Nicole, sounding offended at the idea. "My mom's staying at the hospital for a while . . . She's sick."

"Oh . . . I'm sorry."

Zoey looked to Nicole, who was now shading without really looking at the page. She wanted to say something to comfort her, but couldn't think of what.

"It's OK. She says she's working really hard to get better so she can come home soon."

"I'm sure she'll be better soon, then."

Nicole nodded and turned her attention back to the drawing, which, much to Zoey's surprise, was almost done. She had intended to ask Nicole some questions about the mist once they were finished, but her heart wasn't in it anymore.

"Hey, this looks pretty good, your parts anyway. Mine look like a five-year-old did it."

There was no question in Zoey's mind that if she were to show someone the drawing and tell them that one part was done by a ten-year-old and the other by a teenager, most of them would guess wrong.

"Do you want to do another? I could use the practice."

Nicole looked at their masterpiece with a somewhat pained expression and shook her head. "Can we do something else?"

"Oh, sure. What do you want to do?" asked Zoey, getting to her feet.

"Do you have any games?"

"I don't think so. I mean, I didn't bring any with me." Zoey's words seemed to shake something loose in Nicole's mind. She looked serious as if deciding on something important. "Hey, is everything OK?"

Nicole stared at Zoey for a moment, her head tilted slightly. Then, with no preamble, "Zoey, why did you move in here?"

Zoey's face flushed. This wasn't a topic she'd expected to discuss today. "That's sort of . . . complicated."

"Did something happen to your parents?"

Youch, right to the point.

Pulling herself up to sit with her back against the bed, Zoey studied Nicole. She had pulled herself up to sit, cross-legged opposite her. The mist still outlined her in a faint, silvery glow. Zoey didn't want to talk about her parents if she could avoid it. She got the feeling that any attempt to deflect the conversation would end poorly, though. Nicole was staring at her with such an interested expression that Zoey didn't know how to say no.

"Do you know what it means when someone passes away?" asked Zoey, remembering a time before she had any grasp of the concept herself.

Nicole frowned. "Is that like dying?"

Zoey nodded. "It's another way of saying it. Well, my dad passed away two years ago."

"But what about your mom?"

"She's still alive, but we . . . don't get along anymore."

It was costing Zoey a great deal to keep her expression neutral as she spoke. Saying it out loud only reminded her of how much she missed her mom. Not the one she had now, but the one she used to have. She didn't like to think about it like that, but in some ways, she had lost both of her parents, even though one of them was just a text message away.

"Did you two have a fight?"

"A bunch of them, I guess," replied Zoey, still endeavoring to keep her tone neutral.

"Did you try saying you're sorry?"

Anger flared inside Zoey's chest. She had to remind herself that Nicole was only a kid. Her world was still one where a mother's love was unconditional, one where nothing could happen that was so bad that it couldn't be fixed with an apology and a hug. Come to think of it, Zoey had felt that way herself up until things had started to go bad between her and her mom. Maybe Nicole's mindset was the right one. A mother's love was unconditional, but Zoey's mother was, unfortunately, the exception that proved the rule.

"It's . . . a lot more complicated than that. Saying sorry isn't enough to fix it."

"My brother and dad yell at each other sometimes, but they always say sorry," replied Nicole, her words feeling dangerously close to a lecture.

"It's going to take a lot more than that . . . You know how I asked if your parents were divorced before?" Zoey leaned her head back to stare at the ceiling. "Well, it's kind of like that. It's a lot bigger than a fight.

That's why I'm living here, because my mom doesn't want to deal with me anymore."

The last sentence had slipped out of Zoey's mouth unbidden. It was true, though. If her mom still cared about her, she wouldn't be here having this conversation. Her mom had chosen a path that, despite what people kept telling her, didn't leave room for forgiveness. She could tell that the conversation was making Nicole sad. Although they had only just met, it didn't sit well with Zoey.

"Hey, we're supposed to be having fun, aren't we?" asked Zoey, standing up as if to shake the weight of the conversation away. "You said you liked to listen to my aunt play the piano, right? How about we go downstairs and try to play something?"

Nicole's glum expression transformed into wide-eyed eagerness so fast it was almost comical. She jumped to her feet, sending crayons rolling across the floor.

"Really? You won't get in trouble?"

"Nope," said Zoey, doing her best to mimic Nicole's energy. "I promised my aunt I'd practice today, so you'd be doing me a favor."

"You play the piano?" asked Nicole, overawed.

"Not any better than I color. Probably worse actually. But as long as we're having fun that's all that matters, right?"

Zoey reopened the hope chest and retrieved the small collection of songbooks within. She tossed several of the thinner, more difficult-looking volumes onto her bed before settling on the beginner's all-in-one course. They walked downstairs together, Nicole's jubilation at the idea of playing the piano infecting Zoey as they went.

They sat down on the bench and stared at the first page of the course book. Zoey recognized the squiggly S on one of the staffs as the treble clef from her brief stint of playing the recorder. The backward C on the other hand, she had no clue.

"F . . . A . . . C . . . E . . ." mumbled Zoey, trying to match up the names of the notes with the keys shown by the book.

"You can read music?" asked Nicole, sounding impressed.

"Kind of, this part anyway. Hey, why don't you fiddle around while I try and figure this out?"

It became obvious that Nicole had been holding back until she was asked. Now that she had permission, she plunked out a series of random, discordant notes. It sounded awful, but Nicole was having so much fun that Zoey didn't dare ask her to stop.

As attempting to follow the lesson in the book proved impossible with the noise Nicole was making, Zoey joined in on the improvised piece. The result was a chaotic symphony so loud that she was sure that the trees surrounding Aunt Carol's house were now permanently bird-free. Nicole was laughing, one hand cupped over her ear in some form of defense from the sound they were creating. Before Zoey knew it, she was laughing, too.

"Alright, alright," said Zoey, struggling to have her voice heard over the din. "Maybe let's try to follow the book after all."

The laughter took a while to subside as the ghost of their symphony continued to rattle Zoey's eardrums. With their warm-up out of the way, they began trying to follow the lessons in earnest. Even though it was nothing more than a series of simple warm-ups for her right hand, Zoey found it difficult. It would have been easier if she were attempting this first lesson alone, but not half as fun.

By the time the clock on the mantel struck twelve, they'd made precious little progress through the book. They could identify middle C and climb the notes up through the octaves, but not much else. The black keys remained a mystery.

"I think we tortured this poor piano enough," said Zoey, flexing her fingers.

"I'm getting hungry," replied Nicole. "Do you want to go to my place for lunch? My dad made borscht last night. It's really good."

The thought of going back into the void and experiencing the stomach-churning descent that followed turned Zoey's stomach. But, she'd been wanting to talk more about the mysterious realm that joined their two worlds since Nicole had woken her up that morning. Maybe falling through nothingness would even be fun with Nicole at her side.

"Alright, I just have to think about what to tell my aunt first."

Zoey pulled out her phone. After her conversation with Nicole, the three unread messages from her mom pulled at her. Maybe she'd open them, eventually. Not now at least. She pulled up Aunt Carol's number.

Hey, Aunt Carol. I'm going to go find some place to read outside. I'll be back before dinner.

She hadn't even managed to tuck her phone back into her pocket when it buzzed.

That's OK by me. There's a little park a couple of blocks from the house. I know high school kids hang out there sometimes. Maybe you'll make a friend.

Zoey sent back a thumbs-up. It was hard for her to not feel at least a little guilty over lying to her aunt again. But what other choice did she have? She was about to follow Nicole's lead upstairs when something pulled her up short.

"One second," Zoey strode to the back door and quickly slipped on her sneakers. There were only so many times she could use the whole "grounding" excuse. "Alright, let's go. What did you say we're having again? Broosht?" asked Zoey, joining Nicole on the staircase.

"Borscht," corrected Nicole, laughing. "It's soup. It's really good."

The two of them walked back upstairs with Nicole rambling about plans for the rest of the day. Zoey paused at the spot where the phantom panel at the back of the closet melted away. She knew Nicole had been using the passage between their houses for weeks with no ill effect, but it still made her uneasy.

"Come on, this is the best part!"

Zoey still couldn't decide if Nicole was brave or reckless as the soles of her pink-striped socks disappeared beyond the panel. She took a deep breath. The scent of sugar-spun ozone filled her lungs. Then, with a sigh, she followed Nicole into the mist, glad that she wasn't going alone this time.

CHAPTER FOURTEEN

Float

The trip to Nicole's world went as it had the last time Zoey had taken it. This time, though, the horrible sensation of plummeting was accompanied by Nicole's high, elated shrieking. Zoey yelled right along, but her own cries were distinctly in the realm of panic. They landed on the layer of mist that became solid beneath their feet and crawled through the accompanying square of light.

"Doesn't that scare you? What if something goes wrong one of these times?" asked Zoey, as they made their way down to the kitchen.

"It's not scary. It's magic."

Zoey wanted to argue the point but didn't see much use in it. If that was the way Nicole felt, then that was it. Logic hadn't just left the building, it had never entered in the first place. For all she knew, Nicole was right, it was magic and so it was safe. No, that wasn't right. Maybe it was magic, but it wasn't safe, at least not entirely. Her brief trip outside the mist had proven that.

"I think we might need to be more careful. We don't know much about it."

"But it's fun."

Zoey thought about telling Nicole of her venture outside the fog. What was the point, though? It would only scare her. As long as Nicole stayed inside the house, and it looked like she always did, she wasn't in any danger.

"Don't you wonder where the magic came from, though?"

"Maybe it's always been there? My mom says sometimes real miracles happen. Maybe this is a real miracle."

"It is at least miracle-adjacent."

Nicole screwed up her face. "Adjacent?"

"Oh, it means 'close to.'"

"Like, the stove is adjacent to the fridge?" asked Nicole, pointing to the gas range.

"Exactly."

"Tyler says I'm dumb when I don't know a word."

"He's the dumb one then. You can't know something until you do. Next time he says that try calling him a troglodyte. I don't think he'll know that word," replied Zoey. She hadn't gotten the impression that Tyler spent much of his free time reading.

"What does that mean?"

"It's a fancy way of saying caveman. You know, big and dumb."

Zoey scratched her head in a gorilla-like manner and let out a soft "oook." Nicole guffawed. She opened the fridge, still wearing a smile. She dug out a large container that was filled to the brim with a deep crimson liquid. Zoey supposed it was borscht.

"There's no blood in borscht, is there?" asked Zoey. She didn't think so, but maybe that's just how the people of this world got down.

"What? No!" Replied Nicole, her words broken up by giggles. "It's beet soup. My Baba taught my dad how to make it when he was little. It's really good."

She set the container on the countertop before pulling over one of the slat-backed chairs from the round kitchen table. The chair creaked as she hopped up and began rummaging through the cabinets above.

"Do you need some help?"

"I've got it," replied Nicole, producing two brightly colored plastic cups.

With the cups set beside the soup, she scooched the chair sideways by shifting her weight rapidly from one side to the other. Zoey remembered doing this exact thing when she was younger, but she still felt the urge to steady the back of the chair.

Nicole rummaged around the top shelf on tiptoe. She was pulling down a pair of what Zoey was sure were "the good china" bowls, when her foot shifted and the chair wobbled. As Nicole fell back, she dropped the bowls. She spun her arms in identical windmill motions and managed to steady herself.

The bowls fell in what seemed like slow motion. Zoey reached out a hand to catch them, knowing full well that she wouldn't make it in time. Stupidly, she cried out as if begging the bowls to not smash onto the tile floor.

"Don't!"

She snapped her eyes shut, bracing for the impact. The only sound she heard was Nicole's relieved sigh. Zoey opened her eyes and gasped. The bowls were floating a foot off the ground, unharmed. They were outlined with a layer of mist so thick that it had all but lost its transparent appearance.

An excited laugh left Zoey as the bowls hovered in place. She hurried over to the miraculously unharmed dishware and plucked them out of the air. It was as if they were made of paper, or perhaps filled with helium, moving with only the slightest effort on her part. After a moment, the cradle of mist that surrounded them dissipated, and the weight of the bowls pressed into her hands.

"Did you see that?" asked Zoey.

"You caught the bowls? Thank you! I would have been in trouble if I broke them."

"I didn't catch them, though. They just stopped falling."

Nicole hopped down from the chair and took the bowls from Zoey's hand. She placed them on the counter to join the soup.

"They stopped falling?"

"Yes! I was too far away to catch them. I yelled and then they were floating. It was like the mist caught them."

Nicole screwed up her face and grabbed the neon pink cup from the counter. She held it at chest level then let it fall to the ground. It hit the tile beneath it with a series of hollow, bouncing thuds, rolling under the table before coming to a stop. Zoey picked up the cup and repeated Nicole's experiment. The cup fell, bounced, rolled, and stopped. The mist only swished and swirled around it, as it did whenever anything moved in this world.

"Are you sure you didn't catch them?"

"Yes, I'm sure!" cried Zoey, moved to frustration.

"Oh! Maybe it's because you said don't! Like a magic word."

Nicole picked up the cup once again and dropped it, this time shouting "Don't!" as it fell. The cup thudded, bounced, and rolled. Zoey was about to try the magic word approach herself when a door opened from somewhere upstairs. Footsteps pounded across the floor. Tyler's voice called down to them.

"Hey! What the heck are you doing?"

"We're making lunch!" Nicole was shouting back, but her tone was conversational.

"Doesn't sound like it to me!"

"I dropped my cup!"

"Yeah, like five times! Cool it!"

"You cool it! Don't be such a troglodyte!"

Zoey snorted. Not quite the right usage, but still funny.

"What did you call me?" asked Tyler, his voice moving down the staircase.

"A troglodyte. It means big and dumb like a monkey."

"Who the heck are you calling a monkey? You look in a mirror lately?"

Zoey thought she detected a hint of a smile in Tyler's voice, and going by Nicole's reaction, she wasn't the only one. Even though she knew Tyler couldn't hear her, Zoey whispered her instructions to Nicole, who grinned.

"I can't, they're still broken from the last time you used them."

She was sure she heard Tyler laugh this time. His footsteps reversed course, back toward the second floor.

"You're lucky I'm a nice troglodyte. Now, keep it down."

Tyler hadn't made it to his door before Nicole scooped up the cup and dropped it again. A groan floated down from upstairs, punctuated by the sound of a slammed door.

"OK, maybe let's cut it out with the cup. But really, the bowls were floating," said Zoey, still giddy from the experience.

"I want to see it, though."

Zoey had to snatch the cup from under Nicole's outstretched hand to stop her from repeating the experiment. Tyler wasn't as humorless as she had first thought, but she was sure he'd move onto genuine annoyance if they kept it up much longer.

Ignoring Nicole's offended exclamation, Zoey placed the cup on the kitchen table and sat down in front of it. She picked the cup up and watched the mist swirled to surround it. That was easy, old hat. Next, she pictured the cup leaving her hand.

She could see it in her mind's eye, it rolling out of her hand and being pulled by gravity onto the table below. She wiped the image from her mind. With a clean slate, she painted a new picture: The cup leaving her hand but staying fixed in place. Gravity wouldn't affect it. This was magic, and what chance did gravity stand against a force that made anything possible?

Zoey opened her hand and willed the cup to match the image in her head. Nicole gasped. Zoey let out a cheer of triumph. The cup was floating in the air, bobbing like a cork a foot off the table. Zoey's heart lept. She had half a mind to join in as Nicole jumped up and down excitedly.

The cup bobbed gently before her. She traced a course through the air, stopping with her finger pointing at the sink, all the while picturing its path in her mind's eye. The little pink cup drifted behind the path her finger traced out, as if it were being pulled by an invisible string. When the cup was floating level with the faucet, Zoey forced the image out of her mind. As though the strings had been cut, the cup fell with a satisfying thunk into the empty sink.

"That was so cool!" exclaimed Nicole, making no effort to control her volume.

"It was, but quiet down or Tyler will come back."

Nicole slapped her hand over her mouth. The soup sat forgotten on the counter. Nicole sat down beside Zoey and stared down a set of salt and pepper shakers. Although Nicole's face turned blush, then red from concentration, they didn't move an inch. The mist wafted around the set in passive defiance of Nicole's furiously thought commands.

"Why. Can't. I. Do. It?" asked Nicole, still straining in concentration.

"Maybe . . . because you're from this world? I mean, I can't make things happen just by thinking about them normally. Maybe you could do it over at my aunt's house."

"Can we go back and try?"

"How about after lunch? I want to try that soup."

"You promise?"

"Promise."

It looked as if it pained her a great deal to stop trying to repeat Zoey's trick with the cup, but Nicole went back to heating up their lunch. Zoey, meanwhile, focused on the mist that surrounded her. Just when she had a handle on what it meant, a new wrinkle appeared. This one was far more welcome than the discovery of what would happen if they left the mist at least.

Nicole scooped large ladlefuls of soup into a flowered pot that waited on the stove. It was deep red, like pig's blood. Like Carrie at prom. With no desire for telekinetic vengeance, Zoey's mind wandered to what this new discovery implied.

She could move objects with her mind. No, that wasn't quite right. She could will the mist that permeated Nicole's world to move objects for her. The mist, whose origin or nature was all but unknown. The mist that had leaked out into her world as well, perhaps due to her own meddling. Or, maybe, it had been there all along but she hadn't been able to see it?

Why couldn't she be more like Nicole, to whom the mist was nothing more than a force of pure wonder? Not to be questioned or feared, impossible to understand by its very nature, and, therefore, not to be worried about. After her experience outside the bubble, Zoey was convinced that it wasn't as benign as Nicole saw it. But, did that mean it was sinister? Maybe the truth of the matter was more in the middle, a gray between the black and white of their two opposing views.

"We gotta eat fast, OK? I really wanna go back to your house so I can make things move, too."

The pot on the stove began to simmer, a faintly sweet, earthy smell began to fill the kitchen. Zoey stared at the mist as it wafted over the smooth surface of the kitchen table. What else might it be capable of?

"You really never made anything else happen when you were over at my aunt's house? Anything you couldn't normally do?"

Nicole stirred the soup with her eyes focused on Zoey.

"I don't think so. I'm invisible over there, but I never did anything like that."

"I wonder what all we could do if we tried?"

A sharp hiss from the stovetop interrupted their exchange. The soup, unattended by Nicole, had reached a roiling boil. With a yelp of surprise, Nicole whirled the dial off. She ladled out two large scoops of the crimson soup into each bowl. Zoey made a motion to grab one. This caused Nicole to cry out.

"It's not ready yet!"

Zoey pulled her hand back as if scalded. Nicole scurry to the fridge and rummage around inside. She emerged holding a small container and a bundle of some green herb.

"You need sour cream and dill or it's not borscht."

Nicole dug a third spoon out of a drawer and added a large dollop of sour cream to the soup, sprinkling a dusting of the green herb on top.

"Borscht sure does have a lot of rules," replied Zoey, mirroring Nicole's additions with some trepidation. It wasn't that she was picky, but the combination wasn't something she had a lot of confidence in, especially considering she didn't know what all went into the soup.

"It's not a *rule* rule. It just makes it taste better. Plus, it turns it pink!"

Nicole stirred the sour cream into the soup. It went from a glistening blood red to a light, creamy pink dotted with little flecks of green from the dill. Looking nervous, she looked at Zoey.

"Can you carry it? It's really hot."

Zoey wrapped her hand in a Sea green oven mitt and carried the bowls of soup, one at a time, over to the table. The two of them sat down and, mimicking Nicole, Zoey stirred her soup until it too had turned a pleasant shade of pink. She took a bite. Nicole was right, it was tasty stuff. It had a rich vegetal flavor with a hint of sweetness. A pop of sour played on the tip of Zoey's tongue when she'd swallowed the first bite.

As she was the one who had suggested the soup in the first place, Zoey was surprised to see that Nicole hadn't taken a bite. She was staring at her spoon, trembling with silent effort. Zoey was certain that Nicole was trying to make it levitate.

If she had been able to float the cup by thinking about it, then what else might she be able to do? Zoey fixed her eyes on a spot above the table. The mist there was drifting along whatever phantom current kept it in perpetual motion. She closed off the area in her mind, encasing it in an invisible spun-glass sphere. The mist within the object of her focus stopped its course. It wafted against the invisible barrier Zoey had created, rolling over itself in a dreamy, swirling dance.

"How are you doing that?" asked Nicole, a note of longing in her voice.

Zoey shushed her, determined to keep her mind fixed on her creation. She willed the invisible globe to shrink. The mist drew in on itself, the translucent silver gray growing denser, more opaque. It hovered in the air, now a shining fist-sized gem. Zoey had thought the silvery shimmer that the mist possessed was it reflecting bits of whatever light surrounded it. In its condensed state, it was now obvious that the light was within the mist, rather than without. A soft, silver glow was shining from the glittering gem she'd created. It bathed the section of the table below it with a faint, ghostly light.

Zoey cupped her hand and brought it beneath the shining sphere. A gentle warmth spread from the spot where her hand met its shimmering surface. Although she could feel the smooth surface of the sphere in her hand, could feel its warmth spreading out through the tips of her fingers, it felt hollow, insubstantial. With all that the mist was capable of on its own: bridging their two realities, giving her substance in a world where she ought not to exist, what was it capable of under her instruction? What might it be able to do if only she thought the right things, knew the right words?

An image formed in her mind, pulled from a cherished memory. The orb swirled in place, pulling in more strands of surrounding mist as it turned. It quivered, warbling in Zoey's outstretched hand. Silver rippled into vivid green. Gray shifted to streaks of twisting, spiraling blue. When the last trace of silver faded from view, the orb stopped its steady rotation and fell into Zoey's outstretched palm.

The warmth had left it at some point in its transformation. Smooth glass now pressed into Zoey's hand. Her mouth fell open. She remembered the object that rested in her hand with perfect clarity, though she'd never thought she'd see it again. It was a relic of her childhood. Some delicate, decorative thing that her grandmother had given her dad in the past. A spun-glass gift that lived most of its life tucked away in a box at the back of her parent's closet.

She'd found it one day when her five-year-old self had been snooping around in her parents' room. For whatever reason, it caught her eye in a way that was unrivaled by any of her parents' other hidden treasures. Of course, they had caught her and told her not to play with it, and, of course, she hadn't listened. Whenever the urge to be a bit rebellious hit her, she'd sneak into her parents' room to play with the hidden treasure.

As her parents had predicted, the thing wound up getting smashed to bits, dropped by Zoey in a hasty attempt to tuck it away and flee the scene of her secret crime. Her dad had yelled, she had cried. She remembered crying. Whether it had been because her dad had yelled or over the loss of the object that had fascinated her so, she didn't remember. Seeing it now, whole in her hand for the first time in nearly a decade, caused a lump to form in Zoey's throat.

"That's so pretty!"

Nicole's excited cry pulled Zoey out of herself with a lurch. The delicate glass sphere burst outward. The compressed mist flew over them in a slow-motion explosion. The wisps that had comprised it rejoined the sea that surrounded them.

"Well, it was," replied Zoey, annoyed.

Nicole put both hands over her mouth. "I'm sorry, I didn't know it would break."

Zoey sighed but forced a smile before replying.

"It's alright, I didn't either. I guess you have to focus on it, like when you want to move stuff."

She hadn't realized it until the words had left her, but moving things in Nicole's world had become easier. She'd picked up the oven mitt, carried the soup, and picked up her spoon without so much as a second thought. Why, though? Zoey racked her brain.

"Nicole, when you're over at my Aunt Carol's house, do you have to think really hard to do stuff? Like, when you open doors or sneak cookies?" Nicole looked thoughtful as she ate a spoonful of her soup.

"When I first went over, I couldn't get anything to move. It was kind of scary because the bedroom door was closed and I wanted to get out. But then, I remembered a story my dad read to me with a magic door. So, I said 'Open please fairy knees' and it opened." "What?" asked Zoey, trying not to laugh. "It's from the story!" insisted Nicole. Zoey frowned. Though the words had been different, she'd tried that on her first trip to Nicole's with zero success. Why weren't the rules the same between the two of them?

"So, you have to do that every time you want to open something? What about turning on the TV? I know you've done that."

"Well . . . once I stopped being scared and knew the mist was magic, I didn't need to say 'Open, Sesame' again."

Maybe that was it. She had been afraid of the mist from the get-go, mistrusted everything about the other world. Young and innocent, Nicole's fear had turned to delight at the discovery of the "magic" all around her. Zoey, however, had never stopped fearing the mist, never stopped questioning it. Only once she accepted it a little bit, forgot her fear and moved through the mist with an open mind, had she been able to move objects in it freely.

Zoey opened her mouth to run these ideas by Nicole but stopped herself. If it was true that some level of trust was the key to mastering the mist, then making Nicole question it might cause more harm than good.

"That's not how it is for me, but I think I'm getting the hang of it."

Frustratingly, when Zoey reached out to take another bite of soup, the spoon was heavy once again. She sighed and pictured moving it in her mind's eye until she was able to take another bite. The duality of the situation buzzed in her brain. In order to move things here, she had to not think about the fact that things here didn't move freely for her. A dull pain throbbed behind her right eye. This was enough to give anyone a headache.

"Come on, let's eat fast, I wanna try playing with the mist at your house."

A promise was a promise. Zoey gave a nod of assent and started back in on her soup, head still giving the occasional throb. She tried to view the situation through Nicole's lens. She saw herself stumbling upon the world behind the panel and being excited rather than terrified. Tried to see herself accepting it as a magical world of her very own, rather than a blow to the foundation of how she viewed reality.

Believing on the same level as Nicole was a stretch, to say the least. It wasn't the sort of thing that she could embrace in the time it would take them to empty their bowls. She had to admit, though, she was in a better place to start down that road than she'd been yesterday. Sitting there, eating spoonfuls of the hearty soup, listening to Nicole babble away about everything she wanted to do back at Aunt Carol's house—it had a magic all its own.

CHAPTER FIFTEEN

Friends

Zoey spent the next thirty minutes watching Nicole experiment with the mist. She started off by sending her crayons zooming around Zoey's room with ease, first one by one, then in a cascade of color. After that, she progressed to larger objects. Aunt Carol's amethysts and several of the CDs and books that Zoey had brought with her flew around her room like so many wingless birds.

She finished by making the nightstand beside Zoey's bed float like a balloon and thud against the ceiling before setting it back in place. The look of wide-eyed excitement that spread across Nicole's face when she'd made the first crayon rise off the ground hadn't left her for even a second.

"This is so cool!" said Nicole, her voice giddy with the thrill of her newfound power. "I wonder what else we can do?"

"I don't know, but maybe you should slow down a bit? We still don't know much about the—hey, watch it!"

One of the heftier hardcovers whizzed by Zoey's head, necessitating her ducking to avoid being hit.

"Oh! Sorry!"

"Maybe just the paperbacks? The Stand could do some real damage if it hit something."

Nicole whirled the books above Zoey's bed and let them fall with a series of muffled thuds. A sly grin spread across her face. She pointed to the fluffy cream-colored pillow at the head of the bed, then flicked her fingers in Zoey's direction. Mist swirled around the pillow and it took off toward Zoey's head.

"Hey!" cried Zoey, dodging out of the way with a grin on her face.

Rather than hitting the ground, the pillow zoomed back around, circling Zoey like a down-filled vulture. Each attempt by the pillow was punctuated by a burst of raucous laughter from Nicole. Zoey bobbed and weaved as best she could, but was no match for the fluffy assault. Whenever she thought she'd dodged, the pillow would zoom back in the opposite direction and thump against her.

"You better. Watch Out. Next time. We're at your place," said Zoey between blows. "Annnndddd, gotcha. Ouch!"

Zoey had waited for her moment and snatched the pillow out of the air, forgetting about the cut on her hand.

"Are you OK?" asked Nicole. The sheen of mist surrounding the pillow disappeared back into the general ether.

"What? Oh yeah, it's my hand. It's fine, though, just annoying."

Nicole furrowed her eyebrows in concern, the smile fading from her face. After a brief pause, it returned. "Maybe I can fix it!"

"Do what now?" asked Zoey, tossing the pillow back onto her bed.

"Fix your hand. With the mist!"

Zoey was sure she'd misheard her. "Fix my hand? I don't want to sound like a wet blanket, but I don't think that's a good idea."

"Why not?" asked Nicole, sounding puzzled.

"Well, I . . ." Zoey found she didn't have a good reason for this, other than the fact that they didn't know how the mist worked. "It just seems like a bit of a leap. Floating stuff is one thing. We don't know what'll happen."

"Come on, it's magic! It won't hurt us."

Zoey remembered the crushing fatigue and flickering landscape that she'd experienced the other day. But that had been from leaving the mist, not using it. Uncertain as she was, they'd never understand more about the mist if she kept them from using it.

"I don't know . . ."

Nicole looked up at Zoey with big, shining eyes. "Please?"

Zoey sighed. "Alright. But if I tell you to stop, you have to stop, promise?"

"I promise!" said Nicole, extending her pinky for Zoey to shake.

"So what do we do?" asked Zoey, after sealing the promise.

"You should take your bandaid off," said Nicole, as though she was the authority on such matters.

Zoey couldn't argue the point. She eased the edges of the bandage off her palm before pulling it away in one. The skin underneath it was pale, the cut a puffy lightning bolt that ran from the base of her index finger to the center of her hand.

The mist wafted across her palm as Nicole pulled Zoey's hand closer. She squared her shoulders and glared down at the cut.

"Heal!"

Nothing happened.

"Heal!" This time she accompanied her cry with a dramatic wave of her hand. Still, nothing happened.

"You don't have any idea what you're doing, do you?" asked Zoey, unable to keep the laughter out of her words.

"I can do it!" Nicole glared still more intently at Zoey's hand and, waving her own in a series of swishing motions, cried, "Heal!"

They both stared, as though waiting for her hand to perform a back-flip. Though the mist roved lazily across the surface of her palm, it didn't seem intent on doing anything else.

"Well, maybe that's just not something the mist can do," said Zoey. She was, in part, relieved that Nicole's attempt had yielded no results. A failure where nothing bad happened was a win in her books.

"I really wanted to make your hand better, though," said Nicole, letting go of Zoey's hand so it fell back to her side.

"I know, but it's OK. It'll be better in a few days, anyway."

"I know, but I wanted to help . . ." said Nicole, her eyes still fixed on the cut. "Then it wouldn't hurt when we colored and stuff."

Zoey opened her mouth to reply but stopped short. Her hand felt warm. She brought it in front of her face, her eyes wide. Mist was rushing toward the cut, as though it had become a vacuum. The jagged line shone with the same light that was within the mist, growing brighter by the second. Nicole's face was a mask of focus, her eyes shining with determination.

The mist continued to flow toward Zoey's palm as Nicole's face turned pink from concentration. Heat radiated through the cut as though it were submerged in hot water. She was about to tell Nicole that maybe she should stop when her hand gave a funny spasm and the sensation of heat vanished.

Nicole sighed. Her eyes relaxed, and her expression brightened. "It worked!"

Zoey held her hand in front of her, trying not to gawk. Her palm was unblemished perfection. Smooth and whole once more. For good measure, Zoey made a fist, clenching tightly. There was no pain.

"Whoa . . . you did it."

"See! I told you I could."

"Yeah, I guess you were right," said Zoey, admiring her palm.

"Now it won't hurt your hand when we color," said Nicole, reaching down to pick up her coloring book.

As pleased with herself as Nicole looked, Zoey noticed her wince when she straightened back up. "Is everything OK?"

Nicole shut one of her eyes and put a hand to her head. "My head hurts."

"Oh no, is it bad?" asked Zoey.

"I don't think so. I still want to play," replied Nicole, her smile a little halfhearted.

Zoey looked around the room. The mist was still there, drifting as ever. Was she imagining it, though, or did it look a little thinner than before?

"Is it sort of like a headache around your temples?" asked Zoey, rubbing the spot on her own head.

"Yeah," said Nicole, mirroring Zoey.

Zoey eased Nicole onto the edge of her bed. "How about you wait here and I go get you a snack, and maybe a water, too?"

Nicole smiled back, though it looked in danger of becoming a grimace. "Are there any cookies?"

"Shoot, we just ate the last two. How about I see what else I can find?"

Before Nicole had time to answer, a door opened downstairs and Aunt Carol's voice called out, "Zoey? Are you here?"

Their heads turned toward the sound. "I'm upstairs!" replied Zoey.

"Can you be a dear and come help me bring in the groceries?"

"Oh, sure, I'll be there in a second."

Nicole's shoulders drooped. "Do I have to go home now?"

Zoey nodded. "I have to help my aunt with the groceries, and then I think she wants to make cookies."

Zoey wished she hadn't added that last bit. The look of longing on Nicole's face was all the more tragic, considering her recent request.

"OK . . ."

"Hey, tell you what. How about I ask her to write down the recipe, so I can try teaching it to you sometime. Then you won't have to sneak cookies from over here so often."

A small smile crossed Nicole's face. "OK."

Nicole walked toward the closet, taking small steps that told Zoey all too clearly that she didn't want to go. Part of Zoey wanted to relent and ask her to stay, but a louder, more logical part knew this was the best move. She didn't want Nicole to get bored waiting and come wandering downstairs again, least of all now that she had the power to move things with her mind. Then there was Nicole's headache. She couldn't be sure, but Zoey suspected it might go away once Nicole was back on her side of reality.

None of these facts had occurred to Nicole, it seemed. Her expression was nothing short of heartbreaking as she shuffled toward the closet. Zoey thought she had a point. Aunt Carol's timing had made it more or less a matter of "Thanks for fixing my hand, now scram."

"Come here," said Zoey, crossing the distance between them and pulling Nicole into a hug. "I'll see you tomorrow, OK?"

Nicole returned the hug without hesitation. "I promise I won't wake you up and scare you next time."

"I appreciate that," chuckled Zoey, watching Nicole disappear back into the closet.

When Zoey arrived downstairs, she found several cloth grocery bags already sitting on the kitchen island. She hurried out the back door in time to take the last of the haul out of the back of her aunt's car. Although her hand had been restored to full functionality by Nicole's efforts, Zoey looped the straps of the second bag over her wrist rather than grabbing hold of it.

She set the groceries down among the others already in the kitchen and started unpacking. It didn't take her more than a couple of seconds to realize that she didn't have a clue where anything went.

"Oh, you can put that in the middle shelf of the fridge," said Aunt Carol, walking in to see Zoey holding a large bag of fresh mussels.

They continued restocking the kitchen, Zoey helped by her aunt's instructions. It felt strange, opening up drawers and cupboards, putting things away in someone else's house. She kept having to remind herself that, like it or not, this was her house too for the next . . . Well, she may as well make herself a bit more comfortable with these sorts of things, anyway.

"So, how was the park? Did you make any new friends?"

"What? Oh." Zoey had all but forgotten about the lie she'd told her aunt that morning. She was about to reply that it had been fine, that there'd been no progress on the friend front, when she stopped herself. She couldn't tell her aunt the full truth about Nicole, but that didn't mean she had to be kept secret. "Not really a friend, but I did talk with this little girl who was there."

Aunt Carol finished placing a large amount of lemons in a shallow wooden bowl on the countertop before replying. "Oh, really? What's her name? Maybe I know her."

"Her name's Nicole. I didn't get her last name, though," replied Zoey, glad she could be honest about something.

"Nicole . . . It doesn't ring a bell. What did you two talk about?"

"A lot of little things, I guess," replied Zoey, heeding Aunt Carol's nod and tumbling out an equal amount of bright green limes among the lemons. "She really likes art, and this show that I used to watch when I was her age."

"How sweet. Were her parents there?"

Zoey shook her head. "No, but she said she lives nearby . . . from what she said, she's left alone a lot."

"I suppose ten isn't too young to be going to the park by yourself. I hope she's not left home alone too often, though."

"She's got an older brother that looks after her, I don't think he does a very good job."

After placing a stray box of pasta in the cupboard, Aunt Carol sat at the kitchen table. Zoey joined her at her usual spot opposite. It was nice to get to talk to someone about Nicole, but she couldn't shake the uncomfortable knot of guilt that lying to her aunt was causing.

"Oh, I know how that is," replied Aunt Carol, giving an airy wave of her hand. "My older brother Chris was supposed to look after us younger kids when our parents were out. I don't know if your grandma's ever told you some of the stories of what we got up to back then . . . Well, let's just say he didn't take the job very seriously, either. It's nice that you two were able to bond a little bit. Kids that age can be so sweet."

"She is pretty sweet," agreed Zoey. "Not much of a filter, though."

"I've got a couple students just like that. Did you make plans to see each other again?"

"Well, I think it's more like she made plans with me. I couldn't really say no." Zoey watched Aunt Carol's idly drumming fingers cut lines through the mist for a moment before continuing. "You don't think it's too weird? Being friends with a ten-year-old?"

"Not at all. I think it sounds like it's a cute little summertime friendship."

"When you said you were sure I was going to make friends, I'm guessing you weren't talking about ten-year-olds, though."

"Well, no. But I can't say that I'm surprised by it. You've got a good heart and I'm sure Nicole can see that."

Zoey's face flushed. There it was again, Aunt Carol's inexplicable faith in her. And here she was, telling half-truths left and right.

"So, you said you wanted to bake some cookies today?" asked Zoey, hoping to shift the conversation out of these uncomfortable waters.

"I think I can trust you with at least a couple of my recipes. Just remember who taught you if Nabisco ever comes knocking."

The next couple of hours passed pleasantly enough. The conversation flowed with anecdotes of previous baking escapades and frequent culinary tips from Aunt Carol. It turned out that the unidentified something that Zoey had detected in her aunt's sugar cookies was a hint of almond extract.

Whatever the reason, Zoey was glad that her aunt had forgotten the subject of the supernatural happenings around the house. She still felt a definite twinge over the fact that Aunt Carol still thought Uncle Keith was paying them visits. However, she couldn't bring herself to kill her great-uncle a second time by revealing the truth. For all she knew, both her dad and Uncle Keith were still out there somewhere. Now that she was aware of the mist and all that it implied, she couldn't rule anything out.

The two of them had settled down at the kitchen table, ready to appraise the fruits of their labor, when the sound of crunching gravel perked up Zoey's ears.

"Oh, that'll be your uncle."

The warmth in Zoey's chest, so strong a moment ago, flickered. She reminded herself that her uncle had defended her the other night, or at least, had seemed sincerely concerned about her. He might not dislike her as much as she first thought, but being around him still set her on edge. It was something she'd have to get over. For better or worse, her aunt and uncle were in her life for the foreseeable future.

When her uncle walked through the back door, Zoey received something of a shock. Was it possible, or was that actually a smile on his face?

"You're home a little early today," said Aunt Carol, rising to greet her husband with a peck on the cheek, which for some reason, made Zoey blush.

"Harrison hit the ground running this week so there wasn't a lot for me to do honestly. If he keeps it up, I might be able to retire before I'm in my seventies."

"I'm glad to hear he's finding his footing, but don't make promises you can't keep," replied Aunt Carol, a trace of a smirk on her lips.

"We'll see how things go later this week," said Uncle Will, grabbing a bottle of water out of the fridge. "So what did the two of you get up to today?"

"It's been a lovely day so far. I had brunch with Zoey, then went food shopping, oh, and by the way, they were out of that brand of honey ham you like, so I got black forest instead."

Uncle Will gave an airy wave of his hand as if to say this couldn't matter less. "What about the cookies? Was that Zoey?"

Zoey shook her head. "That was mostly Aunt Carol, I just helped."

"Nonsense," said Aunt Carol. "I think you've got a real knack for baking. You'll be making them on your own in no time."

"Oh, uh, thanks," said Zoey, her face growing warm. From the silence that followed, Zoey took it that it was her turn to detail her day.

"I started practicing the piano, then read in the park for a bit. Then came back here and made cookies with Aunt Carol."

"The piano?" asked Uncle Will, sounding surprised. "That's going to take some serious dedication if you want to make something out of it."

"I'm just sort of messing around, but it's been fun so far."

"Well, I hope you keep at it then. Carol's an outstanding teacher. It would be a shame to let the opportunity pass you by."

"It would be cool to be able to play like her someday."

Aunt Carol beamed from behind her steaming mug of tea. From the look on her face, you'd think that she and her uncle had just become the best of friends, rather than muddled their way through civil conversation for the first time.

"You know, since you're off early it might be nice if the three of us went into town. We could take Zoey to the library so she could pick out something other than those gloomy horror novels. Then maybe we could take her to Hartford's?"

"Hartford's?" asked Zoey, ignoring the jab at her taste in books.

"Oh, it's a wonderful little seafood restaurant downtown. They've got a darling patio that overlooks the ocean."

Uncle Will looked as if he were going to shoot down the idea. Instead, he glanced at his watch and nodded. "It's a little early now, but with the drive into town and the library we could still technically call it dinner I think."

"Won't it be like, five o'clock?" asked Zoey.

"I suppose your uncle and I are getting closer to our senior years. It might be good to get in some practice."

"Should I get changed? I didn't really bring anything fancy with me." She was picturing a place with a snooty maître d' and thought that her jeans and graphic t-shirt wouldn't be a welcome sight.

"It's not too fancy, but maybe pick out something without holes in it," said Uncle Will.

"I think that's the style, Will. Like acid wash jeans but all over."

Uncle Will looked thoughtful for a moment. "Well, maybe we could stop by the mall and pick out something a little less stylish if that's the case."

Zoey wasn't sure if her uncle was making a joke or not, but laughed all the same. "I've got some, uh, less distressed clothes upstairs."

"I should put on something, too," replied Aunt Carol, gesturing to the smattering of dirt and flour on her floral print dress. "How about let's all meet back in the kitchen in, oh, about half an hour?"

The sound of scraping chairs filled the kitchen as Zoey and her aunt rose from the table.

The sun was beginning to droop behind the horizon when they walked back into the house. A few awkward moments aside, Zoey hadn't had a bad time at all. The library was larger than the one in her hometown, and although she'd had to check out some sappy feel-good books, Zoey had convinced her aunt to let her pick up the latest Dean Koontz novel as well.

Dinner had been tasty, though Zoey wasn't sure it was much better than Aunt Carol's cooking. She wasn't sure she could say that she'd enjoyed the time with her uncle, but they had at least gotten along. He was still somewhat severe and a little intimidating as far as Zoey was concerned, but she discovered he did have something of a softer side. This came out especially when he got to reminiscing about his life with her Aunt Carol.

After politely declining her aunt's offer of after-dinner cookies, Zoey made her way up to her room. She was itching to dive into her new novel. She had been about to flop down and lose herself in the pages when she noticed what looked like a folded note resting on her pillow.

Zoey set down the small stack of books in her arms and unfolded the piece of paper. Inside was a hand-drawn picture of herself and Nicole. They were rendered in crayon, making soup in Nicole's kitchen, grins on both their faces. Beneath this affecting drawing were the words, "Thank you for being my friend."

Zoey didn't know how long she stared at the drawing. Her eyes fluttered as she smoothed out the crease from the center and placed it on the bedside table. She hadn't been sure how she felt about Nicole, even after their day spent together. But if Nicole said they were friends, who was she to argue?

CHAPTER SIXTEEN

Texts

With Nicole's card fresh in her mind, Zoey embraced her role as otherworldly babysitter and friend over the coming weeks. At first, she told herself it was simply because of the impossible circumstances that had brought them together, or because of Nicole's admittedly lonely home life, but her heart knew the truth—Nicole had snuck past her defenses and set up shop.

Their days passed in a way that was easy and familiar to Zoey, even if recent years had left her deprived of such friendships. Nicole would, without fail, come wandering out of the closet sometime before noon each day. More often than not, she'd have their whole day mapped out from the word go.

Whenever her aunt or uncle were around, they would spend time at Nicole's place, or else devote themselves to coloring and music in Zoey's room. When they were alone, they spread out into the house proper, playing the piano, having snacks, and playing particularly exciting games of hide-and-go-seek.

The childhood pastime was much more entertaining with the mist as an added wrinkle. Both sides of reality were fair game, so long as they confined themselves to the house. Zoey had insisted on this rule. Sneaking from house to house without the seeker noticing was especially exciting. Zoey had even gotten used to the stomach-churning descent that linked their worlds.

Waiting to be found was its own game, in a way. There was something to be said for being able to tinker with reality while you hid. Changing the mist's color, conjuring small objects out of it, floating crystals, crayons, and stuffed animals alike. They tested the capabilities of the mist like this whenever they were together. The more they did it, the easier it became.

Concerned as Zoey had been initially, Nicole's headache didn't make a reappearance. She couldn't be sure, but she thought her theory had been correct. Using the mist for anything major, like healing her hand, depleted it faster than it could be replenished from the opening between worlds.

The argument was strengthened about a week after their initial meeting. By then, Nicole had extended her experiments to her own body and found that, with some effort and screwing up of her face, she could achieve a state of weightlessness. She'd spent the rest of the day drifting through the air at Zoey's hip as they gamboled through the house. Before they'd parted ways for the day, Nicole had mentioned that she felt dizzy, though she didn't seem too concerned about it.

Zoey wondered if she should be more cautious with their experiments. As the older one between them, she felt it was her responsibility to keep both herself and Nicole safe. The mist's reaction when Nicole had healed her hand had been dramatic, though, a rushing cascade toward the source of Nicole's wish. Nothing they'd done since had evoked such a response. It wasn't a guarantee, but Zoey thought it likely that if one of their experiments proved dangerous, they would know it right away. Contrary as it was to her nature, she did her best to trust that everything would be OK until there were signs that it wouldn't.

Aunt Carol's small collection of new age books was actually proving itself somewhat useful. While Zoey still maintained that their advice about positive thinking and manifesting change through affirmations was largely drivel in the normal scope of things, they acted as a sort of guidebook for utilizing the mist. It had taken Zoey a while to piece it together, but as far as she could tell, the mist worked best when she believed it would heed her instructions. The more she told herself she could do things on the other side, the more things she found she was able to do.

It was on one of these days when there came a knock on Zoey's door. She shared a look with Nicole, who hurried to clear both herself and the large drawing they were working on off to the side. They hadn't yet tested whether her aunt or uncle could see objects from Nicole's world, but it looked like they were about to find out.

"Come in," said Zoey after pausing the CD that had been playing. Her heart fell at the sight of both her aunt and uncle on the other side. For them to come to her room together like this, she was sure it wasn't anything good. "Is something wrong?"

Aunt Carol pursed her lips. "Not exactly, I don't think. Your uncle and I—I mean." She looked toward Uncle Will.

"We don't want you feeling ganged up on, but we thought it was best if we talked to you about this as a unit," said Uncle Will, as measured as ever.

"Talk to me about what?" asked Zoey, definitely nervous now.

Perhaps something of her anxiety showed on her face because Aunt Carol flashed a reassuring smile before continuing in a less flustered tone than before. "We just wanted to have a little talk about how you and your mom are getting along."

Oh no, thought Zoey, *the tone is nice but the words are scary.*

"Oh, OK," said Zoey, trying not to look at Nicole, who was doing her best to make herself small. "Could we talk downstairs though?" She wanted to get Nicole away from this conversation as quickly as possible. It also felt like whatever this was, it would be less intimidating if they weren't standing around her room.

"I think that's a good idea," said Aunt Carol, looking relieved.

Zoey waited for the telltale squeak of the fourth step before she gave Nicole the all-clear.

Nicole looked up at Zoey with wide eyes. "Are you in trouble?"

"No clue," said Zoey. She couldn't think of what she could have done regarding her mom, considering they hadn't spoken since she'd left Ohio.

"Do you want me to come?"

"What? No." Nicole looked as though she'd been shouted at even though Zoey had worked at keeping her tone even. "I mean, I don't know what it's going to be about, and I don't want it to upset you. Stuff between me and my mom isn't usually . . . happy."

Nicole squeezed Zoey's hand, Zoey returning the pressure only half-heartedly. "Maybe it'll be happy this time."

"Maybe," replied Zoey, though she was sure it wouldn't. "If it's nothing major I'll come over after and we can hang out some more, but you've got to go now, OK?"

Nicole looked disappointed but gave Zoey's hand another squeeze before letting go. "Can we finish our drawing if you come over later?"

"Of course. If I can't come over today, then we'll work on it tomorrow. I want to finish that unicorn I was working on."

Zoey waited until Nicole disappeared into the back of the closet before letting go of the breath she'd been holding. "Alright, let's get this over with."

By the time she entered the kitchen, Aunt Carol had laid out three steaming mugs of tea around a plate of oatmeal raisin cookies. Zoey took her usual spot and grabbed hold of her mug. It was hot enough to approach the threshold of painful. Rather than let go, she held it tighter still, letting its heat ground her.

"So . . ." said Zoey, cringing at having to get the ball rolling.

Aunt Carol took a sip of her tea. "Your mom called and had some concerns she shared with us."

"Oh?" asked Zoey. She thought she might know what this was about after all, but wasn't going to offer anything up until she was sure.

"She said you haven't replied to any of her messages since moving in here," said Uncle Will, cutting as always to the heart of the matter.

It was Zoey's turn to take a sip of tea. She let the scalding liquid trickle past her lips as her brain whirred, only replying when she felt she was in danger of appearing obstinate. "There haven't been all that many messages to ignore considering I've been gone for two weeks."

Her aunt and uncle shared a look. Uncle Will opened his mouth to speak, but Aunt Carol got there first. "Why aren't you opening your messages? She's your mother, I'm sure she's worrying about you."

Zoey thought about that. She knew why she hadn't yet responded to her mom but had never voiced it out loud. Her aunt and uncle wouldn't like it, but if they didn't want the truth, then they shouldn't have asked.

"I want her to worry."

"Why would you want her to worry?" asked Aunt Carol, her bangles clattering as her hand went to her chest.

Zoey sighed. They were really doing this. "Because I spent way more time worrying about her than any kid my age should. Do you know how many times I'd be worried she was dead in a ditch somewhere, and then get yelled at for being awake when she got home?"

A silence followed Zoey's words, so dense it seemed to eat up every ounce of air in the kitchen. It stretched on so long that Zoey was about to fill it herself when, much to her surprise, Uncle Will interjected.

"What do you mean? Why would you be worried about something like that?"

Zoey raised an eyebrow. "Why wouldn't I?"

Uncle Will was looking at her with the same expression he'd worn the night Nicole had woken her up. "Zoey, you've earned some trust from us, so please keep that in mind when you answer. What happened between you and your mom?"

"What?" asked Zoey, shocked. "Didn't you ask that before you took me in?"

"We did," said Uncle Will after another shared look with Aunt Carol. "But between what your mom told us, and what you're saying now, something doesn't add up."

"Well I'm telling the truth," said Zoey bitterly. "She'd say she was going out until midnight, then not come home till four and get mad that I wasn't asleep and we'd fight. I said some pretty messed-up things to her after that, though, I can admit that much."

"That's a bit different from the story we were told," said Uncle Will. "What about you skipping school and yelling at teachers?"

Zoey's cheeks flushed. "I was sleeping like crap so some days I'd stay home without telling anyone and, yeah, I snapped at my teachers. It's embarrassing now, but I was just . . . tired and over it."

Though Zoey had told this story to adults before, she'd never seen the look that her aunt and uncle were giving her. Were they on her side? For a while, no one spoke, though Uncle Will shocked Zoey when he reached out and took a cookie for himself.

"Zoey, I'm sorry that happened to you," said Uncle Will. "I can't say I don't wonder if there isn't more to the story, but I can't see why you'd make something like that up."

Zoey couldn't believe what she was hearing and from Uncle Will, of all people. She wanted to say more but only managed to mumble, "Thanks for believing me," as she stared at the mug clenched between her hands.

"I'm sorry, too," said Aunt Carol as she fiddled with one of the bangles on her wrist. "But I don't think ignoring her messages is the right way to go about this."

Zoey shrugged, eyes still locked on her tea. "Probably not, but I don't think I'm ready to talk yet."

"I think that's alright. Part of why we moved you here was because we all thought space would do you two good. But I don't think it should be forever."

Zoey looked at her aunt. "Does that mean I can't stay here if my mom wants me to come home?" She was surprised to hear herself say it, but it was true. Even without taking Nicole and the mist into consideration, she'd gotten comfortable in her life here, or at least found it less chaotic than the one she'd known back home.

"That's—"

"We'll cross that bridge when we get to it," said Uncle Will, cutting across Aunt Carol. "But I agree with your aunt, I don't think ignoring your mom is doing anyone any favors."

Zoey swirled her mug, watching the tea slosh from side to side. "Alright, so what does that mean?"

"I think your uncle and I need some time to talk about it some," said Aunt Carol, looking at Uncle Will, who nodded. "But for now, how about you read what your mom's sent you and try your best to think of a nice reply. We already told her a bit about how you've been doing, but I'm sure she'd love to hear more from you."

Zoey didn't see how she could refuse. It was, on paper, a reasonable request. She didn't think that anything was going to be fixed by a couple of meaningless text messages, though. At the same time, she couldn't think of an argument for how it would hurt anything but her pride to at least try.

"OK, I'll let her know how I'm doing."

"Thank you," said Aunt Carol, fixing Zoey with a smile that only looked somewhat forced.

Tea still unfinished, Zoey pushed away from the table and took a step toward the door. When no one stopped her, she headed back upstairs and shut herself in her room.

She thought of her promise to Nicole but found she didn't have it in her to go for another visit today. Even though the talk hadn't gone as badly as she thought it might have, she was drained. All she wanted to do was lie in bed and wait for tomorrow to come. Since she didn't think that would go over well considering the promise she'd made downstairs, Zoey flipped open her phone and, after a pause, opened the first of the four messages her mom had sent her.

Zoey, I hope the trip was ok.

Let me know when you're settled in.

Don't cause any trouble for your aunt and uncle.

–Mom

"A whole lot of nothing . . ." mumbled Zoey, opening the next message, dated two days later.

Zoey, are you settled in?

I hope everything is going ok.

–Mom

Then almost a week after that.

If you want to be mad at me, that's fine,

But you can't ignore me like this. I'm still your mother.

And finally, from earlier today.

I spoke with your Aunt Carol on the phone,

I hope you'll be in touch soon.

–Mom

Zoey sighed. "Yup, that's on brand," then typed out her reply.

Just got done talking with Aunt Carol and Uncle Will.

Things are fine here, everyone's getting along and I don't

think I'm causing too much trouble. I hope everything

is OK at home. Give Charlie a treat for me.

–Zoey

Zoey clicked send and flung her phone onto her nightstand. *There, problem solved through small talk. Everything's all better now.* She thought, feeling guilty for it the next moment. Aunt Carol was right of course. Ignoring each other wasn't going to fix things, even if it felt satisfying in the moment. If the process of getting some of this hurt out of her heart was to start with some awkward small talk, then she was willing to take that first step, even if she didn't love it.

CHAPTER SEVENTEEN

Expand

Zoey ran her hand across the cool surface of the hardwood beneath her, eyes focused on the mist that swam along the ceiling. The sounds of the program that she was supposed to be watching with Nicole rose up around her. It was some silly animated show that didn't exist on Zoey's side of reality. While she would usually at least feign interest in the show for Nicole's sake, her heart wasn't in it this time. As if on cue, Nicole's voice rang out in a pitch that Zoey had learned to take as a warning sign.

"Zoeyyy, you're not watching."

Zoey pulled herself back into a sitting position and did her best to hitch an apologetic smile on her face. "Sorry, really zoned out there. What'd I miss?"

Nicole wasted no time in babbling on about the intricate problems of the animated characters on screen. Zoey smiled and nodded along as best she could. Try as she might, none of it was leaving any real impression on her. Something in her expression must have given her away to Nicole, who stopped gushing.

"Is everything OK? You look sad."

Zoey gave a noncommittal shrug. "I'm OK."

"My mom says it always helps to talk about things if you're upset," replied Nicole, her attention split between Zoey and the TV.

Zoey thought about that for a moment. It wasn't as if she had anyone else she could confide in. Her problems weren't going to be solved by anything a ten-year-old might come up with, but maybe getting them out would be enough to make her feel better.

"Things in my life are just a lot more . . . complicated than I thought they'd be when I was your age," replied Zoey.

Nicole looked thoughtful before giving her head a little nod. "Are you sad because you're away from your mom?"

Zoey bristled at the question. She wanted to thrust it away, to snap back in defense. She reminded herself that Nicole was a little kid. A little kid who didn't know the full extent of the situation between her and her mom.

"I'm a little sad about that I guess, but maybe more . . . frustrated than anything," replied Zoey, having to search for a child-appropriate word for her feelings toward her situation. "My mom's trying to force me to talk to her, and I don't see the point right now."

In truth, she had hoped that her messaging her mother might have been the first step toward something resembling amends. It had been two days since she'd texted her mom and there had still been no reply. She wasn't sure if her mom was satisfied that she'd exerted her will and gotten her way, or if she was giving Zoey a taste of her own medicine. Either way, it had done little to thaw the frost between the two of them.

"My mom says talking is always good," repeated Nicole, running her hand across the edge of the couch she was leaning against. "Maybe if you talk, you can make up and be friends again."

Zoey smiled sadly. It hadn't been that long ago that she'd thought things were that simple. Or maybe things really were that simple, and she was part of an unfortunate minority that found themselves in a tangled maze of circumstance.

"Your mom sounds like she's a pretty smart lady," replied Zoey, hoping to shift the conversation away from herself.

"She's really smart." Said Nicole, her eyes sparkling "She knows all kinds of things about art and people, and she knows all kinds of stories too because she reads a lot of books."

"Well, when she gets better and comes back home, maybe I can 'meet' her."

Nicole nodded and glanced back toward the still-chattering TV before giving a little jump. "Oh! You don't have to wait for her to come home. I'm going to see her on Sunday. You can come with me!"

"I don't know . . ." began Zoey, thinking of the point where the mist ended in this world.

"Come on, please? It'd be really fun if you came." She jumped up, her uneven ponytail swaying this way and that as she bounced on her heels. "Oh! You said we were going to bake cookies together, too. We can make them and bring them to my mom."

"It sounds nice but think about it," began Zoey, trying to interject some logic into the situation. "How would I even get there? It's not like I can call someone up for a ride."

Nicole stared at Zoey as if she'd said something obtuse. "You can ride in the car with me and my dad."

Zoey was about to point out how that wouldn't work, considering her dad couldn't see or hear her when she realized what Nicole meant. She could slip into the car ahead of Nicole and hitch a ride to the hospital without her dad being any the wiser. It felt strange, and maybe a little immoral, but no more so than her spending time with Nicole almost every day.

Accepting that Nicole wasn't going to let the idea drop, Zoey pulled herself up off the floor and waved her hand. "Come on, there's something I have to show you."

Nicole was all bubbles and cheer as the two made their way down the street toward the mist's boundary. She babbled on about how much fun the visit was going to be now that Zoey was coming. She only stopped her flow of visit-related mirth to comment on how they should play outside more often. Zoey hated the idea of bringing her friend down in such a brutal fashion, but she could think of no other way.

When they rounded the corner that led to the barrier, Zoey took hold of Nicole's hand and slowed their pace. Unable to miss the protective cue, Nicole looked up at Zoey with her eyebrows raised.

"So, the first time I came over here I went on a walk and ran into . . . this."

The boundary of the mist loomed mere feet in front of them. As before, the barrier was only visible because the mist pressing up against it was denser than was normal for this world.

"Oh, that's so cool!"

Before Zoey could stop her, Nicole reached her hand through the other side of the barrier. Zoey's heart lurched before she remembered that the boundary was only a danger to her.

"It does look kind of cool, but it's dangerous," said Zoey with a shudder. Being this close to the barrier was making her skin crawl. "For me, anyway."

"What do you mean?"

Zoey reached her hand as close to the barrier as she could without breaching the other side. "I can't go past here. I think it must be because there's no mist on the other side. I'm not from your world. I came here through the mist, and I guess I can't go anywhere it doesn't."

"Like it's an invisible wall for you?" asked Nicole, sounding as though she were going to suggest that they try to climb it.

Zoey gave her head another shake. "No. I can walk through it just fine, but when I get on the other side . . ." She searched for a way to describe the overwhelming fatigue and crushing dizziness that had overcome her when she'd strayed past it before. "Have you ever heard the expression 'like a fish out of water'?"

Nicole nodded. "Yeah. Fish need water to breathe. They use their gills."

"Right. Well, on the other side, it was like I couldn't breathe. My whole body got tired, and dizzy and . . . Well, I can't go past this spot. So, I won't be able to visit your mom with you. I'm sorry."

Nicole stared at the spot where Zoey's hand had rested moments ago. Her face scrunched up as if she were trying to work out a complicated math problem. She waved her hand back and forth in front of her, eyes fixed on the mist that swirled and twisted around in its wake.

"Hey, Zoey, try thinking really hard about moving the mist."

"What?"

Nicole grinned, a gleam in her eye. "You know how when you first came over here, you said you had to think really hard to move stuff?"

Zoey looked toward the barrier and shook her head, her hair fluttering. "Yeah, but that's di—"

"Well, maybe if you just think really hard about the bubble getting bigger, it will."

The idea struck Zoey as a bit of a long shot, but she couldn't deny that it was at least worth a try. This was, after all, a world where she could conjure any object that came to mind with little more than her own force of will. If it were possible, there was a question of whether it was something she *should* do.

As much as they'd learned over the past few weeks, they still didn't understand the mist when it came right down to it. Would there be consequences for extending the bubble's boundaries? The mist didn't seem to be causing any harm to either of their worlds, but it was possible that was only because it was contained.

Then there was whether this would be like the time Nicole healed her hand. What if she pushed the bubble away, but in doing so, used up all the mist?

The thought of telling Nicole that she wasn't willing to at least try out the idea played at the edge of Zoey's thoughts. She could picture the look of hurt on the younger girl's face, feel her heart fall. There was every chance that she was overthinking this. What was the harm in believing that it was like the magic from the stories of her childhood? It's what Nicole did, and she hadn't run into any trouble yet.

Zoey raised her hand as if she were placing it upon a pane of glass before her. She pictured what she wanted in her mind's eye, willing it to be true. She saw the bubble expanding in all directions, pushing out from a point centered on Nicole's house.

A familiar sensation of strain formed behind her tight-shut eyes, the way it had the first time she'd conjured an object out of the mist. Silver swirled between her and the barrier. It wasn't the same as it had been when Nicole had healed her hand. Rather than disappearing into the barrier as it made contact, it gathered in place, as though there were a second barrier keeping it from escaping back the way it came.

Zoey closed her eyes. The world faded away. The feel of the ground beneath her feet, the warm breeze on her skin, they were meaningless distractions. There was only her and the mist.

Her will reached out as though it were a tangible force. It pressed against the barrier and met its resistance. Screwing up her face, Zoey repeated the series of images in her mind. She told herself that her will was enough to move the barrier, that when she next opened her eyes, it would be to a sea of mist that extended far past its current confines. The barrier shuddered as her thoughts pressed against it. It was beginning to falter.

She saw herself meeting Nicole's mom, felt how happy it would make the little girl who had become so important to her. More than that, she pictured the bond between mother and daughter. It was pure and unshakable, the way such a connection should be. She wanted to see it for herself, to remember what it was like. She wanted to believe that such a thing was still possible.

The force she was exerting sent a tremor rocketing across the invisible surface as the last image roared in Zoey's mind. There was a rushing of air as, all at once, the sensation of resistance before her vanished. Zoey opened her eyes. The world came back to life around her. The sun warmed her skin; the breeze caressed her cheeks, and Nicole whooped beside her. The mist that had moments before been pressed up against an invisible barrier was now drifting lazily forward.

"You did it! That was so cool!" cheered Nicole, jumping up and down in celebration.

Although Zoey agreed, it was only with some effort that a smile crossed her face. A wave of exhaustion had descended on her like a heavy curtain. She felt the same as she had on the days when one of her sleepless nights was followed by a day with a particularly trying gym class.

"Yeah, that was pretty cool," agreed Zoey, contemplating her sudden exhaustion.

"Oh! We can go to the park now, too! It's right down over there!" said Nicole, already pulling Zoey's hand in that direction.

Zoey thought she knew the one that Nicole was talking about. It was likely the same park that she was supposedly spending most of her days at. The idea of going there with Nicole now, however, was something less than appealing. Although it was still early afternoon, the only thing Zoey wanted to do was curl up in bed for a nice, long nap, maybe after a hot bath.

"I'm feeling pretty tired actually."

Nicole's face fell. "What? It's not even lunchtime yet. How come you're tired?"

"I think moving that . . . thing took a lot out of me or something. I was fine before."

"So, you don't want to go to the park?" asked Nicole, her wide eyes downcast.

"Not today," began Zoey, now contending with a dull throbbing behind her right eye. "Besides, the mist looks like it needs time to spread anyway."

Nicole hopped in place and took off like a bullet, sprinting down the street in the same direction as the mist. Zoey smiled. Maybe Nicole should have been the one to try and move the mist. She always had energy to spare. When she was a good way toward the other end of the street, Nicole turned to face Zoey.

"You're right! It's moving reeaaaaly sloooooowly," bellowed Nicole loud enough that anyone nearby was sure to hear. Nicole had accompanied her exaggerated words with some slow-motion waves of her arms that suggested she was attempting to swim through molasses. Tired as she was, it forced a laugh out of Zoey. "Do you think it will go to the hospital soon?"

"Probably, but come back here and stop yelling. People are going to think you're a weirdo!"

Nicole gave a little giggle and tore back down the street toward Zoey.

"I-I'm not a weirdo," she said, the amusement in her voice evident even through the slight panting.

"I didn't say you were a weirdo, I said people would think you're a weirdo. I mean, what would you think of someone who was yelling at nobody?"

Nicole laughed again. "I forgot no one can see you. You're right, that would look funny."

"Come on, weirdo, let's go back home and let the mist do its thing," said Zoey, putting an arm on Nicole's back.

Nicole didn't protest and instead tore down the street back toward her house with the same unabashed mania as before. With no improvement to her exhaustion, Zoey did her best to match Nicole's pace but only managed a lazy jog.

A small voice nagged in the back of her mind. What if the fatigue she was feeling wasn't normal? What if she was going to feel this exhausted forever, as a price for meddling with the laws of the universe? For once, she found it easy to push the worrisome thought from her mind.

The exhaustion wasn't forever; it was merely the aftereffects of the magic, and the magic was safe and good. At least, that's what Nicole would have said.

For all Zoey told herself that she was the smarter one, that her additional years had made her wise, she couldn't help but wonder if that was right. There was no denying that, between the two of them, Nicole was by far and away the happier one. Maybe trusting that the magic was good and safe was a small step toward capturing some of that happiness for herself.

It was only after making an official promise that they'd make time to bake cookies before the visit that Zoey was able to convince Nicole to let her go home early. The house was empty when Zoey walked out of her closet. Thankful that she wouldn't have to contend with anything as strenuous as carrying on a conversation for a while, Zoey ran herself a bath.

As steaming water gushed from the faucet, Zoey fiddled with her phone in her pocket. Her eyes remained fixed on the frothing bubbles now filling the tub. She didn't need to open it to know that her mom still hadn't replied to her message. Try as she might, she couldn't get the thought to leave her mind. What she wouldn't give to be able to push the hurt from her heart as easily as she'd done the barrier in Nicole's world.

Much as Aunt Carol had insisted shutting her mom out wasn't the solution, it had been preferable to the familiar ache that had taken its place. At least before she had been the one doing the ignoring, the one with the power. What was done was done, though. She had extended a hand toward her mom. All she could do was hope she'd return it, even if the chances were slim.

Zoey slid into the water with a sigh, phone left forgotten in the pocket of her jeans, which lay in a heap on the floor. She couldn't do anything about her hurting heart. Hopefully, her exhausted body was another matter. Zoey leaned back and let herself slip below the surface of the water, wishing that she might emerge as someone who didn't feel quite so much.

CHAPTER EIGHTEEN

Baking

I t was through bleary eyes that Zoey set the last batch of cookies into the oven. The whole cookie-baking experience had been more trying than she'd expected. Just getting the oven turned on had been a bit of a process itself. Nicole had waited until the last minute to inform Zoey she wasn't allowed to use the oven without permission.

Since they didn't want to wake her dad on what Nicole said was the one day he slept past eight, they had needed to wake Tyler up. It had taken Nicole some time to convince him to let her use the oven, but she'd gotten there eventually. He'd agreed only under the conditions that she: A.) Let him go back to sleep, and B.) Clean up her mess. They had seemed like simple enough terms at the time, but looking around the kitchen, Zoey was beginning to regret agreeing to that last term.

Though eager to help, it was clear that Nicole had spent even less time baking than Zoey. Between the first two eggs winding up on the floor instead of the bowl and the cup and a half of flour that had been scattered across the countertop, cleanup was going to be no small feat. Even with the looming chore, Zoey couldn't deny that their misadventure in baking was a good time.

"These don't look like your aunt's cookies . . ."

Nicole was peering beadily at the twenty or so misshapen cookies that lay waiting on a wire cooling rack. There was no denying that both the color and shape of the cookies were somewhat different compared to the ones that she'd baked with her aunt only days before. The recipe had been the same and, so far as she could tell through the unfamiliar brands, so had the ingredients. She and Nicole were the only varying factors.

"Well, you're definitely the expert there. You've snuck enough of them from my aunt's house," said Zoey, poking Nicole in the belly.

Nicole gave a shy grin and reached out for a cookie. Zoey had known all along that her resolve to save every cookie for her mom was bound to break.

"We should make sure they taste OK since they look funny."

The logic was there, but Zoey was sure that Nicole's sweet tooth had gotten the better of her. Still, it made sense. They didn't want to give Nicole's mom cookies that might make her even sicker than she already was. The thought lingered with Zoey. Nicole had never said exactly what was wrong with her mom, and Zoey hadn't asked. As sure as Nicole was that her mom was going to get better and come home sometime soon, Zoey couldn't help but worry. She'd known Nicole for the better part of three weeks now, and her mom had been in the hospital the entire time. Whatever she had, it didn't sound easy to recover from.

Thinking of her attempt at a new, more positive outlook, Zoey pushed the thought from her mind. People spent time in the hospital, got better, and left all the time. There was no reason Nicole's mom couldn't do the same.

"So, what do you think?" asked Zoey, reaching for one of her own.

Nicole chewed her mouthful of cookie a couple more times and swallowed. "They're not as good as your aunt's."

Zoey took a bite of her own cookie. Nicole was right. They were crumbly in a way that wasn't all that appealing, and the flavor, though sweet, lacked some of the richness of the batch that she and her aunt had made together.

"They're not, but I think they still taste pretty good for our first try."

"Do you think my mom will like them?"

"I'm sure she will. Even if she didn't, I think it'll make her really happy that you made her something at all. Parents are weird like that," replied Zoey, thinking of all the shoddy gifts she'd given her parents in her younger years. Whether it was a clay mug that didn't hold water or a breakfast in bed consisting of Eggos that were still frozen in the center, the gestures always seemed to make them genuinely happy.

As the last batch of cookies lay cooling among their misshapen brothers and sisters, Zoey glanced at the clock. "Alright, we should start cleaning this up. Then, I need to go back and put in an appearance at my aunt's. You said you're not supposed to go to the hospital until eleven, right?"

"Yeah, but come back before then, OK?"

"I'll do my best, just depends on if my aunt or uncle are chatty . . . and, hey . . . we're for sure not going to be there past like four, right?"

Nicole shook her head, her voice sounding sad. "We usually just stay for a couple of hours. Sometimes, my dad and me go out for dinner after."

Zoey suppressed a groan. She hadn't considered the possibility of anything else after the visit. She was already pushing her luck by using her excuse of reading in the park as often as she was. If she showed up too late, the grace her aunt and uncle were giving her felt sure to evaporate.

"OK, but that can't happen this time. I need to come back here right after."

"The food's really good, though," said Nicole, sounding a little offended that Zoey didn't want that to be an option.

"I'm sure it is, but I can't be too late. I'd get in trouble with my aunt and uncle, then I might not be able to come over anymore," replied Zoey, wanting to make sure Nicole understood the risks involved.

Nicole's eyes went wide at the mention of their visits having to stop. "OK, I'll tell him I want to go home after."

Despite the promise, an uneasy tension remained in Zoey's chest. If Nicole's dad wanted to run errands after the visit, it wasn't like Nicole could stop him. It was too late to back out of the plan now, though.

"Hey, while I'm gone, do me a favor and look up how far away the hospital is. In case I need to walk back." Zoey glanced at the clock again. "I'll try to be back in an hour at most. But first, we really need to clean this place up . . ."

One dizzying descent through the mist and Zoey was back on her side of reality. She gave herself a once over in the mirror, brushing some stray traces of flour from her jeans. She made her way to the kitchen as nonchalantly as she could, taking no effort to skip the squeaky step on her way down.

"Zoey dear, you're up early today," said Aunt Carol brightly.

Her aunt was fiddling with a large earthenware mug, while her uncle sat behind a copy of the Sunday paper.

"I think I fell asleep a little bit earlier than usual last night," replied Zoey, sparing a look at her uncle out of the corner of her eyes.

"Now that you're up, do you want some tea? Maybe some toast? I'm afraid you're going to have to fend for yourself for lunch today. Your uncle and I got invited to brunch with some old friends."

Zoey couldn't believe her luck. Her aunt and uncle being out of the house was going to make the visit a lot easier to pull off. "When you say old friends, do you mean people you've known a long time, or like, old people?" asked Zoey, trying not to sound too pleased with her barb.

A snort came from behind Uncle Will's newspaper. Had she actually made him laugh? Aunt Carol threw Zoey a look of mock warning before letting out a chuckle herself. "I suppose in this case, the answer is both. Susan and I went to high school together, which, now that you point it out, was a lot longer ago than I'd care to admit."

"Wow, that's a long time to be friends with someone," replied Zoey, impressed. Then after a moment's hesitation, "How do you even manage something like that? Didn't you ever grow apart?"

Aunt Carol took a sip of her tea, her face pensive. "I suppose we did grow apart a few times over the years. But it was never intentional on either of our parts. Once we realized it had happened it was easy to grow back together I suppose. Friendships can be funny that way sometimes."

That hadn't been Zoey's experience so far. The friends she'd lost in the last couple of years didn't feel at all likely to come back to her. Then again, maybe it was a matter of Zoey looking at things through her own inexperience. Over the course of a thirty-plus-year friendship, a year or two of distance didn't seem like such an unsurmountable thing.

"So, Zoey, what do you have planned for today?" asked Uncle Will, setting down his paper.

"I thought I might play some piano and then read one of the new books I got from the library."

A look of something that Zoey thought might have been approval settled on Uncle Will's face.

"I'm glad you're sticking with the piano."

Zoey sat down at the table between her aunt and uncle. She wasn't exactly out for her uncle's approval, but couldn't deny she was thankful that he had warmed up to her, at least a little. "It's been fun, and like you said, it would be dumb not to at least try it out, since I've got Aunt Carol to teach me."

"You'll have to pick out a song for us to work on sometime soon, you must be getting tired of scales and warm-ups."

"I could take a look today. Not sure what to look for, though."

"If you don't find anything you like you could let me know some of your favorite songs and I could whip you up a beginner version," said Aunt Carol, finishing the last of her tea.

"You don't have to," said Zoey, shaking her head. "I mean, that would be cool, but it sounds like a lot of work."

Aunt Carol's eyes brightened. "It's no trouble at all, I enjoy doing it."

Uncle Will glanced at his watch. "Carol, we better get going if we don't want to be late."

"You're probably right. Just give me a minute to go find that book I wanted to lend Mary."

Uncle Will let out a sigh, though Zoey thought she saw a smile playing at the corner of his mouth. "Alright, you know where to find me."

It took another thirty minutes for Aunt Carol and Uncle Will to leave the house. Twice they'd almost made it out the door when Aunt Carol exclaimed that she'd forgotten something and rushed back into the house. Zoey waited a while after the gray sedan disappeared down the block before strolling back up to her room.

Zoey flipped her phone open and sighed. There was still no response from her mom. Aunt Carol's words about relationships coming back around tugged at her. Things felt hopeless between her and her mother now, but would time change that? If so, was that even something she wanted?

She snapped her phone shut. There'd be plenty of time to contemplate her dynamic with her mom in the future. Right now she needed to focus on her plans with Nicole, and so, she pushed the nagging thought out of her mind and stepped back into the void.

When Zoey got back to Nicole's room, she found it empty. It didn't take long for her to hear the voices floating up from the kitchen. She recognized one as belonging to Nicole, muffled though it was. The other one was deep and male and could only belong to Nicole's dad.

She followed the conversation to the doorway that led to the kitchen. She was amused to find that, despite having just cleaned it, the kitchen was once more in a state of active distress. From the doorway, she saw a large stack of pancakes sitting between Nicole and a man with deepset hazel eyes, and with flour on his nose.

Zoey recognized him as Nicole's dad, John. She'd only seen him a handful of times before and, even then, it was never for long. He was always rushing from one thing to the next. Home from work for long enough to change before he had to leave for the next thing on his list.

Zoey couldn't help but feel a bit sorry for the man. It couldn't be easy for him, with his wife in the hospital, two kids at home, and a job to hold down. Nicole had told her that Tyler helped with some of the errands. However, Zoey hadn't seen the older boy do much of anything other than check in on Nicole every so often, or shout that he was going out with friends or up to his room.

She was about to walk forward so Nicole could see her when John spoke.

"You're sure Tyler didn't help you with these?" asked John, his pronounced brow furrowed at the twenty cookies that now sat in a large tupperware container beside Nicole's plate.

"Nope! He just turned on the oven and went back to sleep," said Nicole proudly.

John shook his head. "That sounds about right. Well, I can't wait to taste them. Are you suuuure I can't have one before we leave?" John inched his hand toward the sealed tupperware as he spoke. He'd gotten far enough as to have begun peeling back the lid when Nicole slammed her hand on top and snatched it away.

"I want Mom to try them first."

Her tone was firm, as was her expression, though a smile was threatening to twitch up at the corners of her mouth.

"I'm just saying, I know you love your mom's cookies, but when we first got married, I was the one who did all the cooking. If there's a cookie expert in this house, it's me. We want to make sure they taste good."

"You just want to eat them all."

John pushed his stomach out and gave it a hearty tap. "Caught me. When'd you get so much smarter than me?"

"I've always been smarter than you," said Nicole, giggling. "You're a boy."

John's face brightened as he let out a loud, genuine laugh. "You used that one on Tyler yet?"

Nicole nodded.

"What'd he have to say to that?"

"He called me a butthead."

John's tired eyes crinkled. "Well, if you're a butthead then at least you're a cute butthead. He smoothed his wavy brown hair and glanced at his wristwatch. "Alright, finish up your breakfast, then go brush your teeth and we'll be ready to go. We'll be a bit early, but that just means more time with your mom."

"We can't go without Zoey!" said Nicole, the amusement of moments before gone.

"Well, do you know when Miss Zoey will be joining us? We can't wait around forever."

John's tone told Zoey quite plainly that he thought of her as something of an imaginary friend. She couldn't say she blamed him. Even if Nicole had explained the situation to him, it's not like it would make it any more believable.

"She's gonna come back real soon . . . but if she's late, can we wait for her? Please?"

John spared a moment's glance over his shoulder at the messy kitchen. "You know, Nicky, if you want to bring a friend to visit your mom for real, we could work something out."

A look of confusion flashed across Nicole's face for a moment before transforming into one of pure indignation. "I am bringing a friend, I just told you. She's real."

John looked as if he were teetering on the edge of arguing the point, but seemed to think better of it. He gave an apologetic smile and raised his hand as if to wave the uncomfortable moment away.

"Alright, I'm sorry. I'm sure your mom will love to meet Zoey."

"She won't be able to see Zoey . . . but Zoey will be able to see her. I'm really excited!"

"Well, finish your breakfast and be excited in the direction of your toothbrush, alright? " John paused, looking his daughter up and down.

"I'm going to go ahead and veto the cookie dough-covered clothes, too. Maybe Zoey can help you pick out something nice?"

With that, John stood up from the table and, pausing only to give Nicole a kiss on the top of her head, went to work cleaning up the mess made by the pancakes.

Zoey stepped from her spot in the doorway and cleared her throat. Nicole whirled around, greeting Zoey with a grin.

"Dad! Zoey's here, we can go now!"

A slightly exasperated laugh rang out among the sounds of clattering dishes.

"Tell her she's a little bit early, maybe see if she wants some pancakes. There's lots left over."

After checking to make sure that John was occupied with the dishes, Zoey snatched a pancake off the stack and stuffed it into her mouth. This evoked a round of raucous laughter from Nicole. Struggling not to laugh herself, Zoey swallowed the overly large bite.

"Your dad's a pretty good cook. He and my aunt should get together sometime, swap recipes."

Nicole giggled. "Zoey says you're a good cook."

"Well, tell Zoey thank you," replied John, still absorbed with the dishes.

"She can hear you, Dad," said Nicole, as if this were the most obvious thing in the world.

Another chuckle from John. Nicole stuffed the last couple bits of syrup-covered pancake into her mouth and hopped up from the table. Even though she knew full well that John wouldn't be able to hear her, Zoey waited for them to be well away from the kitchen before speaking.

"Your dad seems really nice."

"Of course, he's my dad," said Nicole simply.

A sad smile spread across Zoey's face. It was moments like this where she envied her younger friend. She would have given a great deal to go back to a time when things were as simple as Nicole often saw them.

"So, we just have to get you cleaned up and we're off to the hospital?"

Nicole hopped up the last of the stairs and spun around to face Zoey, walking with her back toward her room.

"I want to bring my markers, too, my mom doesn't have any in her room."

"OK, but I think it'll have to just be you and your mom drawing today. The whole marker moving on its own thing would probably freak her out."

"Oh . . ." Nicole's expression darkened for a moment before springing back to its excited state. "Wait, I know! You can tell me what colors you want to use and then I'll do it for both of us."

"That sounds like a good idea to me. Better than giving your mom a heart attack, anyway."

Zoey sat on the end of Nicole's bed and watched her pick over the various art supplies that lay scattered throughout her room. Happy as she was that their planned visit was bringing her friend such joy, she couldn't dismiss the uneasy knot in the pit of her stomach. "Hey, did you manage to look up how far away the hospital is from here like I asked?"

Glancing up from a pile of half-finished coloring books, Nicole nodded. "The computer said it's a ninety-minute walk. That's not too far, right?"

Zoey sighed. "That's an hour and a half. It's doable, but if we're talking about making sure I'm not late getting back then it's definitely pushing it."

Nicole looked thoughtful before a wide grin broke over her face. "You could fly home!"

"What?" Zoey was sure she'd heard her friend correctly, but that only added to her confusion.

"You can fly over here. You could fly home way, way faster than walking.

"Well, that's an . . . idea," said Zoey, unconvinced.

"It's a good idea! You fly around here all the time."

Zoey thought back on all the time she'd spent bobbing through the air like a half-inflated balloon. For all that Nicole called it flying, she was certain most people would call it floating.

"I'm not sure bobbing home like some weird Zoey balloon is really a good idea."

"Not like a balloon," laughed Nicole, extending an arm in the air, fist clenched. "Like a superhero."

"I guess, as a last resort, I could try and bust out the ol' Super Zoey," said Zoey, mimicking Nicole's dramatic pose. "But, let's do our best to make sure we don't get back here too late, alright?"

Nicole nodded, then returned her attention to her search. By the time Nicole had gathered more art supplies than Zoey thought were necessary for a single visit, John was calling up that it was time to go.

"Alright, got everything you need?" asked Zoey, feeling a bit like her uncle wrangling Aunt Carol.

"I think so . . ." replied Nicole, looking down at the jumble of items she'd collected.

"Let's go then, I'm excited to meet your mom, maybe talk to her about you being a little more organized."

Nicole laughed, causing a couple of crayons to fall to the floor with a clatter. Zoey grabbed a faded pink backpack that was hanging from a hook on the back of Nicole's door and pulled the pouch open. "How about we put everything in here?"

"Oh! That's smart," said Nicole, dumping the contents of her arms inside.

"Do you need some help?" called John's voice from downstairs.

With her backpack slung over her shoulder, Nicole extended a hand for Zoey, who after a moment's hesitation took it.

"We're coming!"

CHAPTER NINETEEN

Lisa

The ride to the hospital, though uneventful, had been somewhat stressful for Zoey. Getting into the car had been as easy as Nicole had predicted it would be. Though Zoey had worried that John might glance back and see the indentation where she was sitting, that worry was quickly dispelled once the car started moving.

Both she and Nicole kept their eyes peeled, scanning for any sign that the mist might not have made it to the hospital after all. They didn't have much of a plan for such a circumstance other than having Nicole scream for her dad to stop, hope he did, and bail out of the car.

Thankfully, no such action was needed. Whatever Zoey had done back at the old endpoint of the mist had worked at least as well as they had hoped. The faint, silvery substance hung in the air, stretching out as far as they could see as they made their way toward the hospital.

The building itself was unremarkable as far as hospitals went. Four stories of concrete and glass rose up amid a series of smaller, similarly built structures. Zoey gave an internal wince as they approached the looming building. She hadn't clocked it until this moment, but the last time she'd set foot inside a hospital was the day her father had died. She'd never been fond of them, to begin with. After seeing her dad broken and bruised with tubes and wires splayed across his body like a network of perverse electronic roots, they were high up on the list of places she'd least like to spend time in.

Still, she was resolved to not let her past haunt her. This wasn't going to be like before. It was a different day, with different people, in a different universe. She would walk out of the place having met someone new, rather than having lost someone precious.

The smell of antiseptic made Zoey's nose wrinkle. That was another thing she didn't like about hospitals. No matter how clean they tried to make it smell, no matter how many bright and cheery pictures they hung in the lobby, this was a place where people came to die.

Stop thinking like that, thought Zoey, resolved to at least try to enjoy herself for Nicole's sake. People get better and leave hospitals all the time.

"I get to push the buttons!"

Nicole broke away from her father, her dirty blonde braid swinging as she ran toward the elevator.

"Hey, remember where we are. No running please," said John, looking somewhere between amused and exhausted.

Nicole skidded to a stop, her worn pink sneakers squeaking against the polished vinyl flooring. An elderly woman in a lopsided purple hat smiled indulgently as Nicole strode past her, arms swinging dramatically at her side as she kept herself from running.

With the elevator summoned by Nicole, the four of them moved inside. Nicole asked the woman in the purple hat which floor she was going to, then pushed the buttons labeled two and four.

After a brief elevator ride, in which Zoey did her best to squish into the corner and take up as little space as possible, she, Nicole, and John all got out on the fourth floor. As they walked down the starkly lit halls toward Nicole's mom's room, Zoey couldn't help but notice the staff that they passed, more than a couple of the scrub-clad nurses gave their party-friendly looks and nods. One tired-looking nurse even stopped typing away at her station to tell Nicole that she liked the bright pink dress that she'd decided on before leaving.

This struck Zoey as a little odd before she realized that it made sense. With Nicole's mom as a long-term resident of the hospital, it was only natural that the staff would get to know Nicole and her father. The thought made her a little sad. Nice as it was that the staff were so friendly to Nicole, being on good terms with a bunch of nurses and doctors wasn't something that happened under the happiest of circumstances.

When they reached room 421, John rapped his fist on the partly closed door before pushing it open.

"Candy striper!"

Zoey paused behind Nicole. Now that she was here, she didn't have a clue what she was supposed to do with herself. Nicole and her father didn't get more than a couple steps into the room when an unfamiliar voice called out.

"There's my girl. Come here and give me a great big hug."

Zoey hesitated at the threshold of the room, looking up and down the hall as if hoping for a sign to tell her what she was supposed to do. Despite the fact that she had been enthusiastically invited along by Nicole, she very much felt like she was intruding on a private affair. Coming all this way to wait out in the hall seemed silly, though, and if she was being honest, she wanted to see what kind of person Nicole's mom was.

Careful not to bump the door as she went, Zoey joined Nicole and John inside the room. She couldn't tell if what she saw made her feel better or worse. The room looked different from what she saw when she pictured a hospital room.

The window shades were thrown open, the early afternoon sunlight pouring in. The need for so much light was readily apparent. No fewer than ten potted plants sat scattered throughout the room. Some were small with bright blooms, while others erupted out of full-sized planters, their verdant leaves drooping under their own weight.

Personal touches weren't contained to plants, either. The otherwise drab, cream-colored walls were covered in a sea of artwork. From doodles and sketches on loose leaf paper, clearly done by Nicole, to full-sized canvas paintings like the ones Zoey had seen in Lisa's studio back home.

The woman sitting in the bed at the center of all this was hugging Nicole with a brilliant, almost pained smile on her face. As touching as the scene was, a knot twisted in Zoey's stomach. She'd seen pictures of Lisa back at Nicole's house. The woman hugging her daughter was, without a doubt, the same one who Zoey had seen smiling back in the photos, but they could have been two different people.

The Lisa in the pictures had possessed a great deal of shiny blonde hair, often done up in a neat braid down the center of her back. Her cheeks had been rosy and full, her eyes sparkling with a healthy glow forever preserved by the snapshot. The woman in the bed looked as though she'd lost at least twenty pounds. Though her face was shining with affection for her daughter, it wasn't enough to disguise the dark circles under her eyes or the cracks at the corners of her lips. She was wearing a silken headwrap, much like the ones that Aunt Carol donned most nights, though Zoey thought it likely that there wasn't much hair left beneath its shiny orange embrace.

The homey vibes of the room couldn't disguise the fact that it was a hospital room at the end of the day. A series of wires ran from Lisa's chest to a machine that was monitoring her vitals, while a bag full of clear liquid dripped into the tube leading to her left arm. Zoey suppressed a shudder. For a moment, she saw her dad in Lisa's place, taking his last breath before the line went flat and he left this world for good.

Don't think about that now, she told herself, She was determined to make this visit a happy one.

"How are you feeling, Lisa? Do you need anything?" John asked.

"I think I've got everything I need right here," replied Lisa, giving the top of Nicole's head a kiss. Then, pausing as if she thought of something important, replied, "I could use a little something sweet, though, maybe you could bring me back a candy bar?"

"I brought you cookies," chirped Nicole, wriggling out of her mom's embrace to tug the tupperware out of her father's hands.

Zoey was quite sure that Lisa hadn't missed the large, cookie-filled container. The look of excitement on Lisa's face struck her as a little over the top, though still genuine. She supposed that was just the kind of thing you did when you were a parent. She remembered how excited she'd always felt to give her parents something that she'd made for them or else bought with money saved from her own allowance. Them matching her excitement had really made those moments special.

"Wow, did you and your dad make these for me?"

"Nope!" said Nicole, pulling the lid off the container with a grin. "It was me and Zoey."

"Ohhhh, the famous Zoey, huh? Sounds like she's a pretty talented girl."

Nicole's already joyful expression brightened. She hopped off the edge of the bed and pointed toward Zoey. "She came with me today. I really wanted her to meet you."

Lisa straightened up in bed and gazed somewhere to the right of Zoey's shoulder. "Well, Zoey, I've heard a lot about you. Thank you for taking such good care of our Nicole."

Zoey was glad that Nicole was the only one who could see her, as she turned a brilliant shade of scarlet. Focused as she was on Lisa, Zoey couldn't help but notice Nicole looking at her expectantly. It took a moment before Zoey realized what Nicole was waiting for.

"Oh, tell your mom thanks. It's been a lot of fun being your friend."

Nicole beamed more widely. "Zoey says thank you, and she really likes being my friend."

It felt odd to Zoey, playing this strange game of telephone. She could only imagine what it would feel like to be in Lisa's position and to find out that her daughter's imaginary friend was anything but. It didn't sound all that heartwarming, more like a horror story.

Nicole crawled back into her mother's bed and joined her in taking a cookie out of the container.

"Hey, I thought you said those were all for your mom," said John, a look of indignation hitched dramatically on his face.

Nicole grinned and took a large bite of the cookie. "You can have one if Mom says you can."

Lisa followed Nicole's lead and took a sizable bite herself. After swallowing her first mouthful, she let out a sigh of delight. "Nicole, these are delicious. Your dad really didn't help you with them?"

"Nope, it was just me and Zoey."

"Well, you two are quite the little chefs. These are too good not to share."

Lisa and John shared a fleeting look that told Zoey they were confirming Nicole's story that she hadn't had any help with the cookies. Once the moment had passed, John strode forward, sticking his tongue out at Nicole as he grabbed a cookie.

"Told you she'd let me have one."

Nicole giggled as her dad bit into his hard-earned treat. They all chewed in silence but for the whir of one of the machines hooked up to Lisa. After he had eaten a second cookie with no complaints from Nicole, John glanced at his watch.

"Alright, I'll just be out running some errands. I've got my cell phone on if you need anything, OK?"

"We'll be fine," said Lisa, wrapping an arm around Nicole.

Still wearing a smile, John snatched another cookie from the container on Lisa's lap. Nicole, who had tried in vain to slap her dad's hand away, was laughing again as he made his way out the door.

"So, what do you want to do today?" said Lisa, kissing the top of Nicole's head. "There's that puzzle that your dad brought last week."

Nicole turned to Zoey. "Do you like puzzles?"

Still aware of how strange this must look to Lisa, Zoey shrugged. "They're OK. I'm down for whatever. I'll only be able to watch anyway."

"Oh, right . . ." replied Nicole. She turned to face her mom, who showed no sign that she thought this behavior odd. "Mom, can we do a drawing instead? Zoey can pick out some of the colors."

"Is Zoey an artist, too?"

Zoey let out a snort that she was glad Lisa couldn't hear.

"She likes to draw with me, but she says she's not very good."

"Do you think she's good?"

Nicole pondered the question for a moment before giving her head a little shake. "She goes outside of the lines when we color sometimes, and when we drew butterflies one time, hers looked like a snake and two blobs. I don't care though, it's a lot of fun to draw with her."

"Hey!" said Zoey, hands on her hips in mock outrage.

"As long as you're having fun, that's all that matters when you're with friends," said Lisa sagely. "Alright, drawing it is then. You know where everything is."

Nicole hopped off the bed and skipped over to a chipped white dresser. She slid open the bottom drawer and, after examining its contents, withdrew a large sheet of paper. She placed it on Lisa's overbed table before returning and pulling out a long, flat box. After reclaiming her spot at her mother's side, Nicole opened the silver lid and revealed a staggering number of colored pencils.

"So, what do you want to draw today?" asked Lisa, pulling out a regular graphite pencil from her bedside table.

Nicole turned toward Zoey with an eager expression. "My mom does the outlines and then I color them in. What do you think we should do?"

Zoey thought back to the paintings that hung in Nicole's house. Her mind went straight to the one of a woman lying in a field of flowers. "How about some flowers? We could use a bunch of colors and make something really pretty to add to the wall for your mom. It looks like she likes plants."

"Yeah!" replied Nicole. "Mom, Zoey says we should do flowers today."

Lisa returned her daughter's smile and set to work. Zoey was amazed at how effortlessly Lisa's hand glided over the paper, leaving a series of beautiful blooms in its wake. For a while, Nicole leaned against her mother, eyes following the progress of her hand across the paper. Once the blank sheet was beginning to look like a monochrome jungle, Nicole pulled herself onto her knees and surveyed the line of expensive-looking colored pencils.

"What's your favorite flower?"

"Lilies, I guess," replied Zoey, never having given it all that much thought before.

Nicole scanned the drawing and frowned. "Mom, Zoey says lilies are her favorites, but there aren't any here."

Zoey was about to blurt out that she didn't want to make any extra work when she was cut off.

"Well, we'll just have to make some for her, won't we?"

A few minutes later, a series of lilies had joined the sea of outlines. Nicole picked out a garish shade of pink and began shading the expertly drawn bloom.

"How did I know you'd start with that one?" asked Lisa, nodding to the colored pencil in Nicole's hand.

"'Cuz it's the prettiest," replied Nicole.

Lisa fixed Nicole with an affectionate gaze before selecting a pale shade of green and began working on some of the drawing's leaves.

They continued on like this over the next hour. Though little was said between Lisa and Nicole, there was undeniable warmth between them. The way they'd glance at each other, then share a smile, or work together on the same bloom without a word between them. When was the last time she and her mother had shared a moment like this, one where there were no bitter words, unspoken or otherwise? When had they last simply enjoyed being in each other's company?

"That looks good, Nicole. You're really getting an eye for contrast."

Lisa had stopped the shading of an orange hibiscus to admire the blush pink rose that Nicole had been working on for the better part of ten minutes. Zoey didn't know much about art, but even she could tell that Nicole was doing more than the average ten-year-old would with the colored pencil. The flower's petals were cast in an alternating pattern of light and heavily shaded patches that gave it the illusion of shadow and depth.

"I've been practicing a lot with Zoey. I showed her one I did with a unicorn with really pretty hair and she said it looked like a professional did it," said Nicole, beaming.

"Well, I don't doubt you'll be a professional one day if you keep at it like this."

Nicole's smile broke into a grin. "Hey, Mom, when you get better and come home, could we do oil painting again? I want to show Zoey, but Dad says I can't, even if he's watching because he doesn't know how to do it."

An odd, almost closed expression settled on Lisa's face. Her eyes, which had moments before been fixed on her daughter, flitted away to instead stare off in the direction of the room's singular window. "Of course. When I get all better, we'll do all the painting you want."

"Do you promise?" asked Nicole, who, oblivious to the shift in her mother's expression, had extended her pinky.

Lisa's gaze shifted back to her daughter, her eyes misted even though she had regained a determined-looking smile. She opened her mouth but seemed to second guess what she was going to say. After giving her head a little shake, she held her pinky up for Nicole.

"I promise when I get better we can paint and draw and color as much as you want . . . But, can you promise me something, too?"

Nicole stopped short of wrapping her pinky around her mom's and looked at her with a serious expression. Zoey knew from experience that Nicole didn't mess around when it came to pinky promises.

"Promise me that, even if your life gets a little sad sometimes . . ." Lisa paused, her free hand gripping the quilt that covered her as if she were resisting physical pain. "I mean, if things get hard, don't give up on art as long as it makes you happy, OK?"

"Why would I give up art?" asked Nicole, sounding confused.

Lisa sighed and stroked a hand through Nicole's hair. "Sometimes, it can . . . be easy to lose sight of things you love when things get tough."

Nicole nodded and wrapped her pinky around her mom's. "I promise."

They sat with their eyes fixed on each other, pinkies locked together when there was a knock at the door. Lisa had only just managed to wipe her misted eyes when a man in a pair of pastel blue scrubs came walking in. He was carrying a covered tray and wearing what, despite the tired look of him seemed to be a genuine smile.

"You know it's Sunday when Nicole is up in the house. How's it goin'—oh, wow, look at that." The nurse was looking at the almost completed drawing with an expression of delight. "Did you do all that yourself? Showing your mom a thing or two." He sounded sincere but followed up his words with a wink to Lisa.

"Honestly, she's getting so good I'm not sure she's going to need me much anymore."

The words had left Lisa cheerfully, though her face turned wax-like a moment later. Nicole, who was busy blushing at her mother's praise, didn't seem to notice.

"Well, I hate to interrupt art time, but I've got to make sure all my patients stay nice and fed. I just need to get your vitals first, though."

Without having to be asked, Nicole cleared the table so the nurse, whose name tag identified him as Bret D., could set the tray down in its place.

"You don't have to take any blood . . . do you?" asked Nicole once the art supplies had been placed on a small circular table opposite Lisa's bed.

"Nope. Just the basics."

Nicole looked relieved as Bret began wrapping a blood pressure cuff around Lisa's arm. The room fell silent as the cuff huffed full of air. "Alright, everything looks good," said Bret a few minutes later, taking his stethoscope out of his ear. "Looks like you need a fresh water and I can get out of your hair."

"I'll get it," chirped Nicole. She slid off her chair and rushed to grab the cup from her mother's bedside table.

"Well, thank you very much, Miss Nicole."

Zoey began rising from her chair but was stopped before she could finish.

"You stay with my mom, I'll be right back."

Zoey eased herself back into her chair. She knew better than to argue with Nicole given the determined expression on her face. A moment later, Nicole had disappeared out into the hallway.

"Who was she talking to?"

"Zoey, her imaginary friend," replied Lisa, adjusting in her bed. "She popped up a few weeks ago."

"Ohhhh, what is she? Mine was a blue turtle named Turbo back when I was a kid."

"She's just a regular girl, as far as Nicole tells me. She's sort of like an older sister."

Zoey shifted in her seat. It was strange to sit there invisible and listen to people talk about her, or the concept of her at least.

"Really? With her imagination, I figured it'd be something more involved than that."

"I think she might be looking for a bit of normalcy," said Lisa, gesturing to her bed. "This hasn't been easy on her."

Bret fiddled with his stethoscope. "I'll bet. Well, I've go—"

"Do you think it's a mistake to not tell her?"

Zoey's pulse quickened. This didn't sound like a conversation she'd wanted to overhear. Bret seemed to be thinking along the same lines. He gave a nervous-sounding cough, his eyes flitting to the door. "I'm sorry, what a thing to ask someone," said Lisa, eyes fixed as though they didn't actually see Bret.

"It's OK," said Bret, who was still fiddling with his stethoscope. "I wish I had an answer. You're sure she doesn't already sort of know?"

A sad smile broke out across Lisa's face. "We were optimistic when I got my diagnosis. The doctor said I had every chance in the world, so that's what we told Nicole. Once Nicole believes a thing, it sticks."

"Oh . . ." said Bret, sounding uncomfortable again.

Zoey rose from her chair and walked toward the door as quietly as she could. She didn't want to hear anymore, wished she didn't hear what she had.

"Shit," cried Zoey, walking down the hall in short, agitated steps. "Shit, shit, shit, shit!"

Now that she knew the truth, she didn't know how she was going to face Nicole. Fury at Lisa erupted in Zoey's chest. How could she go on telling her daughter that everything was going to be OK when she knew it wasn't? Wasn't it a parent's job to prepare their children for the world? How would Nicole being blindsided by the loss make things any easier on her? And now that she, Zoey, knew the truth, it was her responsibility to tell Nicole . . . wasn't it?

Zoey was so consumed by her thoughts that she didn't see the person coming the other way when she rounded the corner. She'd walked right into Nicole, who was holding a plastic mug with a ribbed straw. Luckily it had a lid or else water would have gone flying everywhere.

"Hey!" cried Nicole, rubbing her elbow in an aggrieved sort of way. It seemed as if she too hadn't been paying close attention to where she was going. "Zoey? Why'd you run into me?"

"Sorry, I wasn't looking where I was going. You OK?" asked Zoey, putting a hand on Nicole's shoulder.

"I'm OK," replied Nicole, though she still looked somewhat offended.

"Do you want me to carry that for you?" asked Zoey, then remembering that doing so would mean there'd be a mug floating down the hall, changed course. "I mean, do you need help?"

"It's not heavy," replied Nicole, sounding puzzled. "How come you didn't stay with my mom?"

Zoey's lip twitched. "Oh, uh, I just wanted to stretch my legs. Have been sitting in that chair since we got here."

"Ohhh, OK," said Nicole, sounding as if that made a great deal of sense to her. "So, do you like my mom? She's really cool, right?"

"Yeah, I mean, as far as parents go," replied Zoey, trying to keep her voice even.

"Yeah, I can't wait 'til she's all better and comes back home," said Nicole, speaking openly despite Zoey's motions for her to whisper. An orderly fixed her with a bemused expression as the two of them passed her station.

What would happen if she told Nicole the truth? Would that innocent spark that burned so brightly be snuffed out, forced to wake from her dream-like world of innocence all at once, jaded and scared? Worse yet, what if Nicole blamed her for being the one who brought reality crashing down upon her?

A wave of revulsion swept over Zoey at the thought. How could she be thinking about herself at a time like this? She needed to think about what was best for Nicole. Nicole, who believed in magic. Who saw wonder and goodness in everything around her. Who was sure her mother was coming home soon . . .

They were standing back in Lisa's room far too soon. Bret was on his way out, clipboard held loosely at his side. He flashed Nicole a friendly smile as he passed and thanked her for grabbing the water.

Nicole set the mug beside her mother's table and looked down at what Lisa had been given for lunch.

"That meatloaf doesn't look as good as Dad's."

"Oh it's not," said Lisa, pushing a piece toward a small mound of mashed potatoes, "but it's not bad, for hospital food."

How can you be talking about meatloaf right now?

"Can I try some?"

Lisa speared the piece she'd been playing with. "Sure."

You should tell her the truth.

Nicole took a bite and chewed, looking thoughtful. "It's not as good as Dad's."

"Nope," replied Lisa, after eating a piece herself.

. . . shouldn't you?

"Can we have cookies instead?"

"You can, but I think I should at least try to eat something green today," said Lisa, poking at her steamed broccoli.

Zoey's stomach churned under the weight of the information she was now holding. The smell of antiseptic and hospital food wasn't helping either.

Calm down, she told herself. *You don't have to do anything right now.*

It was true. She could hardly stop Nicole mid-conversation and blurt out what she'd overheard. If that was even what she wanted to do at all. No, for now, the best thing she could do was act normal, smile and nod and get on with the visit. She needed time to think.

"… We used Zoey's auntie's recipe. They don't taste as good, though."

Hearing her name brought Zoey out of her introspection. She forced a smile on her face and looked up in time to see Nicole flash her one in return. Now wasn't the time to contemplate the future. Hating herself, Zoey hitched the most convincing smile she could on her face and pushed thoughts of the truth out of her mind.

Chapter Twenty

Loss

Music was ringing through the house when Zoey stepped back into her bedroom. The notes pressed down on her with the weight of tragedy, unlike any piece she'd yet heard since moving in. She followed the song down to its source, standing to listen in silence, as she had when she'd first heard her aunt play. The dirge continued on, creeping at a mournful pace. It brought to mind the first days after her dad's death. Painted with perfect clarity what she feared might become Nicole's world after her mother's passing. Loss was everywhere today.

She didn't know whether she did it to offer some comfort, or to simply make the notes stop flowing, but Zoey reached out her hand with a tentative, "Aunt Carol?"

Aunt Carol slammed her hands down on the piano, her cry of shock lost among the deafening clamor of discordant notes. "What?! Zoey!" She stood with her hand over her heaving chest, eyes wide.

"Sorry!" cried Zoey, jumping back herself. She hadn't meant to scare her aunt, but honestly, what had she expected? "I, just, you were playing that song, and it was so sad and . . . I wanted to—"

"It's OK, it's OK," said Aunt Carol, now taking deep breaths as she patted her chest. "You've really got a knack for sneaking up on me."

Zoey's face flushed. "Sorry, I didn't mean to . . ." Embarrassment was urging her to head back to her room, but she forced herself onward. "Is everything OK? That song was . . . not what you usually play."

Aunt Carol's expression grew solemn before, much to Zoey's surprise, her lips twitched up into a smile. She must have noticed the look of consternation on Zoey's face because after giving a soft chuckle she said, "I'm sorry, I didn't mean to laugh. I'm just," she paused, looking thoughtful, "flattered that you've paid attention to the songs I play."

"Well, it's kind of hard to ignore." Aunt Carol raised an eyebrow. "No! I mean, I like the songs you play, so I always listen." The urge to run back to her room was growing stronger by the second.

"Well, thank you," said Aunt Carol, the color returning to her face. She ran her fingers along the piano's keys and let out a long sigh. "To answer your question, I'm OK, but you're right . . . That's not the type of song I usually play."

"Do you want to talk about it?" asked Zoey, keen for any conversation that might distract her from the thoughts in her head.

Aunt Carol smiled. "That would be nice."

They turned in unison toward the kitchen. If there was one thing that Zoey had learned in her time living with her aunt and uncle, it was that conversations could always be improved by the presence of tea and treats. With mugs of oolong and a plate of cookies between them, Zoey and Aunt Carol settled down at the kitchen table.

"Did something happen at brunch? Where's Uncle Will?" asked Zoey. She didn't want to say it, but she had noticed her uncle's absence and wasn't sure what to make of it.

"Oh, he and Bruce, that's Susan's husband, went to play a round of golf. Like I said everything's fine, really, it's just"—Aunt Carol interrupted herself by taking a sip of tea. She let out a sigh—" I told you that I've known Susan since high school, right?"

"Yeah, and how high school was a loooong time ago," said Zoey, hoping to interject some lightness to the conversation.

"Yes, much longer ago than I'd like to admit," replied Aunt Carol, her eyes narrowed though she was still smiling. "Well, she obviously knew me all through my time with Keith. She found some old pictures from when he and I started dating. It was so nice to see them. Almost felt like no time had passed."

"Did that upset Uncle Will?" asked Zoey. She thought she might know where this was going.

"What? Oh, no, not at all. Your uncle knows I had a life and love before we met. No, brunch and catching up all went wonderfully. It's just, seeing those pictures, and feeling his presence as strongly as I have lately"—she paused to fiddle with one of her rings—"It was a little overwhelming I suppose."

Zoey wanted to say something comforting, but didn't have the slightest idea of what that might be. The fact that she knew that the presence wasn't her great-uncle Keith kept getting in her way. Rather than words of comfort, the worst possible thing Zoey could think of came rushing out. "How did he die?"

Aunt Carol's eyes grew misty. Her hands twisted the bangles around her wrist before coming to rest on her mug, the same way Zoey's did when she sought comfort from the heat. "An intracranial aneurysm," her words were dry and bitter but brightened slightly. "It was sudden. He didn't suffer."

Zoey reached out. Her arm froze before she gave her aunt's hand a gentle squeeze. This was pain she understood. Her words wouldn't do anything to bring Keith back, but she needed to say them. "I'm so sorry."

Aunt Carol returned the pressure, smiling weakly. "Me too." She took a moment to wipe her eyes on her flowing sleeves. "But like they say, life does go on. And in a strange way, I'm not sure I'd trade the life I have for the one I lost. I still miss him terribly sometimes, but that loss led me to some truly wonderful things."

Healing from hurt. New beginnings from loss. Zoey told herself that they were nothing more than meaningless words. Clichés that belonged confined to the pages of Aunt Carol's self-help books. But did she believe that anymore? If she hadn't lost the only home she'd ever had, she never would have found the one she had now. Never would have met Nicole. Nicole . . . was it possible that she might see new life within the loss that was coming for her?

"Can I ask you a sort of personal question?" asked Zoey, attempting to look her aunt in the eyes, though not quite managing it.

"Of course."

"Well, I was wondering, if . . . if someone could have told you what was going to happen, would you have wanted to know? Even if you couldn't change it?"

Aunt Carol's lips twitched up. "You and I seem to think a lot alike sometimes." She took a moment to take a fortifying sip of tea before continuing. "I used to ask myself that question a lot. It kept me up at night quite often, to be honest. If we had known, what would we have done differently? Certainly, it would have made the realities of his death a bit easier to deal with. Putting things over in my name with his help.

I'd have known whether or not he actually wanted to be buried in that blue sweater I put him in." Her voice sounded in danger of breaking at that last sentence. When she next spoke, however, she had regained her composure. "But, no, I don't think I would have wanted to know."

"Really?" asked Zoey, frowning.

"Really." She surveyed Zoey for a moment, her eyes gleaming. "Do you know what made me come to that decision?"

Zoey shook her head.

"It might sound a little morose, but it happened after my mom got sick." Correctly interpreting the bewildered expression on Zoey's face, Aunt Carol chuckled. "I know, it sounds strange. I don't know if your grandma has ever told you stories about our mom, but the woman was well, a force of nature. She always did and said exactly what she wanted. She spoke her mind a lot more than a woman was supposed to back in those days, and she only got louder the older she got." A genuine smile had broken out over her face as she spoke. She grabbed a cookie off the untouched plate and took a substantial bite. "When she got sick, she didn't let it slow her down for the longest time."

Zoey didn't understand. This story was about her mother dying, but from the way Aunt Carol was talking, you'd think it was her fondest memory. "And that made you . . . not want to know if people were going to die?" asked Zoey, trying to follow what her aunt was saying.

"Oh, sorry, I guess I left that part out." She took a moment to dunk her cookie into her tea before continuing. "She said that the thing she hated most about having cancer, apart from the dying, was how everyone treated her differently."

Zoey scrunched up her face. "Differently how?"

"Oh, people were always getting teary-eyed, or kept trying to remind her of 'better times,' or else just acted uncomfortable around her. She hated it."

"I think I know what she meant," replied Zoey. She hated the looks of pity she'd caught on her friends' faces, even months after her dad had passed.

"Well, she passed years and years after Keith. It was sad, of course, but I knew my mom wouldn't forgive me if I stood around mourning her for too long. After I got on with life a little bit, that's when I realized that I'd found my answer. If I had known Keith was going to pass before he did, I'm sure I would have treated him differently, made him feel unlike himself. I think that would have ruined the last of the time we had."

"So, you think it's always better not to know things like that?" asked Zoey, thinking of Nicole.

"I wouldn't say always, and it's probably different from person to person. But for me at least, I've come to see not knowing as something of an unexpected blessing."

"I think that makes sense . . ." She thought she knew where her aunt was coming from, but wasn't quite sure what to make of it. How would she have felt if she had known her dad didn't have long left in the world? Would she have hugged him more? Have begged him not to go? Whatever she did, she was sure that it wouldn't have escaped his notice. Would he, like his mother-in-law, have hated the fact that she was treating him differently?

Aunt Carol fixed Zoey with a misty gaze. "I know this must be a difficult conversation for you. But I'm very glad we were able to have it."

"Thanks, I am too," replied Zoey.

The silence that followed didn't make Zoey want to inch her way toward the door as it might have in the past. Though her mind was still full of thoughts of what she'd heard at the hospital, talking with her aunt actually cheered her up. A pang of guilt twisted Zoey's stomach. For all she owed her aunt, she was doing a poor job at making repayment.

There was her aunt, always willing to talk with her, no matter how hard the subject might have been. And here she was, letting her aunt keep on believing that her first love might be reaching out from beyond the grave.

Zoey still didn't know what she was going to do about Lisa and Nicole, but she had made up her mind about something else. She had to come clean to her aunt. She needed to do it in the right way, though. She'd have to talk to Nicole first. That part was easy enough, they were due to spend the day together tomorrow. She knew that Nicole would be down for whatever plan she, Zoey, had. She just needed to come up with one first.

CHAPTER TWENTY-ONE

Grief

Zoey was drifting through a sea of darkness, caught somewhere between the realms of sleep and wakefulness. Chill air caressed her face with its cool kiss, while her comforter enshrouded her body in its warm embrace. She was starting to dip back into sleep proper when she realized what had brought her toward wakefulness to begin with.

"Whatisit?"

The room came into blurry focus as Zoey sat up, grumbling in vague annoyance. It hadn't been a dream. Despite her promise to not wake her up like this, a small figure stood silhouetted in the darkness. A hand rested on the edge of the bed, rocking it gently. Zoey was about to growl that Nicole needed to go away and let her sleep when the figure spoke.

"Z-Zoey."

Though she recognized Nicole's voice, it had come out as a soft, anguished mewling. Zoey's senses snapped into focus with alarming speed. Her hand groped on the bedside table before finding the chain that turned on a small, stained glass lamp.

There stood Nicole, barefoot in a pair of pink pajamas with little white clouds dotting them. Her hair was down from its usual ponytail and looking even messier than usual. Most unusual was her face. Her cheerful air was nowhere to be found, instead her features were twisted into an mask of anguish. Though she was quite silent, there were streaks down her cheeks that told Zoey she had been crying, maybe mere moments before.

"Nicole? What's wrong?"

"Z-Zoey," repeated Nicole. "M-my d-dad—h-hospita—m-om—Tylerwouldn'tstay."

Nicole's sob-garbled words only became more unintelligible after that. Zoey was thankful that she was the only one who could hear Nicole on this side of reality. She wasn't sure how Nicole had been able to keep it together while she made her attempts to wake her. Now that she'd started crying, however, there didn't seem to be any stopping it.

"OK, OK, let's just get you calmed down. Everything's OK," said Zoey, rubbing Nicole's back. "Would a cookie make you feel better? I think my aunt has some downstairs." Nicole began shaking her head but stopped midway through. She looked up at Zoey, still letting out the occasional sob, though she had given up on forming any actual words.

"Just wait here for a minute. I'll be right back."

Zoey hadn't taken a full step toward the door when Nicole grabbed her hand in a viselike grip.

"I w-w-want to c-come, t-t-oo." She managed, looking up at Zoey with a fierce determination.

With no real reason to deny her, the two of them crept downstairs. Zoey was relieved to find the kitchen empty when they got there. Having a late-night chat with Aunt Carol while also attempting to deal with a distraught Nicole was not something she felt she had the mental capacity for this late at night. Zoey attempted to have Nicole sit down at the scrubbed table, but Nicole wasn't having it. Instead, they walked to the cookie jar, hands still linked, and looked inside.

"Oatmeal raisin OK?"

Nicole nodded assent, and Zoey pulled a handful of cookies from the jar. She managed to get Nicole over to the table, but when she made to sit down, Nicole shook her head.

"I c-can't s-stay."

A stab of annoyance surged through Zoey, immediately followed by guilt. She knew Nicole wouldn't be acting this way over something minor, but she wished she'd be a little more clear on what was going on.

"You want to go back to your house?" asked Zoey, glancing at the clock and receiving a shock to see that it was almost three in the morning.

Nicole nodded.

"OK, but when we get there, you have to calm down and tell me what's wrong, OK?"

She nodded again and the two of them crept through the silent house.

One dizzying plunge through the mist later, they were standing in Nicole's bedroom. Having never been there so late at night, Zoey was surprised to find a sea of stars dancing on the ceiling when they walked out of the closet. A small rotating sphere sat in the corner, the mock night projected from within. Combined with the drifting mist, it was quite a beautiful sight.

Zoey got Nicole to sit down on the edge of her bed, where she mercifully unclasped their hands and began taking small bites of cookie.

"Alright, what's going on?"

Nicole sat staring off with tear-filled eyes, still suppressing the odd shuddering sob while taking the occasional bite of cookie.

"Nicole, I want to help you, but you need to tell me. What happened? Please."

Nicole took her time chewing before she answered. She took a deep, steadying breath, and without looking at Zoey, managed to speak.

"My dad had to go to the hospital. He said there's something wrong with my mom."

Zoey's heart skipped a beat.

"He just left you here alone?"

Nicole shook her head, her eyes still downcast. "Tyler's here, too. He stayed up with me for a bit, but said we needed to get some sleep . . . and dad would call if anything happened."

Fury replaced Zoey's concern. She'd never given Tyler all that much thought. He'd seemed to her to be a typical older brother, someone who wasn't all that interested in spending time with his sister. It was fair, given that there were a good six years between them, but she'd always got the impression that, when push came to shove, Tyler would be there for Nicole. If that time wasn't now, then when was it?

"How long ago did this happen?"

Nicole looked at the clock and sobbed. "H-hours ago . . . he hasn't called, though, that means everything's OK, right?"

Zoey wanted to say yes, but all she could manage was to sit down and pull Nicole into a hug. In all honesty, she didn't think the lack of contact from John boded well at all. Saying so not only felt cruel but was likely to send Nicole back into a tailspin. Hating herself, she said the only thing she could think of.

"I'm sure everything will be OK."

Nicole glanced up at Zoey and nodded, rocking in place as she did. Zoey wasn't sure if Nicole actually believed her or if she was trying to will the words to be true.

"Do you want to do something to pass the time?" asked Zoey, looking around the room.

Nicole sniffled and taking a last bit of cookie, nodded.

"Alright, what do you want to do? It'll have to be something quiet."

Nicole shook her head.

"I don't know."

The fact that Nicole, who was always up for anything, couldn't pick out something only heightened Zoey's sense of worry.

"How about we get you tucked back in bed and I can read you a story?"

Nicole gave her head a nearly imperceptible nod, sniffing as she wiped her eyes on the back of her hand. Zoey waited for her to climb into bed, then tucked the covers in at her side the same way her parents had done when she was little. She looked over to a set of cubbies covered in hand-painted vines and flowers to match the room's walls.

"Do you have any favorites?"

Nicole sniffed loudly from her bed. "Can you read me a fairy tale?"

Zoey walked over to the cubby and surveyed the books it held. Her eyes roved over several colorful art books before finding a large hardcover volume titled Fairy Tales. She extracted the heavy volume from among its fellows and sat back down on the edge of Nicole's bed.

"Looks like there's a lot in here. Do you know which one you want?" asked Zoey, opening up the weighty book.

Nicole shook her head again. Zoey suppressed a sigh. She ran her finger down the table of contents. She didn't recognize even one of them. This was a different world. Of course the stories wouldn't be the same. Still, she figured the broad strokes of what made a fairy tale must be the same in either world. Since she didn't know a thing about these stories, she figured the best place to start was at the beginning. She turned to the first story, "The Princess of the Alabaster Cavern."

"Alright, let's start at the beginning then . . ."

As Zoey began reading, she was amused to see how similar it was to the ones she grew up on. A beautiful princess was kidnapped by a wicked witch and hidden in an enchanted cave. She didn't think she needed to keep reading to know there was a handsome prince, perhaps atop a noble steed, toward the end of the story. Though she was doing her best to keep Nicole distracted, speaking in loud, animated voices for each character, Zoey could tell that her young friend was only half listening. She knew what the pale, almost blank expression on her face meant. Hadn't she felt that way countless times herself when her mom was out all night?

Zoey paused her performance to think. From the lack of response, it didn't seem as if Nicole minded. What Nicole needed was something new. Something to take her mind off the situation. Old comfortable stories were pleasant in their way, but they weren't exactly engrossing when you'd heard them a million times before. Well, that was easy enough. Any story from Zoey's side of reality would be brand new to her. But would that be enough? She felt so powerless when it came to the situation with Nicole's mom. She wanted to do something special for Nicole. It didn't take long for her to realize that special wasn't out of the question.

"Hey, Nicky?" began Zoey, trying out the name she'd heard Nicole's family use.

Nicole looked surprised but didn't object to Zoey's use of the nickname.

"Yeah?"

"How about we use the mist to do something a little more fun?"

Nicole sat up a little straighter to stare at Zoey with her wide green eyes.

"What do you mean?"

Zoey closed the book and flashed what she hoped was a convincing imitation of Nicole's usual mischievous smile. She shut her eyes and focused on the childhood memories that still warmed her heart. Countless nights spent with her parents reading to her before bed. Peering through one eye, the mist swirled and churned before her, though it refused to take proper form. Squaring her shoulders, Zoey stared at the mist as it swirled just above Nicole's bed. She narrowed the flood of memories down to one. She saw the story in her mind's eye, remembered how she'd felt when last she had it read to her. Warm. Safe. Loved.

The mist twisted and turned in place, drawing in toward the space that Zoey was focusing on. If she squinted up her eyes, she thought she saw the faint outline of something vaguely human-shaped. Then, with a soft pop, the image in her mind materialized.

She stared at the sparkling figure she'd plucked out of the mist, not quite able to believe what she was looking at. The glittering figure hung in the air before her, rotating in place. The hairs on the back of Zoey's neck stood up. She wasn't sure if it was because its face was a blank mask of mist, or that the proportions were otherwise precisely what she saw when she pictured "Cinderella," but something about it unnerved her. It was beautiful to be sure, but almost hauntingly so.

As always, Nicole didn't seem to share her hesitations. She was looking at the figure with an expression of quiet wonder. She reached her hand out, stopping with her fingers less than an inch from the silvery phantom. As if pulled by invisible strings connected to Zoey's thoughts, the figure gave a little pirouette in place, causing a smile to spread across Nicole's face for the first time that evening.

"Alright, I think I've got the hang of this," began Zoey. She had the figure twirl again, then bow, then skip merrily in place.

Zoey went through the story of Cinderella with Nicole watching in rapt attention. With some initial effort, each character got its own distinct mist figure that acted out their part in smooth, graceful motions. The more she got into telling the story, the less she had to think about it. She wasn't sure when it happened, but at some point in the performance, soft music began playing. It came from the mist itself, changing with each scene Zoey narrated.

While it wasn't doing much in the way of getting Nicole back to sleep, it seemed to have gotten her mind away from anxious thoughts. She was all smiles as she watched the silver mist figures act out the story. She even let out a soft "oooh" of longing when the miniature Cinderella spun around, and in a shower of silver sparks, changed from her tattered rags to a voluminous ball gown.

When the tale had been told and Cinderella and her Prince Charming were declared to have lived happily ever after, Nicole demanded another story, then another, and another. After they'd worked their way through Rapunzel, Hansel and Gretel, and Snow White, Nicole's excitement, though still intact, was fighting with the late hour. After Snow White too had ridden off into her own happily ever after, Nicole gazed up at Zoey, looking as though she were fighting back a yawn. When she spoke, her voice was meek.

"One more?"

Struggling to keep down a yawn of her own, Zoey nodded.

"Alright, but you have to try and get some sleep after this one."

With heavy eyes, Nicole snuggled down against her pillows and looked toward the space where the mist figures had vanished mere moments before. Zoey flipped through the store of childhood favorites in her mind, trying to decide which would be most enjoyable for Nicole. It wasn't as though she thought Nicole was at all picky, but she wanted this last story to be special.

She wasn't sure that Nicole realized it, but having the younger girl in her life the past month had been an incredible boon. The bond they'd forged had taken a situation that had seemed like a perilous void of gloom and turned it into something precious. She wanted to pay some of that back.

"Ready?" asked Zoey.

"Ready," replied Nicole, looking back at Zoey with sleep-heavy eyes

"So, believe it or not, our story begins like so many others, in a land far, far away."

Chapter Twenty-Two

Storytime

"Once upon a time, there lived a royal family. A king, strong and caring, who was always willing to lend a hand to those in need despite his high status. A queen, kind and gentle, who was beloved by both kingdom and family alike, though none more than the king himself. Their only daughter and princess of the land was a quiet girl who was still finding her way in the world, but who looked to her parent's example in everything she did."

Zoey focused on the image she'd conjured in her mind, ignoring the small stab of longing that doing so caused her. The mist figures formed one after another. A tall man wearing a crown, a woman holding a scepter, and, finally, a somewhat plain-looking girl, not much taller than Nicole. Zoey took a deep breath and, keeping the story she wanted to tell in mind, began.

"On a day like any other, an ill wind blew through the kingdom, bringing with it a terrible curse. Try as they might, the king and queen were unable to hold back the evil magic and the kingdom fell into ruin.

Where there was once peace and laughter, there was now nothing but sorrow and strife. To spare the princess from suffering under this fate, the king and queen sent her away from the kingdom to live in an enchanted forest. They promised her that one day, once the curse upon the kingdom had been lifted, they would come find her and live as a family once more."

Zoey paused to glance away from the lone figure strolling in place toward a glade of mist-conjured trees. Nicole was watching the scene through bleary, half-open eyes.

"As the king and queen had promised, when the princess made it to the enchanted forest, she was safe from the curse that had befallen the land. But she was all on her own and sad. Safe, but sad. Then, one night when the princess was getting ready for bed in the small home she'd made for herself, she began to hear strange noises. At first, these noises scared the princess, alone as she was. But eventually, her curiosity got the better of her and she went in search of their source."

"This story's kind of scary," yawned Nicole, not sounding the least bit scared.

"It's about to get better, promise."

"She followed the sounds through the densest, darkest part of the forest. Just when she had all but decided to turn back and return to her lonely life of solitude, she found its source. The princess was shocked to see a small figure amid a grove of trees unlike any she'd ever seen before. Though they were the same shape and size as those that made up the rest of the forest, they were each their own brilliant color. Vivid blues, deep rich purples, bright pinks, every color the princess had ever seen, and some she'd never even dreamed of.

"The mist-conjured scenery, which had until this point been nothing but various shades of silver and gray, now bloomed with color. Like gently burning tongues of flame, it grew from the core of each piece of scenery and spread out in all directions. Nicole gave a sleepy "ooohhh" from beside Zoey, and snuggled down a bit more firmly into the bed.

"At the center of these beautiful trees stood a small child, with shining golden hair and pale, glittering skin. The princess remembered the stories of fairy folk the king and queen had told her when she was younger and knew she was standing in the presence of just such a creature. Beautiful as the fae girl and the trees were, the princess couldn't help but feel nervous. She thought about running back to her lonely corner of the forest, but the sight of the fae child looking so happy, surrounded by such beautiful colors, drew her in.

"The princess was afraid to reveal herself, scared that the fae child might run away, or else attack her. She had heard tales of fae creatures who were none too kind. Something in the princess's heart told her that this was not that kind of fae.

"When the princess stepped out from her hiding place, the fae child welcomed her with a smile and a burst of shining color. The princess felt her nervousness melt away at the brilliant smile on the face of the fae child. The two of them became fast friends and spent their days together. The princess told the fae child all about her kingdom and the wonders that it used to hold. The fae child showed the princess the beauty of the forest and the way of the fae folk."

Zoey paused, watching the figures she'd conjured gambol around the edge of Nicole's bed.

"What happens next?" asked Nicole with a yawn.

Sleep was creeping around the edge of Zoey's vision. She let out a yawn of her own.

"I don't really know . . . What do you think happens next?"

Nicole reached up toward the figures, her head drooping. "I think they go back to the princess's kingdom and lift the curse. Then everyone can live happily ever after."

"You know, I think so, too."

Nicole shifted under the covers. Her breathing became deep and steady, her eyes closed above a dreamy half-smile. The mist figures dissolved, their job done. Zoey supposed she should go now, back to her own room and world, but she didn't want to wake Nicole. She didn't know what the future had in store for her young friend, but for now, she was safe and happy. She wanted to let Nicole dream, for as long as the world would let her.

When next Zoey opened her eyes, she was surprised to find the room looking different than it had only moments ago. Warm, early morning sunlight was spilling in around the corners of the drapes still shut tight over Nicole's bay window. The machine that projected stars across the ceiling must run on a timer, as it stood dim and motionless in its corner of the room. Though she was a little stiff from sleeping sitting upright, Zoey felt remarkably at ease as she lay there, her mind still wrapped gently in sleep's lingering embrace.

She wondered what had woken her up, her mind drifting back toward sleep when she heard it again. A series of muffled noises coming from downstairs. This was enough to pull her more fully into the realm of wakefulness, bringing her good sense along with it.

Zoey glanced at the small pink clock that hung on Nicole's wall. It was a little past seven in the morning. As Tyler wasn't likely to be up before the sun under his own steam, John must have returned from the hospital.

Zoey hesitated. She could stay here and find out firsthand what news he was bringing. She was sure that Nicole wouldn't mind. Tempted as she was, that seemed like a conversation she should let Nicole and John have in private.

Slipping off the small sliver of bed on which she'd fallen asleep, Zoey looked down at her young friend. A lump formed in her throat. Nicole looked so peaceful lying there. Her face blank and untroubled, safe from the harsh reality of life in a dreamland of her own creation. It broke Zoey's heart to think of what hardships might soon befall her. Would she still be the same sunny person if the world took her mom from her? Much as Zoey wanted to tell herself that wouldn't happen, that the world wasn't that cruel, she knew better. Discovering the secret of the mist between worlds hadn't changed that fact. The universe was, at the end of the day, cold and uncaring.

With a silent promise that she'd return as soon as she'd put in an appearance back home, Zoey plunged once more into the mist between their two worlds. She was getting back to her feet and wondering if she might not be able to squeeze in another couple hours of sleep when her heart stopped. Her bedroom door was open.

CHAPTER TWENTY-THREE

Truth

Zoey stood frozen, staring at the open door as if it were a gaping maw of some eldritch creature. As far as she was concerned, it might as well be. She racked her brain, going over the events of the night before. Had she closed it when she and Nicole had come back from the kitchen? She had been so focused on Nicole's distress that she couldn't remember. If she hadn't, was there a chance that her aunt and uncle hadn't noticed? It seemed unlikely to the point of absurdity, but it was the only hope she had.

Zoey crept toward the stairs as quietly as she had her first night in the house. Holding her breath, she strained her ears for any sounds coming from below. The vise around her chest loosened its grip. The only things she heard were the sound of her own breathing and the muffled chirps of the morning birds outside. Was it possible she was the first one up? Over the past month, she'd never been awake before either her aunt or her uncle. To the same tune, she'd never been up this early before. Maybe they slept in on weekends?

Zoey headed downstairs, heart thudding in her chest. If there was ever a time for positive thinking to work, it was now. She needed the kitchen to be empty. When she rounded the corner, her heart all but stopped. There was her aunt and uncle, sitting across from each other at the scrubbed wooden table. Both were in their morning clothes and wore grave expressions.

"I think we need to have a little talk, Zoey . . ." said Aunt Carol. Her eyes stayed fixed on the mug clutched between her bony hands.

Every part of Zoey wanted to run from the invitation, back to Nicole's world and away from the scene laid out before her. The only thing keeping her feet in place was the thought of how final such a course of action would be. As dire as things were, there was always a chance that they could be salvaged.

Without saying a word, Zoey strode to the table and sat down.

"So, would you like to tell your uncle and I where you've been? We know you weren't out walking."

Hot prickling guilt welled up in Zoey at the memory of the last time her absence had been noticed. At the time, she'd thought herself clever to have gotten away with it. Now, looking at the disappointment on her aunt's face, she thought she might be sick.

"I wasn't doing anything . . . bad" was all Zoey managed to say.

"You'll excuse me if we find that hard to believe," said Uncle Will. "I can't think of any reason you'd be out of the house in the middle of the night that would be considered "good."

"You didn't even take your shoes. If you were planning on sneaking out, why did you do it barefoot? It just doesn't make sense to me."

"People do a lot of things that don't make sense when they're on drugs, Carol."

"I'm not on drugs!" snapped Zoey, anger coming to her defense, though she knew she had no right to it.

"Then, please," said Aunt Carol, her tone desperate, "tell us where you were."

"I was . . . at a friend's."

Uncle Will shook his head. "Putting aside the fact that we told you we wanted to meet any friends you made, what makes you think going out to see someone in the middle of the night is OK?"

Zoey hesitated. She was being backed into a corner and she knew it. If her aunt and uncle kept pressing, then her entire story would collapse in on itself. Still, the truth was so unbelievable that she intended to cling to her series of half-truths for as long as she could.

"They haven't met, but I did tell Aunt Carol about her."

Aunt Carol looked for a moment as if she didn't have a clue what Zoey was talking about, then recognition spread across her face.

"The little girl you met at the park? Nicole?"

"That's her. She was having a rough night, so I went over to her place to keep her company."

Zoey knew it was hopeless before she'd finished talking. Even if her aunt and uncle believed her, the implications of her story were still highly suspect. In what world was it normal for a fourteen-year-old to go over to visit with a ten-year-old in the middle of the night?

The sentiment seemed to be shared by her aunt and uncle, who exchanged significant looks.

"Zoey, if that is the truth, it's still very concerning. Did this girl's parents know you were there?" asked Aunt Carol, her eyes reproachful.

"Look," began Zoey, trying to sound as respectful as possible. "I know it sounds weird, but it's the truth. Her mom's in the hospital, and she got left alone at the house because her dad had to rush over there."

Aunt Carol wrapped her bony fingers more tightly around the earthenware mug, her numerous rings clinking against its surface.

"How did you even know that she was alone?"

"She called me late last night," said Zoey, improvising wildly.

"Well, if that's true, then her number should be in your call history," said Uncle Will. He extended his hand to Zoey, his expression unfathomable.

"Alright, she didn't call me, but I promise, that's where I was. Keeping a scared little girl company, not out doing drugs or getting drunk or whatever awful thing you're thinking."

"Why should we believe you when we just caught you in a lie?" asked Uncle Will.

Zoey weighed her options. If she kept up the half-truths, she was bound to lose whatever trust her aunt and uncle had left in her. The chances that she'd be allowed to keep living here seemed slim at best. If she told the truth, the results were likely to be the same, but with a stay at the mental hospital before some kind of group home situation. That was, unless they believed her.

She knew she was kidding herself in thinking there was even a sliver of a chance of convincing her uncle. But what about Aunt Carol? She had been planning on telling her the truth. True, the half-formed plan had involved help from Nicole and hadn't factored in her uncle's presence. But what choice did she have?

She forced herself to meet her aunt's gaze, trying to look as sane as possible. Aunt Carol stared back with wide, desperate eyes. Zoey knew she was letting her down. If either of her relatives had truly believed in her goodness, it had been her aunt. Lies had gotten her into this mess. She had to trust that the truth would get her out.

"I know this is going to sound crazy . . ." began Zoey, still keeping her eyes fixed on her aunt's, "but Nicole isn't a . . . normal girl. I mean, she is, but she's not . . . from here."

"Zoey what are you—"

Zoey shook her head. She was determined to get everything out in one go.

"You know how you've been hearing noises? How cookies have been going missing? Well, you were right, you weren't just imagining it, but . . . I'm sorry, Aunt Carol, it's not Uncle Keith, or any kind of spirit. It's Nicole."

"You've been giving cookies to your friend from the park? But, that all started before you even came here."

Zoey teetered on the edge. There'd be no going back after this, but she didn't see what other options she had. Delaying it wouldn't make it any easier. In one long, breathless ramble, Zoey told her aunt and uncle everything that she'd kept secret from them. Once she started, she found it impossible to stop. Not for Uncle Will's frequent grunts and motions to interrupt, nor for her aunt's increasingly bewildered expression.

She told them about the first time she'd discovered the hidden panel in the back of her closet. She told them about the mist and everything it could do. But, most of all, she told them about Nicole. How they'd met. She told them how having Nicole to talk to had made her feel more herself than she had in years, and how she'd come to regard her as something more precious than a mere friend.

". . . and I know it all sounds absolutely batshit crazy, but I promise, it's all true. You have to believe me. You can't send me away. She's my friend and she's losing her mom. She's scared and sad and I need to be there for her."

Though she had always known that her aunt and uncle wouldn't believe her story, the look that they shared when she had stopped talking still sent a pang through her heart. It told her quite plainly that they were, in fact, wondering what they'd gotten themselves into by inviting Zoey into their house.

"Zoey . . ." said Aunt Carol, her voice sounding like something someone might adopt at the bedside of a very sick friend. "You don't really believe all that, do you?"

"Is it really that much crazier than thinking there was a cookie-eating spirit?" said Zoey, a bit more harshly than she intended. "I mean, doesn't it explain that whole thing?"

"I'd sooner believe Carol's ghost theory than the story you're trying to sell us."

Zoey was about to snap back when the sound of hurried footsteps came from upstairs. They all looked up at the ceiling just in time for the telltale groan of the fourth stair.

"What was that?" asked Aunt Carol.

Zoey had just enough time to register that even Uncle Will looked concerned by the sudden outburst of creaking when Nicole rounded the corner. If she had appeared distraught last night, it was nothing to how she looked now. Her face was twisted into an expression of such anguish that she hardly looked human. When she saw them sitting at the table, Nicole let out a long, pained wail that Zoey thought might have contained her name.

"Nicole? What's wrong?" asked Zoey, not caring that all this was happening in full view of her aunt and uncle.

So pale that she might have actually been a ghost, Nicole shook her head and threw herself into Zoey's arms. Zoey returned the hug, rubbing her back in what she hoped was a soothing way. Some part of her mind registered Aunt Carol asking what she was doing, but it wasn't enough to pull her focus from her anguished friend.

"Nicky, is she . . . OK?"

Nicole shook her head against Zoey's chest and mumbled something that sounded like, "I have to go."

"What, where?"

After a long pause in which she did little more than shiver in Zoey's arms, Nicole managed to choke out, "To say goodbye."

Zoey wrapped her arms more tightly around Nicole. "I'll come with you."

Nicole returned the hug, nodding in a haphazard way into Zoey's chest. Zoey took a step toward the door when something pulled her back. Looking back, she saw that "something" was Uncle Will. He had grabbed a hold of her wrist, a blazing expression in his eyes.

"You're not going anywhere."

"Will!"

"Let go of me!" yelled Zoey. She tried to pull her wrist free, but her uncle's grasp was too strong.

"You're not going anywhere until we figure this out. You're sick, Zoey. You need help we can't give, but we're going to get you to the people who can."

Spurred on by her uncle's words, Zoey flailed still harder against his grasp. It was no use. He was stronger than her and determined to keep her where she was. Before Zoey could make a fresh attempt at reasoning with her aunt and uncle, Nicole went flying from her side. She raised her hands and, with all the strength she possessed, shoved Uncle Will hard in the chest.

"Zoey is not sick!"

Uncle Will's eyes went wide as he stumbled backward, his grip on Zoey's wrist, loosening long enough for her to pull it free. Without Zoey to steady him, Uncle Will fell to the hardwood floor with an agonizing crash. Zoey didn't know what shocked her more. The sight of her uncle splayed on the floor, or Nicole, who still stood with her hands in front of her, panting through gritted teeth.

"Will?! What happened?" cried Aunt Carol, rushing to his side.

"What do you mean what happened?! Your niece attacked me!"

Uncle Will slapped away Aunt Carol's extended hand and got to his feet. His chest was heaving, his face red.

"She didn't. You stumbled back like you were shoved, but Zoey was pulling away from you."

"Well, if it wasn't her, then who the hell was it?" snapped Uncle Will, his usual controlled manner shattered.

Zoey glanced at Nicole, who was staring at her uncle, face still contorted with rage. "Show them."

Nicole didn't need to be asked twice. She stared at the table, eyes blazing. The four chairs that surrounded it flew out in all directions. Each one slammed into a different wall with a series of clattering bangs. After shaking violently for a moment, the table shot up in the air. Aunt Carol's half-drunk mug of tea flew off in a high, spinning arc and fell to the ground where it shattered. Aunt Carol screamed. Uncle Will looked as if he might faint.

Still glaring, Nicole let the table fall to the floor, where it landed with a crash that shook the entire kitchen.

"W-what was that?" asked Aunt Carol. Her voice was high and breathless as she clutched at the pashmina around her shoulders.

"I told you, Nicole's real. She's here and she needs me, so I'm going to go."

Uncle Will, shocked into silence, stared at Zoey with wide eyes. He reached his hand toward Zoey as if he were going to try and stop her again, but pulled it back. Was he frightened of Nicole?

Zoey took Nicole's hand and marched out of the kitchen. Hot tears threatened to spill out of her eyes with each step. She couldn't believe she was about to walk out of another home for the last time. This was supposed to be a temporary thing, a place for her to stay before she put it behind her. Why then, did it hurt so much? At least this time, she was certain she was walking toward a place where she'd always be welcome, even if only by one person.

They had gotten to the top of the stairs when the sound of clattering bangles made Zoey pull up short. She turned around to find Aunt Carol standing at the foot of the stairs. Though one of her hands was still clasped to her chest, she spoke in a clear, ringing voice.

"Please, promise you'll come back when you're done with whatever the two of you need to do."

They held each other's gaze for a moment, fawn-brown meeting misty-gray with a look of disbelief. Zoey's voice caught in her throat, but she managed to nod her head. Aunt Carol, too, seemed to be at a loss for words for the first time since Zoey had met her. She contended herself with pulling her pashmina more tightly around her shoulders.

Zoey squeezed Nicole's hand before turning back to her bedroom. The two of them walked together in silence, back into the mist. Whatever awaited them on the other side, they'd face it together.

CHAPTER TWENTY-FOUR

Goodbye

They tumbled out of the crawlspace as one, Zoey's mind still reeling from the scene in the kitchen. She shook her head and shoved the thoughts down inside her. Her feelings could wait, Nicole couldn't. No sooner than they had stepped into Nicole's bedroom, there came a gentle tapping at the door.

"Nicky, are you ready?" John's voice came through the door, faint and exhausted. Nicole, who was still white as a sheet, gave her head a shake. John knocked again. "Nicky? Do you need me to come in?"

Nicole shook her head again, seeming to forget that her father couldn't see through walls.

"Nicky, you need to answer him."

Nicole started to shake her head for a third time but caught herself. "I have to get dressed."

There was a silence from the other side of the door before the sound of John's footsteps traveled down the hall. The quiet of Nicole's room pressed hard against Zoey's ears. Now that the adrenaline had all but left her, Zoey was all too aware of the grim task that was laid out before them.

"Hey, Nicky, you need to get changed out of those pj's. How about we find something." Zoey hesitated for a moment before continuing, "Something your mom would like?"

". . . OK," said Nicole in the softest voice Zoey had yet heard her use.

Still trembling, Nicole rummaged through her dresser. Occasionally, she'd pull something partway out to get a better look at it. Each time she did, she'd shove back whatever it was with a frustrated huff. This continued for some time, Zoey hovering behind her, unsure of what to do. Eventually, Nicole grabbed the collar of what, at first glance, appeared to be a plain, white shirt. However, when she pulled it out, Zoey saw that every inch of the garment had been stained some other color. Some of the splotches of paint were old and faded, as though someone had, at one point, tried to restore the shirt back to its original white.

"Can I wear this?"

Zoey swallowed hard, willing herself to keep her eyes from misting over any more than they already were.

"I think your mom will like seeing you in that."

Nicole managed something resembling a smile. She turned back to her dresser and after a few more moments of digging, pulled out a pair of equally splattered jeans. After swapping her cloud-covered pajamas for the outfit they'd picked, Nicole hesitated, then sat on the edge of her bed.

"Zoey, do you know what happens when someone dies?"

Zoey sighed, giving her head a slight shake. "I don't . . . No one does, really."

"That's what my dad said . . ." Nicole screwed up her face. "He said, when someone dies, they leave their body behind. He said, without their body, they can't be in pain anymore. Is that true?"

"I think so."

"But, you don't know where they go after that?" asked Nicole, the pleading in her voice unmistakable.

"I don't . . . but like your dad said, I don't think there's pain or anything after you . . . leave your body."

Nicole shook as tears welled up in her bright emerald eyes. Zoey wrapped her arm around her. It was all she could think to do.

"I don't want my mom to—go away," sobbed Nicole, her voice breaking before she could get the entire sentence out.

"I know," replied Zoey, her own voice in danger of failing. "It's not fair. Parents . . . shouldn't leave their kids like this."

Before Zoey knew it, tears were running down her cheeks. She wasn't sure what they were for. Grief for Nicole. Sad memories over her own loss. There was anger in there, too. Anger at the universe for being so unfair. Things like this shouldn't happen. Children shouldn't have to say goodbye to their parents. They shouldn't have to be hardened by things like this, to grow up before their time. Not because of drunk drivers, or some disease that doctors were too stupid to cure.

Zoey didn't know how long they sat there, holding on to each other, the tears flowing hot and fast. She wasn't sure who was comforting who by the time they stopped, leaving a hollow feeling inside Zoey's chest. She wiped her eyes with the back of her hands and stood up. They couldn't hide away in here. If she had learned one thing over the past two years, it was that there was no going back, or freezing time, no matter how badly you wanted. Time marched on, and the only thing to do was march right along with it.

"I think it's time to go."

Nicole got to her feet and extended a hand to Zoey. They walked downstairs, their hands linked until they reached the living room. Tyler and John sat waiting, neither looking at the other.

Tyler was dressed in a pair of jeans and a plain black shirt, looking both better groomed and more downcast than Zoey had ever seen him. His look of sadness was nothing compared to his father's however. John looked as though he'd lived a hundred years since Zoey had last seen him, the bags under his bloodshot eyes dark trenches of sorrow. Zoey was sure his stony expression was holding back feelings that she didn't want to contemplate.

Both men turned their heads when they entered the room, though, of course, they only saw Nicole. Tyler's expression remained unchanged, while a look of something close to annoyance flickered across John's face. It was almost immediately washed away as a wave of tears spilled out of his already misty eyes.

"Is this OK?" asked Nicole, gesturing to her paint-splattered outfit.

John sniffed and wiped his eyes. "Your mom will love it."

"Looks good, squirt," added Tyler, sounding as if he had a bad cold.

Nicole attempted a smile, though didn't quite manage it. Without saying anything, John and Tyler rose from their seats and made their way toward the front door, Nicole following in their wake.

When they reached the silver minivan parked in the driveway, Nicole opened the back door. Zoey clambered in as quietly as she could. It wasn't necessary. Zoey suspected she could have opened the door herself and neither John nor Tyler would notice today.

The ride to the hospital was silent. Each occupant of the car had spent it staring ahead blankly. This was somewhat worrying as John was the one driving. He seemed to be functioning on a deeply ingrained autopilot, however, and the trip was as smooth as any car ride Zoey had taken.

Although the hospital was the same one that Zoey had been to only last week, it felt different to her. The people bustling around the first floor seemed to move more slowly, their expressions grave. Even the music that played in the elevator sounded vaguely sinister, though Zoey was sure it was as cheerful as always.

When the doors slid open on the fourth floor, no one in their party gave any sign of moving. The elevator doors started to close again, necessitating John to stick out his arm to stop them.

They shuffled out of the elevator and made their way to Lisa's room in silence. When they reached the door, John turned to face Nicole. He got down to her level and pulled her into a hug.

"Your mom's in there just like always, but she's going to look a bit different," said John once he'd pulled away.

Nicole was looking at the door through shimmering eyes. She trembled as she asked. "Different?"

"You know how she was hooked up to those machines? The ones that gave her fluids and kept track of her heartbeat?"

Nicole nodded.

"Well, she's got one that's helping her breathe now, so there'll be a clear sort of mask over her face."

Nicole's lower lip trembled. "Will she be able to talk?"

John's hand clenched into a fist at his side. "The doctors have given her some medicine to help keep her comfortable, so she's going to be pretty sleepy. She might not be able to talk, but I'm sure she'll be able to hear you."

Nicole nodded but kept her eyes fixed on the door as though it might reach out and bite her at any moment. Zoey gave Nicole's shoulder a reassuring squeeze. The gesture went unnoticed, as the younger girl continued contemplating the door. John seemed to be giving Nicole time to respond, but as the seconds stretched into minutes, he continued on.

"Do you want to go in?"

Nicole kept staring for another couple of seconds, then turned to Zoey as if she might have the answer. Zoey gave her shoulder another squeeze. This was something Nicole needed to decide for herself. After a long pause, Nicole stepped forward and took her father's hand.

They filed into the room, with Nicole and John leading the way. This time Zoey didn't wait to follow the others in, though a moment later, she wished she had. Though John had forewarned them, the sight of Lisa still made Zoey want to turn and run from the room. There were too many wires. Too many tubes. The scene was too much like the one that had served as the backdrop to her final goodbye with her father.

Lisa's bed had been lowered from its previous upright position, leaving her lying on her back, head propped up on two pillows. The new machine was whirring beside her, rhythmically following the rise and fall of her thin chest. Her skin was so thin as to be translucent and hung on her frame too loosely. How had she degraded so much in less than twenty-four hours?

"Mom . . . ?"

Nicole's voice was so soft that Zoey doubted Lisa would have heard her even if she had been awake. Nicole reached out, stopping short of touching her mom's hand. She looked to her dad as if to ask for permission. John nodded through streaming eyes as Tyler wrapped an arm around his shoulder. Nicole called out for Lisa again, louder this time. When she didn't respond, she grabbed her hand and gave it a gentle shake.

". . . Mommy, can you hear me?"

This time, Lisa stirred. Her head rolled in Nicole's direction. It was clear that some part of her was there with them, but whatever they had given her to keep her comfortable in her final days seemed too strong for her to overcome.

"S-she can hear you, Nicky," John croaked out, his lower lip trembling. He stepped beside Nicole and stroked the back of Lisa's hand. "Lisa? Nicky's here, you can hear her, right?"

Lisa's head moved toward the sound again, an almost imperceptible groan escaping her cracked lips. Her hand twitched and searched for Nicole's. Their fingers intertwined.

This is wrong, thought Zoey, her jaw clenched. *Parents shouldn't leave kids this way.*

It was the scene with her father all over again. All the pretty words and tears in the world couldn't change the fact that Lisa was dying. And once she was gone she was never coming back. Worse yet, when she left, she'd take a part of Nicole with her forever, despite it being the last thing she'd want to do to her child.

The world shuddered. Zoey's stomach lurched as if she'd missed a step down a flight of stairs. The universe wasn't fair. That was an immutable rule and always had been . . . Or, at least that's what she'd thought before meeting Nicole. There weren't supposed to be other worlds, and yet, here she was. People weren't supposed to be able to lift things with their minds or conjure objects just by thinking about them, but she had done those things and more. If the universe said that it was time for Lisa to die, what would happen if she, Zoey, told it no?

The mist never looked more beautiful to Zoey as she focused her mind. She pictured Lisa as she'd seen her yesterday. Sick but awake, fighting to get better, with the end not so close in sight. A ripple ran through the air. The back of Zoey's neck prickled. She saw in her mind's eye the self-portrait of Lisa. A beautiful, healthy woman amid a field of pink flowers, her whole life ahead of her. The mist churned violently, then as if she had become a magnet for the stuff, began rushing toward Lisa.

A smile on her face, Zoey forced the image of a healthy, whole Lisa to grow clearer in her mind. She saw the cancer that racked her body shrinking, retreating, being unmade by the force of her will. The mist flowed faster. It rushed toward Lisa like water cascading down a stream. The world began to blink. Her lungs struggled to take in gasps of the now too-thin air. She was a fish out of water, but she refused to turn back.

Panic threatened to overwhelm Zoey as the mist picked up speed. It rushed to Lisa like a sea of raging, silver rapids. What she was doing was bigger than anything she'd done before. It demanded more of her. More of the mist that was her sustenance in this world.

Zoey clenched her jaw and fixed her eyes on the family before her. She could feel their hearts and minds crying out for the dying woman in front of them. No, not the dying woman. The woman who was about to make a full recovery.

The mist outside the hospital was churning and raging in its course toward Lisa. Though Zoey's body ached, she urged it ever onward. What was the cost of a single life? How much of the mist would it take? Be it every last speck, then that was what Zoey would give to her wish, her promise to Nicole. She wasn't going to lose her mother. Not like this.

Zoey's lungs screamed for air, her muscles ached, though not as much as her heart. She sensed the price she was paying, even before her hands had become something less than solid. She pushed the fear rising in her chest aside. The air in the room was clean and clear, free of mist. It had all been poured into Lisa along with Zoey's fervent wish, and the last of her strength.

Something splintered inside her. Her knees buckled and, though they crashed against the hard linoleum floor, there was no pain. Nicole turned around at the sound in time to catch one last glimpse of Zoey, a smile spread across her face, before she vanished. Before she was nothing.

CHAPTER TWENTY-FIVE

Bonds

Zoey groaned. The light making its way through her eyelids told her it was time to get up, but the siren song of five more minutes was calling her name. She wasn't in danger of being late, anyway. Her dad always intervened before then.

"Hey, Zoey, time to get up. Don't want to be late on your first day."

Right on time, thought Zoey.

Stretching, Zoey opened her eyes and tried to will herself to take the monumentally difficult first step out of bed. What was it her dad always said? It only hurts for the first five minutes, then you have the whole day to enjoy? Well, that might be true, but whenever she was faced with those initial minutes, she always felt that she'd rather just stay in bed.

"Alright, geeeeettttt up," cried Zoey, sitting up and sliding out of bed in one motion. Her dad was right, she didn't want to be late on her first day of high school.

After blinking away the specks of light that accompanied her rapid ascent, Zoey stretched, gazing around her room. The outfit she'd picked out last night hung on the back of her desk's chair. She wasn't the type of girl to agonize about this or that outfit on a day-to-day basis, but she wanted to get this first day right.

A shower and breakfast seemed in order first, though. No one was going to want to make friends with a smelly Zoey. Mercifully, she wouldn't have to rely on bringing in a whole new crop of friends. Though eighth grade had been the last year she'd spend with some of them, she would retain a handful of the ones she'd made in middle school, seeing as a good number would be going to the same high school as her.

With this cheerful thought to bolster her spirits, Zoey strolled toward the smell of breakfast coming from down the hall.

"Thought you were going to hibernate right through freshman year there, Zoe-bear."

Zoey rolled her eyes. She wasn't sure where the name "Zoe-bear" had come from, only that she had tried to retire it sometime around her eleventh birthday. Her parents were good enough about refraining from using it around her friends, but it still cropped up from time to time whenever they were feeling nostalgic.

"Yeah, well, you always said you thought I was smart enough to skip a grade, maybe this is the year."

Her dad chuckled as he slid a plate of bacon and eggs in front of her. "Trust me, the next four years are going to go by fast enough. You don't want to go skipping them."

"I think that's just something old people say. It's high school, it can't be that much different from middle school."

Zoey's dad let out a noise of mock indignation. "Old? Clair, your daughter's being a bully."

"Well, she's in high school now, I guess it was inevitable for a bit of her mean girl to come out," said Zoey's mom, pausing in the act of buttering her toast. "She has a point, though. You're officially the father of a high school student today, I think that makes you old."

"And what does that make you?" asked Zoey's dad, still wearing a look of playful indignation.

Her mom tossed her chestnut curls. "With how young I look? An older sister I think."

"Mom," groaned Zoey, barely managing to keep herself from rolling her eyes.

"That's a cute top you laid out, by the way, mind if I borrow it later?"

"Mom!"

Her mom and dad laughed and, after a beat, Zoey joined in, too. Her parents were weird, even embarrassing sometimes, but she had to admit, they were pretty cool as far as adults went. Not that she'd ever tell them that.

"Concerning bullying habit aside, I've gotta say, your *old* dad's proud of you. High school freshman and soon to be top of the class."

Zoey couldn't help but smile. "I don't know about top of the class, but I still get a reward if I get good grades, right?"

"Ice cream cake?" offered her dad, now sitting at the table with his own plate.

Zoey speared the center of her egg and dunked a piece of toast in the runny yolk. "I was thinking more like something with four wheels. Goes fast. Most kids get one in high school."

Her dad stared at her for a moment. It was a look she'd seen before. It often preceded a speech about how he couldn't believe how grown up his little girl was getting.

"You've got at least another year before that, and you'll have to get some pretty good grades to enter into car-reward territory," said her mom.

"And, you lost some points there with 'fast.' What I think you meant was 'safe and reliable for getting from point A to B in one piece,'" added her dad.

Zoey rolled her eyes. "Yeah, yeah. Safe and sound, as long as I don't have to drive the Mommobile."

For a while, there were no sounds but the clicking of cutlery against plates and the lilting melody coming from the kitchen radio. Said radio was perpetually tuned to one of two stations. One that played nothing but hits from the '70s and, when Zoey had her way, 105.8, a station that mercifully only played songs from the last decade. Therefore, it was strange that the song filling the room was some classical piano piece.

"What's with the music?"

"Guess they're branching out," said her dad. "It wouldn't hurt us to get a bit more culture."

Zoey shrugged and attempted to devote herself to the food remaining on her plate, but the music pouring out of the radio kept pulling her back. The slow, lilting melody filled her with a longing that she couldn't quite describe. Cultured or not, it wasn't the way she wanted to start off her first day of high school. It had taken her weeks after middle school graduation to get over her rose-colored-glasses-induced sadness over leaving that part of her life behind.

"Anyone mind if I change the station?"

Taking the lack of response as the go-ahead, Zoey flipped the station over to 105.8. They caught the last few bars of a bouncy pop song before the DJ announced that up next was Debussy's "Clair De Lune." Zoey had just enough time to frown in confusion before the same dreamy piece began playing.

Before she could remark on the odd occurrence, something purple flashed across the corner of her vision. She spun around to face it, but only saw her parents sitting at the table as they ate their breakfasts. There wasn't a trace of purple to be found.

"Something wrong there, Zoe-bear?" asked her dad.

A chill ran up Zoey's spine. A half-remembered memory played at the edge of her mind. A name danced at the tip of her tongue. She pushed both sensations away.

"No, just not feeling music this morning," she replied, flipping the radio off.

The next thing she knew, breakfast was over and it was time to get ready for the rest of the day.

As she stood at the front door, showered and dressed in her carefully curated outfit, she couldn't help but feel a bit nervous. Much as she knew high school wasn't the end all, be all of life, she was uncomfortably aware that the next couple of days would go on to shape the coming four years.

"Don't worry, honey. You're going to have a great day," said her mom as she stood next to her dad with watery eyes.

"Yeah, I guess, but . . ." She paused to wipe her clammy palms against her skirt. "What if I don't make a single new friend?"

"Well, in the extremely unlikely event of that happening, your mom and I could always pose as a couple of cool foreign exchange students and be your friends, boost your cred." He grinned at Zoey before letting his face fall dramatically. " Oh wait, I look too old for that, don't I?"

"You're really not going to let that one go, are you?" asked her mom amid Zoey's fresh round of groaning.

"Hey, ruggedly handsome dads have feelings, too, you know."

Zoey rolled her eyes. A smile crept over her face despite her best efforts. She gave her mom a quick hug goodbye. When it came time for her to pull away from hugging her dad, she instead squeezed more tightly.

"Wow, haven't gotten a hug like this since you turned teen," said her dad warmly, returning the hug with interest.

When Zoey pulled away, she was mortified to find her eyes had misted over. She blotted the tears with a tissue pulled from her purse. She did *not* want to show up to school looking like a drowned raccoon.

"Alright, I'll see you after school, I guess."

"Have a good day," replied her mom.

"Remember," said her dad, adopting a thick Russian accent, "super cool high school seniors Sergi and Tatiana are just a phone call away."

Not deigning to reply to her dad's latest bout of nonsense, Zoey waved her parents goodbye and made her way down the street.

The sunlight that poured down from the cloudless sky caressed her skin with its gentle warmth. The air was perfumed with the smell of grass and late summer blooms. Every so often, she'd pass other kids, no doubt on their way to school themselves. Some walked alone, like her, others in small groups of three or four. None of them looked like they were old enough to be in high school, though. She supposed all the juniors and seniors were heading there by car, but she had hoped she'd run into some other freshmen along the way.

She had walked past a small group of giggling elementary school-aged girls when it happened. Shocking pink flashed at the edge of her vision, and she could have sworn she'd heard one of the younger girls call her name. When she whipped around toward the group she'd passed, she found that not only had none of them called out to her, but she was the only person on the block.

Zoey shook her head. Maybe it had been a mistake to stay up reading those last few chapters of Salem's Lot last night if she was so tired she was already zoning out. It didn't take long before she'd made her way out of the residential blocks and into the more lively downtown area that housed, among other things, the high school. She glanced at a large mural on the side of an old brick building as she went. She'd passed it countless times before, a scene of a sunrise over a field of wheat.

It happened again. A flash of pink. The sound of a young girl calling out her name in a high, clear voice. Zoey turned her head this way and that, looking for the source of either the voice or the garish shade of pink, but found neither. She quickened her pace. Whatever was going on, she was sure it would go away when she got to school. She'd be too busy to worry about strange flashes of color, phantom voices, or to contemplate why she knew the name "Debussy" when she knew she'd never heard it before.

As she neared the school, she began seeing what she clocked as fellow freshmen here and there. They had the same nervously excited air Zoey was hoping wasn't too evident around herself. They walked toward the school amid groups that moved with a little more confidence, chattering among themselves or calling out to others they spotted after a summer apart.

By the time she was outside the school itself, the scene was wall-to-wall teens. The other freshmen looked particularly young amid the seniors, who may as well have been adults as far as Zoey was concerned. She stared at the looming building. Her stomach felt as though she'd had frogs for breakfast rather than pancakes.

With a deep breath, Zoey readied herself to walk forward into the next chapter of her life. She just needed to take a breath, find her smile, and tell her feet to move forward. She'd been looking forward to this for weeks. So why was she frozen in place?

"This isn't right . . ." said a voice that Zoey was shocked to find was her own.

A flash of color, green this time, amid the sound of squealing tires and shrieks of mirth. It sounded as if some hot shot had done a burnout in an effort to impress their friends. Why then, did the sound make her feel like bursting into tears and running as fast as she could in the other direction?

A flash of purple.

The sound of a piano and the smell of patchouli.

A flash of green.

Her dad's voice reading her bedtime stories.

Green again.

The sound of screeching tires and shattering glass.

Zoey threw her hands over her ears and shut her eyes tight, hunching over with a groan. What was going on? Why wouldn't it stop? Why wouldn't they leave her alone?!

Though her eyes were shut tight, there was a flash of pink once more. This time, the voice said her name with a soft desperation rather than shouting it. She could feel something tugging gently at her wrist as if there were a balloon on a string there.

When she opened her eyes, the drab gray of the sidewalk came into focus beneath her, along with a glittering pink strand around her wrist. The strand was caught somewhere between transparent and barely opaque, shimmering in an ethereal way.

Zoey reached out to touch the strand. Her hand both passed through it and carried it with her, like trying to touch a stream of bubbles at the pool. When her hand passed through the strand, she saw a small blonde girl that she didn't recognize. Images flashed before her mind. She and the girl drawing in a room that looked like a jungle. Banging away on a sleek grand piano. Visiting a woman in a hospital bed.

She ran her hand through the strand again. This time the young girl was grasping around the floor of the same hospital room, as though she were trying to pull someone through the linoleum. Her eyes were filled with tears, though Zoey had the strangest idea that the girl should have been happy instead. Hadn't she just been given a gift?

Wait, where did that thought come from?

The girl scrabbling around on the floor looked toward a pair of men standing behind her and cried out. "Zoey's gone!"

Zoey lurched back as if she'd been hit in the face with something heavy. Nicole! She remembered! She saw herself standing in front of the woman, no, not "the woman," Lisa, as she lay dying. She saw herself willing fate to be changed, then disappearing from that world. If she wasn't in Nicole's world, and she wasn't in her own, then where was she? Was this a punishment or a reward for what she'd done? Or maybe it was neither.

With the spell that surrounded her fading now, she saw the pink strand wasn't the only one wrapped around her wrist. There was a whole rainbow of colors, in every shade she could have imagined. Some glittered as brightly as Nicole's, while others shimmered and flickered faintly.

No matter how bright or dim they were, they extended off her wrist and up into the churning mist above her. All except one.

It was two shades of green, one forest, the other a vivid emerald. It ran from her wrist, up her arm, and across her shoulder toward the center of her chest. At the spot atop her heart, it vanished. No, not vanished. That was where it became one with her. Tracing her thumb along it, Zoey's mind flooded with memories of her father. Walks on crisp fall days, his voice reading her favorite stories more nights than she could count, and most of all, the feeling of safety she could always find in his arms.

The memories roused her cloudy mind to clarity. They were precious, and more importantly, real. This mist world around her was not. She knew what she needed to do.

Zoey straightened up and turned around. She was unsurprised to find not the path that she'd taken to school, but her own house. Downtown had evaporated, leaving only the simple two-bedroom home amid a sea of silver. She steadied herself for a moment, thinking again of what her dad said about waking up. She held the idea close to her heart as she walked back inside her childhood home.

The inside of the house had changed in the short time since she'd left for school, or wherever it was she'd actually gone. The walls were bare, the furniture reduced to little more than a couch in the living room and a table in the dining room. It was like she'd walked into a minimalist stage production based around her home life. It didn't matter to her, the scenery wasn't why she'd ventured back.

"Hey there, Zoe-bear, back from school already?"

Her dad was standing in the kitchen with his back to her, hands bustling with something she couldn't see.

"Yeah, it was a short day," said Zoey, trying to keep her voice from trembling.

"You too old for an after-school snack?"

Something in Zoey twisted, threatening to break. How many chances would she have again?

"A snack sounds nice, Dad."

The next second, her dad turned to face her with a sandwich and a side of chips in hand. Ham with cream cheese and pickles, something she hadn't been able to bring herself to make since . . .

"Well, first day of high school, you've got to have some stories."

Her dad sat down at the kitchen table and set a plate at the spot across from him. He smiled at Zoey as he waited for her to take a seat, a sandwich of his own laid out before him. Zoey hovered at the point of sitting down. She knew that if she did, it would make what she was planning to do even harder. She compromised by taking a bite of the sandwich while standing. It tasted like her childhood, like happier times.

She couldn't stop herself from staring at her dad as he dug into his own snack. He looked exactly as she remembered, right down to the flecks of gray among the brown around his temples and his slightly crooked nose.

"Something on your mind?" asked her dad before the silence had stretched on too long.

"You're not really you . . . are you?"

Her dad's smile faltered, a look of mild confusion taking its place. "Who else would I be?"

Zoey sighed, glancing at the dark green strand running up her arm.

"I mean, you're you, but I don't think you're *you* . . . you."

Her dad's form flickered, revealing a silhouette of mist for the briefest of moments. The smile fixed back on his face brought to mind the vague, airy grins of beauty contestants.

"What are you talking about? This some hip new lingo I'm not caught up on?"

"You don't remember what happened on March sixth, two thousand and two, do you?"

He flickered again.

"I don't think you want me to know the answer to that. That's not why you made me."

Zoey's stomach churned, her vision swayed. She took a deep breath. She needed to keep it together.

"These all go to someone don't they?" asked Zoey, gesturing to the gossamer strands extending from her wrist. She didn't wait for him to reply, "But this one . . . yours, it doesn't go anywhere. Does that mean you're not . . . out there somewhere?"

"Where what goes to the who now?" asked her dad, tilting his head.

Zoey dug her nails into her palm. "Answer me. Does that mean he's not out there somewhere."

The mask slipped further. His features blurred, tendrils of mist furled out around the edges of his face.

"I don't know anything you don't know, Zoe-bear."

Zoey's fist trembled. "Don't call me that! You're not him!"

"I'm not, but you wish I was, don't you? And isn't that what you learned about the mist? If you wish it, it can be real?"

Zoey's heart ached. He wasn't wrong. A part of her longed for him to be real. She'd even settle on falling back into the dream-like state in which she'd awoken in this world. Would that really be so bad? To forget? To live in this land of make-believe for the rest of her days?

"What happens if I stay here?"

"Whatever you want," replied the hollow dad.

"But, it won't be real."

"Won't be real," it intoned blankly.

The painful longing in her chest was threatening to spill over now. She ran her hand along the sparkling green. She saw her dad helping her with her homework, felt joy flare in her chest when he'd brought Charlie home. She trembled. A sob caught in her throat.

"So that's it?" cried Zoey. Her face grew hot. Her legs carried her forward in a furious march. What little remained of her house dissolved away, leaving her floating in a sea of silvery nothingness." I'm just supposed to go, ohhhhh, you're right here in my heart wherever I go? Sure! That makes it all fucking better!" She turned on her heel to come back the way she came.

The mist figure tilted its head, spurring Zoey onward.

"It's great that I'll never get to talk to you again! It's totally fucking fine that mom couldn't deal without you and just stopped functioning!

It's all OK because you're alive in my memories!" Zoey was screaming now, her voice growing hoarse from the force she was exerting on it.

"Oh, wait, no, that makes it a thousand times worse! I don't *want* you to be in my heart! I don't *want* to remember you if you're just . . . gone!" she stopped her furious pacing and whipped around to face the mist figure. "How?! HOW COULD YOU LEAVE ME!?"

Zoey's voice broke. She fell to her knees, tears flowing down her cheeks. The mist churned. Grief poured out of her in an unending torrent. Her body shook from the force of her sobs, her thoughts a muddled sea of agony. She hated her dad. He should have reacted quicker, tried harder to hold on. Anything to not leave her. She hated him for being so weak. So . . . human.

She didn't know how long she lay there sobbing, only that when it began to die down, her throat was raw, her body numb.

Her hand found the streak of green running up her arm and clutched it. "I'm sorry . . ." she said in a ragged whisper. She wiped her eyes on her arm, not willing to let go of the fragment of her father.

Her hand swayed, wrist pulled by the same invisible force as before. Still clutching her forearm, Zoey glanced up toward the glittering strands that glided out into the mist. Sparkling purples, oranges, blues, yellows, every color she'd ever seen, all twisted together with her favorite shade of green. Not quite the same shade as her father's. An emerald child of his forest green.

She watched a blue-green strand sway. It was flickering and frayed, bright one second, faded the next. She hesitated for a moment, but let go of her forearm to bring her hand through the strand. The scent of rose perfume. The first time she'd ridden a bike. Popcorn and movies on rainy days. Memories of her mother.

The strand shimmered among the sea of color. Of Nicole-pink, and Aunt-Carol-purple, a steely blue she knew belonged to Uncle Will, each one braided with her own shade of green.

What would it be like, as they were severed one by one through the course of time's relentless march? Reduced to a bond that led not to another person, but to her own heart. How many times could she survive that? What was the point in making more ties, more connections to the world when they were all fated to be severed? Was it perhaps better for them to just fade away instead?

She could do it. Stay here and watch them flicker out one by one. Or maybe she could recreate her fantasy world. Maybe she could even wipe her mind clean so that she might never realize she was living in a playland of her own imagination. What then, though? She'd be safe from pain, but empty and . . . she'd be alone.

She would never know if the bond between her and her mother could have been restored, never see Nicole and Lisa happy, healthy, and together. How many other bonds would never be forged, simply because she was afraid of them being severed? What was the saying? Better to have loved and lost? Zoey had always thought that it pertained only to romantic love, but now she wasn't so sure.

Zoey put her hand on her chest and took in a deep, shuddering breath. She focused her mind. A tremor traveled through what remained of the mist figure before it dissolved back into the sea from which it had been conjured.

"I love you, Dad . . ." she whispered, her eyes fixed on the strands leading off into the distance. "But, I can't stay here."

With one last look at the braided trail of green that led to her heart, and, taking comfort in knowing that it would always be there, Zoey followed the others back to life.

CHAPTER TWENTY-SIX

Restored

The world materialized around Zoey in a rush of color and sound. When her ears stopped ringing and her eyes brought the world into focus, she was standing in the exact spot that she'd been in before she vanished from the world. The scene before her had changed, however. The bright summer's day had been replaced by the still darkness of night, and Nicole, John, and Tyler were nowhere to be seen. Gone too was the machine that had been helping Lisa breathe. Lisa herself was still there, though.

Zoey's heart leaped. The woman lying asleep in the bed looked closer to the one she'd seen in the photographs around Nicole's house. No longer cracked skin and painfully visible bones, she looked to have put on a good deal of weight since Zoey had last seen her. Her face was calm and peaceful as she slept, her breathing untroubled and even.

Had this remarkable change come about in mere hours? That was as long as Zoey felt she had been gone, at least. She checked the date on the whiteboard hanging from the wall, which also announced the name of Lisa's night nurse. Her stomach lurched. She had been gone for over a week. It would make things more complicated going forward, but overall, it was a small price to pay for bringing Lisa back from the brink.

Zoey took a moment to let the night wash over her. This stillness was one that she knew well. A world for her and her alone. One that was real, and not some illusion of the mist. Zoey strolled around Lisa's room to take in the art that adorned the walls, examining each one in loving detail.

Her heart smiled to see that the floral piece that she had watched Nicole and Lisa work on had been added to the collection. There were other fresh additions that told Zoey that Nicole had seen her mom since her brush with death.

One was a work in crayon, depicting a small pink creature dancing among a multicolored forest. It was cute, to say the least, and more artfully done than she could ever manage. It was the other one that made Zoey gasp, however. It was her in watercolor. A strange ethereal creature with her features, blurred and beautified, surrounded by billowing silver. Had Nicole described these things to her? Or had Lisa seen this with her own eyes somehow? Maybe when people talked about seeing a white light, what they were actually seeing was into the mist?

Touched as she was to have made the wall, Zoey was eager to get back to Nicole. She hadn't taken two steps from Lisa's bed when a voice rose up behind her.

"You're back, thank goodness. Nicky was so upset." Zoey froze. She must have been hearing things. Zoey took another step toward the door when, again, the voice spoke, more loudly this time. "Don't go yet, please?"

Unable to deny it any longer, Zoey turned to find Lisa sitting up in her bed. She was squinting through the semi-darkness directly at Zoey.

"You can see me?" asked Zoey, taking a step closer.

Lisa nodded. "Yes, but you're . . . it's like you're made of—"

"Mist?" supplied Zoey.

Lisa furrowed her brow. "Like moonlight reflecting *off* of mist. You're glowing, but . . . I can barely make you out."

"Well, uh, is this better?" asked Zoey. She took a step forward.

"You're still . . . I saw you before, glowing . . . blurry, but I thought it was the drugs. And your voice . . . it sounds like it's coming out of an old radio." Lisa extended her arm as if to see if Zoey was solid, but fell short. Zoey bridged the gap and placed her hand on top of Lisa's. ". . .What are you?"

Zoey smiled, remembering her first encounter with Nicole. "I'm just a kid."

"That's what Nicky says, a girl from another world," said Lisa, still with her hand beneath Zoey's.

"I know it sounds crazy, but yeah, that's right . . ."

When their hands parted, a glittering strand shone between them. It was a brilliant orange, the color of sunrise, spun together with Zoey's own shade of green. It shimmered between them, drifting on the phantom breeze that kept the mist in motion, before fading from sight.

"What was that? Is that how you saved me?" asked Lisa.

"No, that one's sort of new to me, too." Zoey paused. Her eyes darted away before she continued. "I think they lead to people we care about."

Lisa studied Zoey for a moment, frowning. She appeared to realize this and gave what looked like an attempt at an apologetic smile. "Sorry, this is just all so . . ."

"Batshit crazy?"

Lisa laughed. "That's a good word for it."

Zoey glanced at the heart monitor and back at Lisa. "So, you're all better now?"

Lisa laughed again. "You sound like Nicole." She nodded, a smile spreading over her face. "I feel good enough to go home. I think the doctors are only keeping me here because they don't understand how I got better."

Zoey let out a long sigh. "That's great. I mean, not that they're keeping you here. Just, that you're better." She'd known it all along, but hearing it from someone else was a tonic she didn't know she'd needed.

"I think they're running out of tests, to be honest. So I should be home soon."

Home, thought Zoey as guilt burned in her chest. She shifted in place and glanced toward the door. "Well, uh, I should get going there, uh, home, I mean. If I've really been gone for a week, my aunt must be freaking out."

"Wait, don't go. I still need to—" Lisa took a deep breath and straightened in her bed,

looking Zoey in the eyes. "Thank you—"

"You don't need to . . ." interjected Zoey, her cheeks flushing.

"I do though. I know I wouldn't be here right now if it wasn't for you. It's more than that,

though." Lisa's eyes traveled to the drawings on the wall before finding their way back to Zoey. "Thank you for being such a friend to Nicky through all this."

"I'm the one who's glad she's been a friend to me," said Zoey. "It's been nice to have someone who . . . likes me for a change."

"You feel like you're a pretty easy kid to like," said Lisa simply.

Zoey shrugged. "Honestly, at this point, I think it's just Nicole and my aunt."

"I might be a little biased considering what you did for me, but I think you can count me on that list, too."

"Thanks for saying that . . ." said Zoey, her face growing hot. "I really should go, though. You know, let Nicole and my aunt know I'm OK."

"How are you going to—you know, I think I'll just assume you know what you're doing."

"I'm not sure I'd go that far, but I manage."

Zoey crept out of Lisa's room and down the hall, only running into a sleepy-looking nurse typing away at a workstation. She glanced up when the elevator doors opened to collect Zoey, but much to her relief, went right back to her work. It was good to know that her trick with the mist had only resulted in Lisa being able to see her, and not the world as a whole.

Cool night air washed over her when she walked through the glass doors in the lobby. As much as she enjoyed the stillness of the night, the thought of spending the next hour or more walking back to Nicole's house was not a particularly welcome one. It wasn't as if she could call a cab, though, so she might as well get going. She had only taken a couple steps when an image popped into her mind. Nicole, posing with one fist thrust high above her, the other on her hip. Smiling, Zoey brought the image to life in her mind, and, for good measure, copied Nicole's superhero pose. Then, her feet left the ground.

A scream rang out through the air as Zoey plummeted several feet toward the ground before being able to right herself. As confident as she had been that she had mastered the mist, her flight to Nicole's was proving more turbulent than she had envisioned. The mist was coiling out in every direction, but she thought it looked thinner than it had before her disappearance. She had used a great deal of it to heal Lisa, so maybe the mist was still replenishing itself. Not letting the idea trouble her too much, Zoey focused instead on getting where she was going.

"When there's a smile in your heart," Zoey sang to herself, trying hard not to think about how high up she was.

When she reached Nicole's house, she floated up to the bay window that looked into the younger girl's room. She reached out her hand and knocked gently. The resulting noise rang out like a gunshot in the otherwise silent night. After several beats and with no sign that Nicole had heard her, she knocked again. She flinched as the sound reverberated through the deserted street.

She was about to knock for a third time when a pair of hands parted the curtains enough for an eye to peek out. Nicole threw open the curtains and let out a sound that was somewhere between a scream and a sob. She glanced at the ceiling above her and clapped her hands over her mouth. After a moment where it looked like she didn't dare to draw breath, Nicole lowered her hands.

"Zoey?" she mouthed.

Smiling, Zoey pointed down and made the motion of turning a door handle. Nicole nodded and scampered from the room. Zoey let herself grow heavy and touched down on the porch just in time to get tackled by a teary-eyed Nicole.

"What happened? Where did you go?"

Zoey could tell that Nicole was trying to keep her voice low but wasn't quite managing it. She returned the hug, too tired to hold back. Or maybe it was that she'd grown past such things.

"It's sort of a long story, and I want to tell you all about it, but we need to be quiet."

Nicole pulled away to look up at Zoey, her eyes overbright. "It's been a whole week. I thought maybe you . . ."

"I know, I'm sorry, but it didn't feel that long to me where I was." She looked around the empty yard, then back over Nicole's shoulder. "Come on, let's go inside. I don't want to get you in trouble."

Nicole led them into the foyer. She turned to Zoey, who shook her head and motioned upward. They slinked their way upstairs, Nicole looking as if it were costing her a great deal not to bombard Zoey with questions. When they made it back to Nicole's room, her self-restraint failed. She pulled Zoey into another painfully tight hug.

"I thought you left forever."

Zoey returned the hug, doing her best not to tear up.

"I know, I'm sorry," she said. She didn't know where to start. "Hey, I saw your mom, she looks like she's doing really good!"

Nicole's face brightened as she released Zoey. "She's all better. Dad says the only reason she's still in the hospital is because the doctors are making extra sure the cancer's all gone."

"That's what she said," replied Zoey, who, catching Nicole's look of surprise a moment later, smacked herself on the head. "That's right, you don't know. Nicky, she can see me now. Well, sort of. She said I'm all blurry to her."

Nicole's eyes widened. She ran over to her cubby and after rummaging around, pulled out a piece of paper and handed it to Zoey. It was Nicole's rendition of the drawing of her that hung in Lisa's room.

"My mom said she saw a beautiful angel in the hospital. She said she told her that her daughter still needed her. I knew it was you!"

"Oh . . ." began Zoey, remembering the painting she'd seen in Lisa's room. "I guess that was me, but I'm no angel. I mean, do you see any wings?"

"You were flying outside my window."

"That was your idea to begin with, remember? Super Zoey," said Zoey, striking a pose.

"So, how did you make my mom better?"

"I thought that was obvious. I used magic." Nicole's eyes grew wide. Zoey could tell that she wanted to hear the whole story, and she wanted to tell it, but Nicole wasn't the only one who was owed an explanation. "I'm not sure I need to ask, but do you think you're up for sneaking some cookies? I think a story like this needs some snacks."

CHAPTER TWENTY-SEVEN

Together

A chill ran over Zoey when she and Nicole stepped out of the closet and into her room at Aunt Carol's house. Even though it had only been a week, Zoey couldn't help but think the room looked forlorn. Or, maybe it was just that she was feeling guilty over how she'd left things with her aunt and uncle.

She and Nicole made their way down to the kitchen, not taking any particular steps to remain quiet.

"OK, you wait in the kitchen, I'll go get my aunt and then we ca—"

For the second time that night, Zoey was on the receiving end of a hug that almost knocked her to the ground. Awash in a sea of patchouli and bangles, she struggled to take a breath that didn't make her head spin.

"Oh, I knew you'd come back! How are you? What about your little friend, is her mother OK?"

Zoey mumbled an unintelligible response into her aunt's shoulder blade while trying to extricate herself from the hug. Seeming to remember that Zoey needed air to survive, Aunt Carol let her go and bustled back into the kitchen. "Do you want some tea? Some cookies? Have you been eating?"

"Actually, some tea and cookies would be great, but could you get an extra mug for Nicole?"

Aunt Carol froze with the kettle in her hand, eyes darting around the room.

"Your little friend? She's here?"

"Yeah, she's right over there," said Zoey, feeling very much like a little kid with an imaginary friend.

Aunt Carol pulled another mug from the cabinet, her hands trembling. "I just can't believe it. I always believed that there was something out there, but I never thought I'd have someone from a whole different world in my kitchen. Do you know what kind of tea she likes? Or, what kind of cookies? I guess she must like them all if she's been the one sneaking them. Oh, I wish I could see her myself."

Nicole was looking at Zoey's aunt with her eyebrows raised, her cheeks a little flush. Zoey gave her a reassuring pat on the shoulder and whispered, "She's a little strange, but she's a really nice lady, trust me."

"What was that, Zoey dear?"

"Oh, I was asking Nicole what kind of tea she likes."

Nicole shifted in her seat, looking wearily at the kettle. "I don't like tea."

"She doesn't really like tea."

"Oh, how about hot chocolate then?"

Judging by the way Nicole's face lit up, Aunt Carol had found a suitable alternative.

Nicole's face lit up. "With marshmallows?"

Zoey relayed the message. Aunt Carol had been right, it would be a lot easier if she could see and hear Nicole. She didn't know what she could do on the seeing front, but as far as being heard . . .

"Wait here a minute," said Zoey. She dashed to her uncle's office, grabbing a pen and notepad from his desk before returning. She placed them on the table in front of Nicole. "Alright, now if Nicole has something to say, she can just write it down. How does that sound?"

Nicole pondered the question before picking up the pen and scribbling, "OK."

Aunt Carol's jaw dropped at the sight of the pen floating in mid-air. Zoey stifled a laugh. She had never seen that happen to someone outside of cartoons. Her aunt rallied quickly however and went back to bustling around the kitchen as though nothing had happened.

"So your name's Nicole? How were you able to come over to our world? Can everyone where you're from do things like that? How did you move all those things the last time you were over?" asked Aunt Carol, barely pausing between her questions.

By the time the three of them were seated around the table, Zoey felt that Nicole and her aunt could hardly be classified as strangers anymore. Nicole took all Aunt Carol's questions in stride. Whether it was the fact that she had provided her with some pretty tasty food or the amount of interest she was showing in her, Nicole seemed to have taken a shine to her aunt.

Zoey could tell Aunt Carol's list of questions about the other world had by no means been exhausted, but as they sipped their drinks, her aunt gazed at her expectantly.

"Alright, so after we left here last week . . ."

Her aunt and Nicole didn't make a peep as she relayed the events of the last trip to the hospital. Zoey had done her best to glaze over the emotional scene that had prompted her to heal Nicole's mother but spared no detail when it came to describing the mist world. It had all been so surreal that she felt she needed to hear it out loud to truly wrap her head around it.

It cost her a fair bit when she reached the part about her final conversation with her hollow dad. She left out some of the more colorful language she'd used but kept the feelings intact. She wanted them to know that they were a big reason why she was able to pull herself out of that world.

"So, can you still see them now? Those magical threads?" asked Aunt Carol in a hushed voice once Zoey had finished.

"No," said Zoey, shaking her head, "but I know they're still there."

"And Nicole, your mom's all better?"

Nicole scribbled "Yes" across the paper.

The watery smile that had been fixed on Aunt Carol's face for most of Zoey's tale quivered. Zoey thought she knew why, but didn't know how to bring it up. Luckily for her, Aunt Carol wasn't the reserved type.

"I can't tell you what it means, knowing that even after someone's gone, they're still with us, in their own special way. I've always wanted to believe that, but never really . . . Well, now I know for sure . . ."

Aunt Carol spared a moment to dab her eyes on her opulent bathrobe. This gave Zoey a much-needed opportunity to wipe her own.

"So, that's everything. After that, I wound up back in the hospital and went to Nicole's house, then came here."

"I'm so glad you knew you could come back to us."

"Well, you told me I could, so . . ." said Zoey, trying not to throw her gaze away from Aunt Carol's watery expression. Unbidden, a question bubbled to the forefront of her mind. "Did my mom ask about me while I was gone?"

"Oh, she did," began Aunt Carol, looking somewhat bashful. "I feel so bad about lying to her, but, well, it was your uncle's idea."

"What was?"

"Well, we told her that you were volunteering at a camp for troubled youths, and they had a no-cell phone policy." Aunt Carol paused to look at Zoey, rushing on when she saw her look of surprise. "It wasn't really a lie. I mean, Nicole's family was troubled, and you helped them get better."

"I just didn't expect Uncle Will to cover for me."

"Oh no, your uncle!" said Aunt Carol, leaping up. "We should wake him up and tell him you're back home."

The fact that her uncle had told an outright lie to cover for her wasn't lost on Zoey, but the thought of having to retell her story was not at all appealing. Something of this thought must have registered on her face, however, as Aunt Carol sat back down and sighed. "I suppose I can tell him myself, you look like you could do with a good night's sleep."

Gratitude rushed through Zoey. She knew she'd have to face her uncle and, at the very least, apologize for the dramatic way in which she'd left last week, but she was glad that she didn't have to navigate that tonight.

"I think I need to get Nicole back to her house first. We don't need her winding up on the nine o'clock news."

Aunt Carol gasped. It occurred to Zoey that her aunt hadn't considered the lateness of the hour. Aunt Carol hurried them out of the kitchen in a clatter of bangles, though Nicole still managed to grab a final cookie as she went.

"You'll come over tomorrow?" asked Nicole as they stood in front of the closet in Zoey's bedroom.

"As long as my aunt and uncle let me, but now that they've met you, I don't think that'll be a problem."

Nicole let out a little cheer and pulled Zoey into a hug, which Zoey returned gratefully. "I love you, Zoey, I'm really glad you're back."

Zoey must have left the part of her that would have recoiled from such a sentiment back in the fake misty world because she didn't hesitate before replying, "I love you too, Nicky. I'll see you tomorrow."

CHAPTER TWENTY-EIGHT

For Now

"Maybe I should have picked an easier pattern . . ."

Nicole giggled from somewhere to Zoey's right. "You said you made these before."

"Well, yeah, but I was younger than you the last time I did," replied Zoey. She kept her eyes locked on the diagram she was trying to follow. "It doesn't help that someone wanted four different shades of pink."

"Yours is all green and I finished it yesterday," said Nicole, finishing off in a sing-song tone.

"I'm gonna kick your butt . . ." mumbled Zoey. After a few more moments of fiddling, Zoey sighed, set down the complicated braid she was working on, and closed her copy of *101 Crafts for Kids*. "Whose bright idea was friendship bracelets anyway?"

"Yours."

"Oh, right," replied Zoey, flexing her fingers. "Well, I'll get yours to you in four to five working days, just give me time." Zoey uncrossed her legs and flopped onto her back, looking up at the star stickers on Nicole's bedroom ceiling. She gave a wave of her hand, filling the plastic press-on flowers with a soft golden light. They shone brightly for a moment before flickering and, one by one, reverted to their previously lightless state.

Zoey glanced to her side, hoping that Nicole hadn't noticed the shorter-than-intended light show. Fortunately, her attention was elsewhere.

"Mom's awake!" she cried excitedly, following a series of creaks from out in the hallway.

Zoey pulled herself up off the floor and followed Nicole. Sure enough, there was Lisa, wearing a bathrobe and the slightly dazed expression of someone who'd just woken up. Nicole threw her arms around her mom and pulled her into a hug.

"I thought you'd be here Zoey," said Lisa, stifling a yawn. "Seems like whenever you spend the day, I get to sleep in a bit."

"Ten is sleeping in late?" asked Zoey.

Lisa rolled her head from side to side as though to clear it of any lingering sleep. "Once you're a mom? Mornings tend to be all hands on deck."

"Dad says you still need lots of rest."

"That man," said Lisa with a dramatic sigh. "If anyone needs to slow down and get some rest, it's him. I'm the one who spent the last couple of months in bed."

Nicole frowned at the mention of her mother's stay in the hospital. Zoey thought she knew why. Her mother looked well to the point of robustness. Aside from her head of fine blonde peach fuzz, it would be easy to forget that she was ever sick in the first place. It had been less than a week since Lisa had returned home from the hospital, though, and Zoey was sure that Nicole was worried that it might all go away.

"But, you're all better now, right?" asked Nicole, her tone worried.

"All better now," assured Lisa, kissing the top of Nicole's head. "Just like yesterday, and tomorrow, and the day after." Nicole sighed and released her mother from their hug. "Can we work on the story?"

Lisa smiled. "Tell you what, you and Zoey go get things set up, and I'll be there after I put on a pot of coffee."

Nicole grabbed Zoey's hand and pulled her toward her mom's studio. Life had been restored to this room. The air was no longer stale, the supplies freed from their state of chilly organization. Sketchbooks lay scattered around the room amid a sea of paints, charcoal, and brushes.

Zoey recognized the sketchbook they were looking for and plucked it from among the others. She smiled as she flipped through it. Each page depicted a scene from the story that she'd dreamed up for Nicole. It was still a little weird to see herself on the pages, transformed into a fairy tale princess by Lisa's hand. She had no issue seeing Nicole as the colorful fairy child, though.

"Alright, I have the sketches. You wanna grab the finished pages?"

Zoey turned to find Nicole holding a sketchbook of her own, her eyes fixed intently on its pages. From the look on her face, Zoey knew what was inside it. Sure enough, the page Nicole was staring so intently at was one of Lisa's sketches of her, Zoey. The particular sketch showed little more than a hazy, humanoid outline. If Zoey didn't know that it was supposed to be her, she would have guessed at an oddly shaped cloud.

"It's not fair . . ." said Nicole, eyes flitting to the mist that enshrouded them. Just as the day before, there was less of it hanging in the air than ever.

"I know . . ." said Zoey, her voice somber. She placed a hand on Nicole's shoulder. "But it doesn't look like there's anything we can do about it."

If Zoey was being honest with herself, she'd known that they were heading in this direction from the first night she'd come back from her self-made dream world. She didn't know if it was always fated to be this way, or if her intervention with Lisa was the cause. It didn't really matter. The fact remained that their time together was coming to an end, and they both knew it.

"Do you think it will ever come back?" asked Nicole through watery eyes.

Zoey took a deep breath. "I don't know, but I hope so."

"I don't want you to go away," whispered Nicole.

"Me either . . ." replied Zoey through the lump forming in her throat. "But remember about the strings I saw in the mist? We'll always be connected by them."

Nicole nodded slowly. "It's not the same, though."

"I know. But, hey, we don't need to be sad about it right now. We can still see each other for a while at least." Nicole smiled, but it didn't look very convincing. "Plus, you've got a lot to look forward to. We've still got time to finish the book, and you're starting sixth grade in a couple of weeks. That's a big deal!"

"And you're talking with your mom more, too. That's good, right?"

It was true that her mom had started to text more regularly. She hadn't offered up any sort of apology, but she had said she was proud of Zoey for her supposed work at the camp. In return, Zoey had done her best to reply to her mom's messages as soon as she got them, and even reached out on her own a few times. She had hoped that she'd be able to forgive her mom in one after seeing Nicole almost lose hers. It hadn't worked out that way so far, but she felt like things were starting to warm between them, if slowly.

"Yeah, we're getting along better," said Zoey.

"And your uncle's being nicer, too?"

"Oh yeah," said Zoey, holding the sketchbook at her side. "It's a little freaky actually. Now that he knows I wasn't lying about you he's more on my side about my old homelife stuff. Doesn't think I'm such a bad kid after all. I think Aunt Carol's more relieved about that than I am."

"That's good," said Nicole, her eyes fixing again on the sketchbook in her hands.

"Come on, let's put that away and get the story pages. We've gotta work hard on it if we want the princess and the fairy to live happily ever after, right?"

Nicole hesitated. Her eyes lingered on the sketchbook a moment longer before she snapped it shut. "Right."

Nicole picked up the half-finished picture book from atop a stack of paint cans and turned to leave the room, her hand outstretched. Zoey knew that there would soon come a day when the passage between their two worlds would close, that their time together would come to an end. But that day wasn't today, and she was going to enjoy what she had, for as long as she could have it.

Robert J. Halliwell was born in the magical land of Canada during the age of butterfly clips and jelly sandals. He spent his formative years watching spooky movies and being jealous of Belle's library from Beauty and the Beast. Many people don't know Robert is married to an American Cyborg or that he's secretly in possession of the two cutest cats in the world. He can often be found playing Dungeons and Dragons, knitting, or struggling to keep his garden alive.

robertjhalliwell.com